Asa Shinn Boyd, J. Henry Boyd

Poetical Works of Asa S. Boyd

Asa Shinn Boyd, J. Henry Boyd

Poetical Works of Asa S. Boyd

ISBN/EAN: 9783741118111

Manufactured in Europe, USA, Canada, Australia, Japa

Cover: Foto ©Andreas Hilbeck / pixelio.de

Manufactured and distributed by brebook publishing software
(www.brebook.com)

Asa Shinn Boyd, J. Henry Boyd

Poetical Works of Asa S. Boyd

POETICAL WORKS

—OF—

ASA S. BOYD;

TOGETHER WITH

AN ALLEGORY OF THE JOURNEY OF LIFE;

AFFECTIONATELY DEDICATED

TO HIS WIFE AND CHILDREN,

AND

DESIGNED FOR THE GOOD OF THE GENERAL READER.

With Selections from the Writings of J. H. Boyd.

BALTIMORE, MD.:

PUBLISHED BY ASA S. BOYD,

Author of Modern Mnemotechny; or, How to Acquire a Good Memory.

328 N. FREMONT STREET.

1886.

PRINTER,
JOS. E. HUSBAND,
BALTIMORE.

ELECTROTYPERS,
CHAS. J. CARY & CO.,
BALTIMORE.

PREFACE.

The contents of this volume were written under various circumstances, and at various times and places; running through a period of over twenty-five years. Some were written beneath bright skies, and some beneath lowering clouds; some in seasons of sorrow, and some in hours of rejoicing; some in tears of grief, and some in tears of gladness; some in the quiet grove—fanned by heaven's zephyrs—and some in the crowded city—amid the jostling throng; some in the balmy morn, some at sultry noon, some in the shades of evening, and others in the lone midnight hour, and others, even at the advent of the morning star! Some were written when the author was but a boy, and others amid the cares of busy manhood; and all, I trust, under the shadow of the wings of the " Son of Righteousness; " softened by the dews of Hermon, dripping from the olive branch of peace — nourished by the " Root and the offspring of David."

The most of the poems were written for the comfort, encouragement or amusement of myself, family and friends, without any thought of ever having them published, or seen outside of the circle of my friends.

Some of them have appeared in newspapers from time to time; and many requests have been made of the author to have them published in book form. An appreciation of their merits has been frequently expressed by many—convincing the author that it is his duty to offer them to the world, which he now does, hoping his labor will not be lost; and that the sower and reaper may rejoice together.

The writer will feel well repaid if he can lift the weight from any burdened heart, and bring to view the bright side of the pictures in the darkened chambers and hallways of life, and lead any who are longing for light and liberty, love and peace, in smooth and pleasant paths, to higher plains and holier.

On the latter pages of the book there will be found some selections from the writings of J. Henry Boyd, a deceased brother of

THE AUTHOR.

CONTENTS.

J. H. BOYD'S WRITINGS.

POETICAL WORKS

—or—

A S A S. B O Y D.

"*LET YOUR LIGHT SHINE BEFORE MEN.*"

SHOULD moon or star refuse, by night,
To shed on Earth its borrowed light,
It seems the Sun would hide its face,
Or God remove it from its place.

So with the light shed on my heart,
Should I refuse it to impart,
It seems that God, though He be love,
Would hide His face, or me remove.

Though I with star may not compare,
Or with the moon, more bright and fair,
Yet I should in my place appear
As true as they—in greater sphere.

Some thirsty soul may seek the brink
Of that pure well from which I drink,—
May faint and lie beside the way,
While I go drink from day to day.

One star of all the shining host,
May cease to shine, and not be missed
By greater, but some feebler one
May miss it, as the moon the sun.

So I with feebler light than Pope,
Or Paul, or Milton, may not hope
Upon the world such light to blaze;
Yet I may shed some fainter rays

On eyes too weak to look upon
The glory of the noonday sun,
Or trace sublimer beauties through
The azure vault of ether blue,—

May stand beside life's darkened way,
At early noon or close of day,
Or when the night with dew is damp,
And wave my faint and flickering lamp.

The highest stars which deck the sky,
Cannot be seen with naked eye,
While those more near, with feebler light,
May cheer and beautify the night.

So, as in humble paths I go,
My light may fall on those too low
A glimpse of those bright stars to gain,
Which shine upon a higher plane.

The light to me my Lord hath given
To cheer on earth and guide to heaven,
Should I beneath a bushel hide
To smother,—none to cheer and guide?

My heart has often glowed and swelled
With light,—all gloom and doubt dispelled,—
Which never met the longing eye
Of those to me most dear, most nigh.

And now, if God, who gave in love,
Will not the "candlestick remove,"
And take away the light he lent,
I'll let it shine, though now far spent.

Unlike the man who in the ground
His talent hid, in napkin bound,
May I be at the Lord's return;
And with my talent others earn:

For if no other one I gain
The Lord may not let it remain;
And should I with it gain but one,
Doubtless my Lord will say, " Well done."

And now the water by the way
And crumbs which dropped from day to day,
I'll gather up, and trust God's grace
Will all that lacks, again replace.

My bread I'll on the waters cast,
And trust 'twill all be found at last;
Safe, gathered on Life's lengthened tide,
Or surely on the other side.

The seed we by the wayside sow,
May lie beneath the drifted snow,
And seem to us as lost or dead,
But yet the roots reach down and spread,

And vernal showers, and sun and shade
Will bring to view the springing blade,
And summer's sun and summer's rain
Will bring at last the golden grain.

The sower may not live to reap,
But ere the harvest fall to sleep,
Yet God's grace, like descending dews,
Will life into the seed infuse;

And other hands the fruit will reap—
If seed be good, if soil be deep,
And worldly cares and birds of prey
Choke not, nor take the seed away,—

Not only reap, but also sow
From seed first cast beneath the snow;
Then, Oh, how well to see no tares
Are sown to reap in coming years.

And though the sower may not stay
To see the fruits along the way,
If sown in faith, he joys to know
It will in fields immortal grow;—

And also joys to know at last,
That every snow and storm and blast
That fell upon life's well tilled field
Will bless the fruit, increase the yield.

Now, as your steps I gently lead
By running brook, through dell and mead,
And fruitful field, and shaded grove,
Each step, I hope, some good may prove.

But, if perchance, some song of bird
Be not so gay as some you've heard,
Or fruit so sweet, or flower so fair,
As some which scent the summer air,

Condemn them not, for 'mong life's throng,
Some never heard so sweet a song,
Or ate such fruit, or saw such flowers,
Or water sipped 'neath shaded bowers:

For those these words are penned and pressed;
To those this volume is addressed;—
To all who may within it find
Comfort or strength for heart or mind.

From all the seed my hands may sow,
I trust no thorn may ever grow
To pierce, or cause one pang or sigh,
Or tear to fall from any eye.

But that the olive and the vine
May 'round some bleeding heart entwine,
Their oil may soothe some troubled breast,
And on its placid waters rest!

CRITICISM.

IT has appeared in every age,
That thoughts which some men most engage,
And seem as wisdom in their eyes,
Is but for man to criticise.

There's Milton, with his thoughts sublime;
There's Campbell, with his flowing rhyme;
Or, if we take a larger scope,
There's Byron, Tennyson and Pope,

And others—we might name a score,
Who bring to light much hidden lore;
Perhaps each thinking he knows best,
Is food or fun for all the rest,

Who watch with envious eye each day
To pounce upon and pick their prey,
To see some chance—some evil hour,
And vulture like, their prey devour.

At Johnson's works, how Cobbett laughs!
Picks out whole lines and paragraphs,
Turns out the dark and faulty side,
That others, too, may them deride,

He holds them up to public gaze,
That he may get the critic's praise,—
Which seems to give as much delight
As guiding others in the right.

He takes his literary axe,
At every word and sentence hacks;
Declares it is all bad syntax,
And all that he asserts are facts.

Another critic now appears,
Who Cobbett's work to pieces tears;
He makes some song, or jingling rhymes—
Sings " Cobbett is behind the times."

About the time this critic ends,
Another one on him descends;
And laughs, as Cobbett laughed, and tries
To show his faults to other eyes.

Another critic comes along—
Declares this man is in the wrong;
He writes a book, and hard he tries
To show his faults, wherefores and whys.

Then some one else, of greater ken,
Points out the faults of all these men,
Says, " To the world I'll give the light,
For they are wrong and I am right."

Then some one else, of great pretence,
Says, "Any man of common sense
Can see these men are far astray;
Mine only is the proper way."

And so it is with all the race;
Each thinking he is most in place,
Sees other's faults, but cannot see
His own—though he may honest be.

This being so, shall we expect
The critic will no fault detect
In what we advocate, or when
We write or speak our thoughts to men?

Though some men cannot build a house,
  'Twould not be wrong to try,
If, after trying once or twice,
  They build it by and by.

Not every man can write a book,
  Or hold a crowd spell-bound,
And if they could there would be few
  To plough or reap the ground.

But if a man has good to tell—
  Tho' works in shoes or clothes—
It seems he would be doing well
  To tell whate'er he knows.

Some have to do the roughest work;
  Some have to do the fine;
Some mould the mineral into coin;
  Some dig it from the mine.

Some have to work in wool and hemp,
  And some in sand and brick,
Some have to teach the A B C's
  While some teach reading Greek.

A man who uses plow or spade
  May be a man of ken,
And one who uses plane or saw
  May sometimes use the pen;

But, if in using now and then
  He should not quite excel,
He should not be condemned by those
  Who use it oft and well.

But we should feel, for it is true,
  That all on all depend,
That each one has a work to do,
  And each a hand should lend.

Some have to work by patterns made,
  Whilst some devise and plan;
The world is wide, there's work for all,
  Let each *do what he can.*

But we should never thrust aside
  Our fellows; and ignore
The good they do; their wrongs deride,
  And bid them *do no more.*

Yet it will often do us good
  To show our faults; for we
Are often blind to many wrongs
  Which others plainly see.

HAVE WE NO WORK TO DO?

WHEN we, with vision bright, behold
The Shepherd fighting for the fold;
And see the wolf, in rage and pow'r,
The lambs all ready to devour,
As from the fold they lose their way,
Or from the Shepherd go astray,
And while the sheep, with trembling feet,
For safety to our arms retreat,—
    O! can we fold our arms and stand
    Unmoved, and lend no helping hand?

Shall we see men in crowds descend
The road that must in ruin end,
And for assistance hear them cry;
And leave them there to moan and die;
While we hold folded in our hand
The guide unto that happy land,
Where life and peace and joy and rest
Dispel the grief of every breast?
    Shall we look on and not assist,
    And still profess to follow Christ?

Shall we, whose burdens are made light,
See others toiling with their might,
With heavy yoke—by sin oppres'd,
While we've been freed, and made to rest
With Him who said, (and truly spoke),
"Come unto me, and take my yoke"?
Who spake as no man spake before;
What none could bear, for us he bore,—
  Shall we look on, and not as much
  As even with "one finger touch"?

Shall we behold our brother thirst
For waters which so freely burst
From out the Rock that never dries,—
Of which who drinks thirsts not, nor dies,
Or see him hungering for bread,
  Without the which the soul is dead,
While at the fount we drink, and know
The tree where fruits immortal grow?—
  Will He who fed the fainting throng,
  Say we have acted right or wrong?

Shall we stand by and idly look,
When, for our sins our Master took
His cross? (O, see Him Calvary's mount ascend!
There bleed and die,—his murderers' friend!
And there, while dying hear Him pray,
"O Father, take their sins away!")
And yet refuse our cross to bear,
Or in the Christian fight to spare?
  Should we not run the Christian race?
  Our love and prayers, our foes embrace?

Oh! see Him weep; and hear Him pray,
"O, Father, take this cup away!
Yet not my will but thine be done,
For this came thy obedient Son."
Then hear His Father's voice on high,—

"My Son, through love for man you die!"
Oh! can we hear His groans, and see
His tears, and say, " 'Twas not for me?"
   No, we will work with heart and hand,
   And follow at our Lord's command:

Yes, follow Him, like Him we'll live:
Free we've received; we'll freely give;
We've of the tree of life been fed;
We'll give the hungery " living bread."
And all we find, by sin oppress'd,
We'll point to Him who us has blest;
We'll love Him, his commands we'll keep;
We'll prove our love; we'll feed his sheep:
   Like Him, if need be, we will die,
   To meet and live with Him on high.

HOPE AND CAUTION.

'TIS Hope or Caution all along
   The path of life that checks or cheers;
Hope smiles, or sings some cheering song,
   While Caution sighs, or weeps, or fears.

Hope, *without* Caution, travels on,
   And never stops to count the cost,
Thus, starting on some brilliant morn,
   Is in the evening darkness lost.

Caution, *alone*, with timid heart,
   Sees in the future no bright star;
So, on the road she fears to start,
   Or starting, does not travel far.

But, hand in hand, they both progress;
   Hope leads, while Caution guards the way:
Thus, they each other's journey bless,
   And travel on, both night and day.

Hope builds her castle in the sky,
  While Caution chinks or props the wall;
Hope's object is to rear it high,
  While Caution guards against its fall.

Hope fires the engine—puts on steam,
  And drives ahead without a fear;
While Caution does of dangers dream,
  And plods alone far in the rear.

Then Caution looks far in advance,
  Tells Hope to stop, or slack her speed;
Hope turns to Caution with a glance,
  But still the warning does not heed.

Caution cries out, with fear and dread,
  " There's danger, Hope! O, stop! come back ! "
Hope looks not back, but drives ahead;
  Then stops, by running off the track.

Hope hoists the sail to catch the breeze,—
  Nor does she danger e'er discern—
When sailing o'er life's troubled seas,
  While Caution watches at the stern.

Hope rushes boldly to the field,—
  Fears not the cannon's loud report;
While Caution, from the foe concealed,
  Protects herself behind the fort.

Hope plows the ground and sows the seed;
  While Caution builds the fences high,
Pulls out the thistle, brier and weed,
  Or fears, perhaps, the crop will die.

Caution oft draws her purse-strings tight,
  That what she has she may retain;
Hope lets them loose, that by its flight,
  It may return with double gain.

Caution oft fears that want may blight;
    So, seldom gives, befriends, or lends:
Hope says, "The end will all be right;"
    Gives and indorses notes for friends.

Hope thinks perhaps she'll win the prize:
    So thinking, put her chances in;
But Caution never throws the dice,
    Unless she's pretty sure she'll win.

Hope eats and drinks whate'er she craves;
    But Caution has an eye to health,—
Eats what is best, the rest she saves,
    And adds unto her stock of wealth.

In health, Hope never fears disease;
    While Caution fears at every breath,
Some pestilential, evil breeze,
    May sow in her the seeds of death.

In sickness, Caution fears to die,
    And of the future has much dread;
While Hope sees joy beyond the sky,
    Or rest among the silent dead.

Thus, each one is a saving trait;
    One saves from danger, one despair:
And when we meet at heaven's gate,
    They both will help us enter there.

And when they meet in that bright land
    Where all life's ills shall pass away,
They'll take each other by the hand,
    And to each other thus will say,—

"O Hope, bright Hope! thine is the hand
    That led me to these realms of day!"
"O Caution! thou didst by me stand,
    And guarded me whilst on the way!"

Then let us these two traits unite;
  They'll take us through this "vale of tears:
And in death's dark and gloomy night,
  Bright Hope shall banish all our fears.

* * *

FRIENDS.

WHEN first we enter on the stage
Of life, and in our part engage;
Before our infant feet can walk,
Or hands can work, or lips can talk,
O, then, how much does all depend
Upon the care of some kind Friend.

And when in childhood's sunny days,
We join our mates in mirthful plays,
And seek companionship in youth,—
O, then, how much we feel the truth,
That much our happiness depends
Upon the kindness of our Friends.

And when in manhood's busy strife,
We meet the sterner ills of life,
(For good and ill will be our lot,
Tho' wise may be our choice or not;)
Tho' we need borrow not, nor lend,
Sad is our lot without a Friend.

And when our lot we strive to bless
With wealth, but fail to find success,
And still we strive and toil the more,
But fate or fortune keeps us poor;
Oh, then, our hope at last must end
In poverty, without a Friend!

When wearied by the cares of home,
(For none so blest but cares will come)
When every thing 'gainst us appears,
And sad and silent flow the tears,
Then surely all our joy must end,
Without some sympathizing Friend.

When death and sickness throw their shade
Across our door—our home invade,
And fill our fireside with gloom,
Or take our lov'd ones to the tomb,
What anguish then our bosom rends !
Oh, how we feel the need of Friends !

When in some strange and distant land,
With none to take us by the hand,
And as 'mong strangers there we roam,
And turn our thoughts toward our home,
What joy to lonliness it lends,
To know that there we still have Friends:—

A brother or a sister dear;
A wife, who sheds the loving tear;
A doting father, or a child;
Whose tender heart is unbeguil'd;
A mother, who in prayer oft bends:—
How lov'd, how dear are all these Friends.

When years of care and toil have fled,
And time has silver'd o'er our head,
And in our furrowed cheeks is traced
The marks of storms we oft have faced,
And our frail form so feebly bends,
What comfort then to still have Friends.

And when our race on earth is run,
And all our work below is done,
And when we look to worlds more fair,

And know but One can take us there,
It does all other joys transcend,
To know that we have such a Friend.

Now if we would have Friends in life.
To cheer us in our toil and strife,
And help us onward day by day,
While passing through life's rugged way,
Our aid to others let us lend;
To others let us be a Friend.

If in a world of joy and bliss,
We hope to live when done with this;
There meet the Friends we love so dear,
With whom we have to part while here;
Let us our life, our labors spend
For Him who lived and died our FRIEND.

------◆------

"AND WE BEHELD HIS GLORY."

"And the Word was made flesh, and dwelt among us, (and we beheld His glory, the glory of the only begotten of the Father,) full of grace and truth."

SUCH glory as no earthly king
    Had ever seen, or monarch known,
Or eye of prince had e'er beheld,
    Around the path of Jesus shone.
        "And we beheld his glory!"

In Him unite the high and low—
    Weakness and strength together meet;
The highest joy, the deepest woe,
    Want, wealth, and" grace and truth " complete.
        "And we beheld his glory!"

Though in a manger with the beasts,
  He came to us in humblest birth,
And seemed of all to be the least,
  Yet He was Lord of heav'n and earth.
    "And we behold his glory!"

With not a place to lay his head,
  He was the poorest of the poor;
Yet He was richest of the rich,
  And brightest crown and robe He wore.
    "And we beheld his glory!"

He was the meekest of the meek;
  Although exalted to the skies:
He felt the weakness of the weak,
  And yet broke satan's strongest ties.
    "And we beheld his glory!"

We see Him resting at the well—
  And asking drink to slake his thirst;
While from Him sweeter waters fell
  Than e're from crystal fountain burst.
    "And we beheld his glory!"

He hungers waiting for the bread
  Which his disciples go to buy;
While He is life—the living bread,
  Which man may eat and never die.
    "And we beheld his glory!"

We see five thousand hungry souls
  Half famished from the want of bread,
While He had neither scrip or purse,
  Yet from his hands they all were fed.
    "And we beheld his glory!"

He had no palace for his guests,
  Nor table rich, to charm their eyes;
But humbly on the grass He sat,
  While He had " mansions in the skies."
    "And we beheld his glory ! "

We see Him weep with those who wept,
  As there He stood beside the grave;
His spirit groan'd for him who slept,
  Although He knew his power to save.
    "And we beheld his glory ! "

He calls ! and at his voice comes forth
  The sleeping dead from out the tomb;—
Faith banishes all doubt and grief,
  And gladness drives away the gloom.
    "And we beheld his glory ! "

And so, when sinners, dead in sin,
  And bound about, and cannot see,
He has the power to break their bands,
  And give them life, and set them free.
    And they'll behold his glory !

We hear him in the garden pray,
  In deepest anguish—all alone,—
"O Father, take this cup away !
  Yet not my will, but thine be done."
    And heav'n beheld his glory !

Oh ! how He gloried in that hour
  When the seventy to Him came,—
Said, " Lord, e'en devils lose their pow'r
  When we rebuke them in thy name."
    "And we beheld his glory ! "

" I've glorified Thee on the earth:
  And now, O Father, glorify
Me with the glory, ere my birth,
  I had with Thee in worlds on high!"
    "And we beheld his glory!"

From heav'n a sweeter message came
  Than ever came from God to man;—
"On earth I've glorified thy name,
  And it I'll glorify again!"
    "And we beheld his glory!"

Beneath the cross His back He bow'd;
  And did beneath his burden groan:
But on the cross He bow'd his head;
  Then, O, what glory 'round Him shone!
    "And we beheld his glory!"

We see Him lying in the grave
  As mortal man—as lifeless clay;
But O, we see God's power to save,
  When the stone is roll'd away!
    "And we beheld his glory!"

'Tis sad! 'tis dark! as there He lies,—
  His friends despond with one accord;
But O, what glory meet their eyes,
  When they behold their risen Lord!
    "And we beheld his glory!"

Did not their hearts within them burn,
  When in the way He met them there;—
Blest, left, and said He would return,
  And mansions for them would prepare.
    And they'll behold his glory!

When we are sad, with care oppress'd.
  Then we may meet with Him in prayer;
And in his presence we'll be blest,
  And see his glory here and there;
    And e'er behold his glory !

"ARISE, AND LET US GO HENCE."

WHEN the supper was ended, the hour come nigh—
    Christ sat with the twelve, where the last bread he
      broke !
  As He spoke of the sop, each said, "Is it I ? "—
    O, what words of sorrow the troubled Lord spoke !

When He sopped the traitor went out.   It was night !—
  The Scripture fulfilled, in the deed he had done;
The hearts of the chosen felt deeply the blight,
  But the glory of God shone bright in His Son.

" O, be not afraid, neither troubled," said He;—
  He felt all the sorrow that saddened each face,
" In my Father's house many mansions there be;
  And thither I go to prepare you a place."

But some of them doubting—their hearts filled with dread--
  Could not see the way to those mansions of bliss;
While others, more trusting, confidingly said,
  "Lord, show us the Father, and it will suffice."

" So long I've been with you, from day unto day,
  Yet dost thou not know me, nor my Father see ?
I am the life, and the truth, and the way;
  And none to the Father can come, but by me.

" If ye love me, then my commandments ye'll keep,
  And I will be with you, and in you will live;
And though for a season ye sorrow and weep,
  The Father I'll pray—He'll the Comforter give.

"And now tothe Father, who sent me, I go;
  My peace I leave with you, (not in the world's sense);
I soon will return, then the Father you'll know,
  And we'll abide with you.—Arise and go hence."

From these blessed words what a lesson we learn,
  As our journey we tread through the desert below,
We'll not linger long where the scorching sands burn;
  But "Arise and go hence," where the sweet waters flow.

When troubles beset us, and sorrow and gloom,
  We will not sit mourning, in doubt and despair;
But reach to the heights where the bright flowers bloom,—
  "Arise and go hence," where the skies are more fair.

When we with misfortune are compassed about,
  And tears of deep sorrow fall thick at our feet,
We'll reach to the hand that is ever stretched out,—
  "Arise and go hence," where He waits us to meet.

When done with temptations—resisted them all,
  And ridden o'er temper and time's sordid sense,
How glad we will list to the words, as they fall
  From the lips of the Master,—"ARISE AND GO HENCE."

-----•-----

THE GOOD SHEPHERD.

"And I will give unto them eternal life; and they shall never perish,
neither shall any *man* pluck them out of my hand."

BEHOLD the "good Shepherd!" How faithful and true!
  Regardless of danger, or labor, or cost.
He seeks without ceasing, the wilderness through,
  Till he finds every sheep that is scattered or lost.

He leaves (though he loves them) the ninety and nine,
  To search for the one that is lost and alone;
"My Father, he gave it to me, it is mine,"
  He says: "though it left me, it still is my own."

And oh, what a joy to the Shepherd it gives,
  To find it—tho' trembling with hunger and cold!
He feared it was dead; but now knows it still lives:—
  On shoulder he takes it again to the fold!

Likewise there's more joy with the angels, they say,
  When a sinner returns to the Shepherd of souls,
Than o'er ninety and nine which went not astray:—
  How tenderly it in his arms he enfolds!

Yes, Arch angels wonder! and Seraphs behold!
  And, oh! what a rapture fills heaven's domain,
When wandering sinners return to the fold,—
  Abide with the Shepherd and sin not again.

There'll be but one Shepherd, and be but one fold:
  The Shepherd won't flee, and no wolf shall appear:
The sheep shall not suffer with hunger or cold,
  Nor tremble nor scatter with terror and fear.

The voice of a stranger the sheep will not hear;
  (For none shall there enter to give them alarm;)
The voice of the Shepherd shall bring them all near,
  And he will watch o'er them, and keep them from harm.

There clear running rivulets never go dry,
  And sweets fields of verdure shall never get gray;
No cloud and no shadow shall darken the sky;
  "No night shall be there;" but one bright endless day.

And there they will rest in that bright, happy land;
  He'll call them by name; and they'll come at his call:
And none shall be able to "pluck from His hand,"
  Nor hand of the Father: He's "greater than all."

CHRISTMAS.

'TWAS Eighteen hundred years ago,
  When on the world did dawn
A light which dim shall never grow:—
  A beatific morn;—

When angels with their song began,—
  "Good news to all we bring:
Great peace, on earth,—good will to men,"
  Through all the earth shall ring!

A Babe is born in Bethlehem,
  Let heav'n the gift record;
Let all the earth, let every man
  Receive Him, King and Lord.

Let heavenly host in highest strains,
  To God all glory give!
Tho' man be dead, and darkness reigns,
  In light he now may live!"

"Jesus," that new born Babe was called:—
  He shall his people save
From sin; and those by death enthrall'd
  He'll ransom from the grave!

When first he entered on his work
  The powers of hell arose:—
He weilded well the sword of God,
  And conquered all his foes.

A victor while in life he liv'd;—
  In death victorious died!
Yes, devils trembled and believ'd
  When he was crucified.

Through death, the pow'r of death shall die,
   And death shall loose its sting.
The boasting grave,—where millions lie—
   Its spoils to Christ shall bring!

Yes, death, the last and strongest foe,
   To him shall yield its power;
And sorrow's tears shall cease to flow,
   And death shall be no more!

Yes, eighteen hundred years ago,
   This glorious day begun!
Its light shall on and ever flow;
   And ne'er shall set its sun.

Though clouds may oft obscure its skies;
   And sin oft sorrow brings;
" The Sun of righteousness shall rise,
   With healing in his wings.''

Then let us praise our Saviour's name!
   Rejoice ye sons of earth!
This is the day the angels came
   With tidings of his birth!

Let all then hail this Holy day;
   Let gifts be freely given:—
This is the Day that earth received
   The greatest gift of heaven.

"*JESUS OF NAZARETH PASSETH BY.*"

WHAT is it breaks upon my ear?
  Whence is the tumult?　What the cry?
It seems to come more near and near:—
  "Jesus of Nazareth passeth by!"

Lo! Jesus now is passing by;
  Arise, ye blind! receive your sight:
Come, trust in Him; on Him rely:
  He'll turn your darkness into light.

Yes, Jesus now is passing by;
  Around Him how the people crowd!
And though they bid you cease your cry,
  Still unto Jesus cry aloud.

Behold! He stops, and bids you come;
  And says, "What will you have me do?"
Now let your wants to Him be known,
  And He will bless and comfort you.

Arise, and go with all thy might;
  Make Him your first—your only choice;
Say, "Lord, restore to me my sight;"
  And He will listen to your voice.

And should your garments cause delay,
  As to Him through the crowd you press,—
Oh, throw them, throw them all away;
  He'll clothe you with his righteousness.

He'll wash the stains of sins away;
  He'll give you garments pure and white;
And all the debt you owe He'll pay,
  And on your hearth is "new name" write.

He will not only sight restore:
　He'll make the lame and leper whole;
The healing balm He'll gently pour;
　He'll soothe—He'll cure the sin sick soul.

Tho' you your substance all have spent,
　And on the husks of sin you've fed,
He will forgive, if you'll repent,
　And feed you with the living bread.

Oh, come to Him while He is nigh:
　You have no friend as dear as He!
He'll be your friend until you die,—
　Your friend through all eternity.

Oh, sinner, come without delay,
　Come, make His holy path your choice:
Perhaps no more He'll pass this way,
　Perhaps no more you'll hear His voice.

Then, come to Him while now He stands:
　No more like Him will e'er pass by;
He'll bless you—take you in His hands,
　And bear you to His home on high.

WHY WE PRAISE THE LORD.

"Oh, that men would praise the Lord for his goodness, and for his wonderful works to the children of men;"

PRAISE, O praise, our dear Redeemer!—
   Praise the Father; praise the Son!—
We will praise Him now and ever,
   For the glorious works He's done.
Praise, O praise, the God of heaven;
   Praise Him all ye hosts above:
Praise on earth to Him be given!—
   Praise Him for his wondrous love!

We will praise Him, for He made us;
   And when we from Him did stray,
Come to Him again, He bade us—
   Said He'd meet us in the way.
Praise Him, for his word has told us,
   E'en when we were dead in sin,
His strong arms would feign enfold us—
   Take us to his fold again.

Praise Him, for He sent to save us—
   Sent his dear—his only Son:
Free the precious gift He gave us,
   Oh! what more could He have done?
Yes, we'll praise our dear Redeemer:
   For He left his home on high;—
Liv'd a life of love and labor;
   And for us did bleed and die.

Praise Him for his love unbounded!
   Praise Him for his matchless grace!—
Saw us faint, and weak, and wounded—
   Came to suffer in our place.
Praise Him, for our feet He's taken
   From the pit of mire and clay—
Plac'd them on a "Rock" unshaken—
   Turn'd our darkness into day!

Praise Him, for when we were dying
  For the want of "living bread,"
And on our own strength relying,
  He our fainting spirits fed!
Praise Him, for when we were thirsting,
  He beheld us near death's brink,
Show'd us water freely bursting
  From the Rock, and bade us drink!

Praise Him, for when we were blindly
  Groping through the gloom of night,
Then He came to us so kindly,
  Touched our eyes and gave us sight.
We will praise Him, for He's told us
  In his ever blessed word,
That his eyes always behold us,
  And his ears our cries have heard.

But the work for which we praise Him
  Most of all,—his life He gave
To destroy the sting of dying,
  And the vict'ry of the grave!
Praise Him, O, adore and wonder!
  Was such love e'er known before?
See Him burst death's bands asunder—
  Open wide the prison door!

Praise his name! for He has told us,
  They who live, and do believe,
Though the arms of death enfold us,
  Shall eternal life receive.
Then we'll praise Him while here living!
  Yes, we'll praise; and serve and love,
When immortal life is given—
  Praise Him with the hosts above!

I WILL RETURN.

"Return unto me and I will return unto you, saith the Lord of hosts."

WHEN men were dead in sin, the Lord
   Looked down from heaven above,
And said " 'Tis time that they should see
   And know my wondrous love.

I sent my Prophets, one by one,
   But men would not believe;
And now at last I'll send my Son,
   Perhaps they'll Him receive."

Then to his only Son He said,
   "Are you prepared to go
And desecrate that sacred head,
   That man my love may know?

Must you unto the earth descend,—
   Your life a ransom give
To prove to man I am his friend,
   And show him how to live"?

And then said Christ, "O God! I come,
   As it is writ of me:
I leave my high, my heavenly home,
   That man the way may see."

And when on earth the Lord appeared,
   The angels did rejoice;
And my faint heart, which long had feared,
   How glad to hear his voice!

I've often lean'd upon his breast;
   I've oft knelt at his feet,
By day, by night, in Him found rest;—
   My joy it seemed complete.

But now my faith, it has grown weak;
  I've left the heavenly way;
The praise that's due I cease to speak,
  His word fail to obey.

The light which in my bosom shone,
  And which the Lord had said,
I unto others should make known,
  I 'neath a bushel hid.

Alas! from Him I've wandered far,
  Where once I was so near!
I dimly see hope's guiding star,
  Which used to seem so clear!

The fruit on which my soul once fed
  Still hangs upon the tree;
The cross on which my Saviour bled
  Still stained, still stands for me!

I'll go and fall before his face;
  I'll ask Him to forgive;
His love, so sweet, I will embrace;
  I'll eat life's bread and live.

From Him no more I'll go astray,
  My vows I'll now renew:
His holy word I will obey,
  Unto the end be true.

At morn and noon to Him I'll pray,
  At eve his praise I'll sing.
He is the life, the truth, the way,—
  My Lord! My God! My King!

His wondrous love I will proclaim,
  That love which makes us free;
That light I'll fan into a flame,
  That all the world may see.

"MEET me in the morning, Mamma,"
  Were the words of a darling boy,
The only son—away to school—
  His widowed mother's hope and joy;—

A telegram contained the words,—
  The first her Willie ever sent;
With pride and joy she read it o'er,
  As 'bout the house all day she went.

She read, and showed it to her friends,—
  To each and all who called that day,
And as she read it, now and then,
  She'd wipe love's starting tear away.

And some suggested she should hang
  It o'er the mantle in a frame,
That all who come could read it o'er,
  And see beneath it Willie's name.

At length upon a scrap book leaf
  She pasted it, with the intent
That he in years to come might read
  The telegram which first he sent.

Just one year he had been away,—
  Ne'er before so long from home—
And sent the message on the day
  Before the morn he thought to come.

All that long night—but half asleep—
  The mother's heart in dreams of joy,
Looked to the morn she hoped to meet,
  And to her bosom clasp her boy.

At early morn, before the sun
  Had sent his rays across the plain,
She rose, and preparation made
  To meet her Willie at the train.

But just before the time to leave,
  A hasty rap came to the door;—
Another telegram was there;—
  Not like the one the day before.

The mother with her eager hands—
  Her nervous frame could scarce keep still—
Opened and read these startling words,
  "Come quickly! Willie's very ill!"

She started for the early train;
  And for the time could scarcely wait:
She met her darling boy that day,
  Yet, met him! but just met too late!

He lay, unconscious on his bed, .
  And seemed not her to recognize;
She bent her form down close to his,—
  Looked in his loving, half closed eyes;

She spoke, and called him by his name,
  When these sweet words he faintly said,
"Meet me in the morning, Mamma."
  His eyes then closed; his spirit fled.

Ah! mother, grieve not for your boy;
  But lift your soul where his has gone;
And though you meet no more on earth,
  You'll meet him where 'tis always morn.

Though here you hear his voice no more,
  Nor look into his loving eyes,
He calls from where the skies are bright,
  And fairer than Italian skies.

In many a sad and lonely hour,—
  While tears give to your sorrow vent,—
You'll read the message on the leaf;—
  The first and last he ever sent.

You'll twine around your mourning heart,
  The message, like a broken wreath,
And gather up the memories fresh,
  And bind them with the name beneath.

And when these eyes no more can see
  These words—obscured by evening's shade—
Then in a greater book you'll read
  Your name and his,—no more to fade.

No message from a dying boy,
  Will ever turn your joy to pain,
Nor o'er a death-bed will you bend,
  To give the parting kiss again.

As morn and noon and night roll 'round
  To you may these words ever come:
"Meet me in the morning, Mamma;—
  Meet me in the morn at home.

The message I from heav'n may send,
  You may not place upon a leaf;
But on the tablet of your heart,
  To cover up the marks of grief.

I have here sweeter lessons learn'd
  Than e'er my earthly teacher knew,
And when you come, my dear Mamma·
  Then I will tell them all to you."

SPEAK KINDLY.

SPEAK kindly, speak kindly, there's sorrow and care
Enough in the world which we now have to hear.—
Off bitter enough in our pathway will fall;
Then don't spoil the pleasant and sweet with the gall.

Speak kindly, speak kindly, don't pile on the wood,
With fire already too hot to be good.
When the fire burns low, and we scarce can keep warm,
Don't drive the shivering ones out in the storm.

Be kind to the children,—their hearts soft and young,—
Are oftentimes pierced by the thorn of the tongue:
Don't speak to them harshly, or torture with fear;—
For often a kind word will dry up a tear;—

Though oft they be wayward in deed or in word,
O, let not your bosom with anger be stirred;
For gladly, perhaps, when they're wiht you no more,
You'd hear their sweet voices—see them romp as before.

Be kind to the aged, whose wrinkled brow bears
The marks of long years, and of sorrows and cares:
When we, young and playful, they kindly caressed,—
Our hearts to their bosoms so tenderly pressed !

Speak kindly; speak kindly; speak kindly to all:
Let no angry words from your lips ever fall;—
They seldom do good, while they often give pain,—
And oft, when we cannot, we'd take back again.

LIFE.

"What is your life? It is even a vapor, that appeareth for a little time, then vanisheth away."

OUR life is like a shadow brief, that quickly passes by;
Or like the grass that's green to-day, to-morrow mown
    and dry;
  'Tis like the vapor which the sun drives from the
    morning air,
  Or worldly pleasures, oft whose tracks are trodden
    by despair;

'Tis like the flower of a day, that flourishes at morn,
Which, when the evening shadows fall, its beauty all is
    gone;
'Tis like the vivid lightning's flash, or meteor of the skies:—
Before we get a perfect view, its brilliant beauty dies;—

'Tis like the spray upon the sea, or like the ocean wave,—
Just as we think 'tis springing up 'tis buried in the grave;—
'Tis like the stone thrown in the lake, that sinks from
    mortal sight,
Or washes on the distant shore, all polished, smooth and
    bright.

Life's deeds are like the ripples smooth, that circle it around,
That widen on and widen till they reach the distant bound:
They'll flow on and flow ever, when this mortal life is o'er,—
Out on the sea with depths unknown, the sea without a
    shore.

Then cast the stone in gently, that the ripples smoothly
    glide,
And not go grating harshly as they reach the other side;
But polished, tried and fitted—of every shape and size—
To build the house eternal, with its mansions, in the skies.

BE NOT DISMAYED.

THE morning sun is oft obscured,
  And that of noon-day dimly seen,
Yet hope lights up the evening sky;
  With setting sun—bright and serene.

'Tis not the brightest, sun-lit day
  That brings refreshing to the flow'rs;
'Tis when the evening shadows fall,
  'Tis 'neath the reign of darkest hours.

Oftimes the fairest flow'r of morn,
  Bathed in the dew—kissed by the sun—
Will lose its beauty ere the noon,
  And wither ere the day is done.

While climbing up the hill of time,
  Its height may hide the star of hope,
Whose brightness will our brow enwreath
  While passing down the gentle slope.

While some are toiling up the way,
  They by the hundreds may be passed,
But ere they reach their journey's end
  They may be first—the first be last.

The fastest runner in the start,
  Not always with the prize is crowned,
But they who run with steady zeal,
  May victors in the end be found.

Yet we will press towards the mark,
  With all the strength that God hath given;
And if we fail to grasp the prize
  On earth, it will be won in heaven.

SONG OF THE MORNING.

The following was written on a bright Sunday morning in June, between sunrise and breakfast hour, when all Nature seemed to be saying, "It is a good thing to give thanks unto the Lord, and to sing praises unto thy name, O Most High: to show forth thy loving kindness in the morning."

O HAPPY! happy! morning, for the sun is shining
    brightly,
  And the birds are singing sweetly in the trees;
  And the flow'rs they are smiling at the rays that
    kiss them lightly,
  While the willow's waving gently to the breeze.

CHORUS.

But these are only shadows of the beauties which are
  beaming
  Far beyond the blue, and golden studded sky;
For, from that land of glory we now only have a gleaming:
  But will see it in its beauty by and by.

The sheep are gently grazing, and the little lambs are
  skipping
  In the shadows which reach far upon the plain:
The cows are wending slowly, while the herbage they are
  nipping,
  As they pass along the heavy shaded lane.

The dew-drops on the leaflets, like bright diamonds are all
  glowing,
  And the bees are bringing honey to their store;
Through green and waving meadow, see, the babbling
  brook is flowing,
  As it strikes its note of music 'long the shore!

Then who cannot be happy when all Nature is united:
  And its beauties and its blessings 'round us throng?
The thoughtless, and the thankless, and despondent, are
    invited
  To help to swell the chorus of the song.

Surrounded by these blessings, which so beautify the
    morning,
  We'll go gladly to the labors of the day;
And through the noon and evening, we'll behold a brighter
    dawning,
  Which will guide, and cheer, and bless us, by the way.

But church-time is approaching, and the bells will soon
    be ringing:—
  Don't you hear their sweet and merry "ding-dong-del?"
Ten thousand happy voices are united now in singing,
  As the anthem and the chorus loudly swell!

THE CUP AND SAUCER.

Lines to my little granddaughter Jennie, on receiving from her a
Cup and Saucer, February 4, 1885.

MY little Granddaughter, the pleasant surprise
You gave me last eve, to these verses gave rise.
The beauteous colors, so blended and twin'd,
While pleasing the eye, bring up to the mind
That little hot-house of buds tender and young;—
Warmed by affection,—from which this gift sprung;
The green and the orange, the purple and gold,
Hang thick at the doorway, and keep out the cold.

May the bright Sun of Love ever shine through the pane,
And the streams of affection fall soft as the rain;
May the eye of discretion look well the beds o'er,
And the hand of protection keep guard at the door.
As oft as this Cup I shall raise to my lip,—
As oft as the thirst-quenching water I sip,—
Of the giver I'll think with affection,—I hope,
More lasting than emblems entwining the cup.

May your heart keep as pure, and your pathway as bright,
As the saucer and cup, with the ground-work so white;
May the vine of affection the young and the old
Unite, as the vine does, the purple and gold.
The colors are varied, yet all sweetly blend,—
So life will be varied from now to its end!—
But though they may vary they cling to the vine,
So may truth's endless chain all your virtues combine;

And like the gold bandage around the Cup's rim,
May Love's golden chain ever bind you to Him
Who of all was most humble—most holy of all;
Yet drank of the cup which was bitter as gall.
And may you remember the sweet words He said,
When He drank of the cup, and with thanks broke the
        bread,
And be one of those who shall feast on His love,
And drink of that cup in His kingdom above.

THE WATER OF LIFE.

"In the last day, that great day of the feast, Jesus stood and cried, saying, "If any man thirst, let him come unto me, and drink."

O FATHER! kind Father! my faint spirit thirsts
For th' water of life, which unceasingly bursts
From the pure crystal fountain—the river which flows
To wash away sin, and to heal all its woes.
I ask not the depth of this river so clear;
But Father, dear Father! O, let me come near,
And drink of the water, which runs o'er its banks,
For this my faint heart will rejoice and give thanks.

The true and the faithful, the pure and the good,
May drink of the depth of this unebbing flood;—
May feast of thy bounty, may eat of the bread
With which thy large table so richly is spread:—
I've tasted its sweetness; I've been at the feast,
I've sat with thy guest, though of all them the least:—
But I do not ask for,—though faint and so poor,—
The best of thy blessings, the choice of thy store.

But Father, dear Father! for this I would pray,
O, let not my feet wander so far away,
That I'll hear not thy voice, nor see thy bright face,
Nor feel the sweet joy of thy comforting grace.
If thou art my Father; if I am thy child,
O, let not my weak heart by sin be beguil'd;
But let my feet follow the Master divine,
Till the love of His heart be reflected from mine.

For this, gracious Father, for this would I pray,—
To make me more watchful, more zealous each day;
More gentle, more patient, and ever increase
In praise and thanksgiving, in prayer not to cease;
To hush my complainings; to dry up my tears;
To fill me with trust, and to banish my fears;
To bear and forbear, to forgive and endure.—
All this may be done by life's water, so pure!

This life-giving water I need every day,
To cleanse and to strengthen, along life's rough way;
I need it at morning; I need it at noon;
I need it at evening, as night needs the moon;
I'll need it, I'll need it, in life's latest hour,
So fresh, full and free, with its comforting pow'r!
I need it each moment; thou Lord knowest how
I need it, I need it, I need it just now!

O, give me life's water, sin's passions to cool,—
The sweet crumbs which fall from thy table so full;
That faith may grow stronger; that sight may grow clear,
Thy presence more precious, and heaven more near:
O, raise up my soul by the pow'r of thy grace;
Each day let me sit in some heavenly place,
Till strong in thy might, by thy grace I shall soar,
To drink of the depth of thy love evermore!

O, Father, I now feel the water, so sweet!
Refreshing my heart, giving strength to my feet:
I feel thy soft hand, as so gently 'tis press'd;—
The life-giving water spring up in my breast.
Abide with me, Father; don't leave me to-night!—
The stream of thy love, with its rapt'ous delight,
Flow over my heart, and continue to flow,
Until it is whiter and purer than snow!

Through Jesus, the Life, and the Truth, and the Way;
We come to Thee, Father, from day unto day:
There's no other fountain to which we can go
And drink living water, but Christ, here below;
And no other name among men hath been giv'n,
Whereby the dead soul can be raised up to heav'n,—
Whereby we may gather around the great throne,
And drink of that fountain to mortals unknown!

BEAUTY.

SURFACE beauty soon shall fade:
   Its luring charms shall pass away;
The youthful blush shall leave the maid,
   When bends her form, and hair grows gray.

Then if no other beauty lies
   Within the casket of the heart,
When outward beauty from her flies,
   All beauty from her then must part.

But should all outward beauty fly
   From those with whom dwell love and truth,
These graces still look through the eye,
   And hold the charms they won in youth.

ELCOME TO EIGHTEEN HUNDRED AND EIGHTY-FOUR.

OH, welcome, welcome, Eighty-four!
  Of thee we hear, but cannot know,
If from thy hidden hand shall pour
Upon us grace, or want, or woe.

But still we hail with joy thy birth,
  Since thou art of that ancient line
Of monarchs now beneath the earth—
  The last, the nearest kin of thine.

Though nearest kin, no two, alas!
  Together ever dwell on earth,
Or meet but once, then quickly pass:—
  They only meet at death and birth.

We know not if bright flowers shall bloom
  Along the path thy feet shall tread,
Or whether thorns, and blight, and gloom,
  O'er us thy unseen hand shall spread.

We know not if thy skies shall frown
  Before the shadows eastward fall,
Or whether when thy sun goes down,
  Bright golden beams shall gild thy pall.

We know not if upon thy thigh,
  Thy glitt'ing sword is half unsheath'd,
Or whether o'er thy placid eye,
  The vine and olive branch are wreathed.

We think we see around thy head,
  The morning twilight's gilded rays;
And as the path of time you tread,
  We hope for bright and peaceful days.

We think we see a smile serene,
  As morning breaks upon thy face;—
The gloom of night no longer seen,
  As streams of light the shadows chase.

And now we feel thy presence near;
  To thee our doors we'll open wide;
No evil from thy hand we'll fear,
  But we will trust thee—though untri'd.

We've lived beneath the gracious reign
  Of other monarchs of thy line,
And found the joy outweighed the pain;
  And trust we'll find the same 'neath thine.

We've felt the bitter and the sweet;
  The beating storm and cheering sun;
And still expect through life to meet
Both good and ill, till life is done.

At thy approach the bells we'll chime,
  As chimed the bells of eighty-three;
Be lifted up ye gates of time!—
  Swing back and make the entrance free!

Ye ceaseless wheels of time roll on;
  Vibrate thou pond'rous pendulum!
Move 'round ye hands, point out the morn,
  Which tells of brighter days to come.

We trust our faith will not prove vain,
  Nor vain the hopes our bosoms store;
Then gladly we repeat again,
  Welcome, welcome, eighty-four!

AN ACROSTIC.

ONG all the gifts with which we meet,
Young babes appear most dear and sweet.

Like little angels, from above,
In search of hearts to fill with love;—
To cheer sad hours of lonliness;—
To warm our hearts, and labors bless.—
Like spring-time buds and blossoms fair,
Enchanting by their beauties rare.—

Germs of pure innocence and love;
Robed in raiment from above.
Are they not " minist'ring spirits sent ? "
(Not *given* us, but only *lent*).
Does not the Word say, " Treat them well,"—
Do for them while with us they dwell ?
And we their little steps should train;—
Unknown how long they may remain:—
Guard them in all their helpless hours:
Heaven has made this duty ours.
Then we should try, while them we have,
Each day to show them how to live.
Repaid are all who *rightly* give.

In asking good, I would implore,
Dear Babe, on thee the choicest store.
And on thy head may blessings pour.

Virtue with modesty, candor and truth,
Inspire thy young heart in childhood and youth.
" Remember thy Maker in youth," it is said:—
God, He will prepare a bright crown for thy head.
In all of thy journey He'll never forsake
Nor leave thee, nor from thee thy crown ever take.
In faith and obedience, lean on his arm;
And He will be with thee and keep thee from harm.

Patience will bless thee when trials assail;
Religion will keep thee, though all else may fail:
Industry gives competence, oftentimes wealth.
Caution and prudence add much to thy health.
Embellished are they, who these precepts obey.

Be kind then, Dear Parents, to Baby, and pray,
Yourselves to be able to show it the way.

And think not, nor say not, "There's time, we will wait."

So thinking, so saying, it may be too late.

But let it not draw all thy heart from above.
O, never forget Him who sent it in love!
You should not—as some have done—wait till the *tie*
Departs from the *earth*, and then calls from the *sky*.

————————◆————————

IN BLESSING WE ARE BLEST.

IF we'd take flowers in our hands,
As passing through life's desert sands,
They'd cause some saddened heart to glow—
Some eye which never saw them grow.

If we would lend a hand to guide
The drifting souls on life's rough tide,
'Twould bring to many a wander'r rest,
And make our voyage doubly blest.

If we can sing some cheering song,
As on life's road we pass along,
It comfort may, and gladness bring,
To those who cannot walk or sing.

"DON'T FORGET US, PA."

On a Sunday evening, in May, after accompanying my daughter and her husband a short distance on their way to church, I left and bade them good-bye, to leave the city on Monday morning, and in doing so, as we parted, my daughter spoke the words under which these lines are written.

"DON'T forget us, Pa"! were the last words that fell
On my ears, as parting I bade them farewell.
'Twas on the street corner, the last Sunday eve
In May just past, when I of them took leave.
'Twas my daughter who spoke them, standing beside
Of him who with her's had his destiny tied.
Each of whom promised that while life should prolong,
To cherish and nourish that love—then so strong.

Each heart to the other had not only vow'd,
But in God's holy house together had bow'd,
As drops of pure water fell soft on their brow,
And angels, with gladness, recorded the vow.
'Twas thither, when parting, they wended their way,
To listen and learn, and to praise and to pray,—
To eat the hid manna which God has prepar'd,
And drink from the cup which His bounty had shar'd.

"Don't forget us, Pa"! 'twas so plaintive, and yet
She could not have thought I would ever forget.
What! a father forget?—From love's memory part,
While pictures hang fresh on the wall of the heart?
By "Don't forget us," then, what could she have meant?
Was it thoughtlessly said, or with earnest intent?
To me did the words all their meaning impart,
As they from her lips, fell soft on my heart?

The sentence was brief, but its briefness was fraught
With blossoms which burst from the small buds of thought;
Which grew till the bush was so full, not a few
Dropped off and fell soft where the tiny buds grew.
Yes, brief were the words, yet they reached to my heart;—
Forged a link in the chain which time cannot part;—
Dropped a seed in the soil, which quickly took root,
And grew to a tree, which is dropping its fruit.—

But did she design that it ever should spring,
Or blossoms should bear, or fruit ever bring?
Or was it chance seed, which she dropped from her hand
Unnoticed, which fell on the soft fertile land?
On the soft fertile land, not rocky and bear,
Exposed to the to the sun and the fowls of the air;
But in the deep soil where the roots are kept wet
And tended by Him who will never "forget."

But where did she gather the seed she let fall?
Was it sown in her heart when life's twig was small?
And did the spring's sunshine and summer's soft show'rs
Cause the young buds to swell—to burst into flow'rs?
May sunshine of hope and the showers of grace
All darkness and doubt from her bosom erase.—
May the flowers of thought—like the sweet scented rose
Which sweetness receives from the bush where it grows—
Their sweetness receive from the Master divine,
The offspring of David, the "*root*" and the "*vine!*"

May the streams of God's mercy—loves flowing tide,
Keep clean her heart and his who walks by her side;
And ebb not, except to bring back to the shore,
The waves of God's love, as profusely they pour.
O, may these waves roll till they every heart reach,
And wash them as white as the shells on the beach;—
Till millions of millions be washed in His name,
And roll back the white waves as pure as they came!

"Don't forget us, Pa," but faintly express'd
The unspoken thoughts,—at which quickly I guess'd—
That when we were parted, and I went to prayer,
On the wings of my heart I to heaven would bear,
In kindly remembrance, a strong, earnest plea,
That they from all sin and temptation be free—
That God's Holy Spirit—blest heavenly dove,
Would bear down to them, on the wings of his love,
Some message of mercy—some kind word of cheer,
And strength to endure till the end shall draw near;—
Confirming the sweet truth, that virtue is gain—
That their labors of love have not been in vain.
O, Father of mercies, we pray Thee to let
Such blessings descend that they will *not* "*forget !*"

And I will remember each sweet, balmy May—
The month of the flowers—the *Twenty-first* day;
The day when her Mother—now parted—gave birth
To the newly-born infant, then ushered on earth.
And oft may this May-day its visits repeat,
And bring with it memories sacred and sweet—
The birds and the flowers, and mild azure sky;
All telling us plainly that summer is nigh.

And, if I forget not, 'twas also in May,
A bright balmy morning on God's holy day,
You laid on His altar the love of your heart,
And in His good work you resolved to take part.
May the thoughts of that happy day often revive—
The sweet bread of heaven your soul keep alive—
The flowers which oft have been strewn in your way.
And the seed you have sown on each Sabbath day,
All tell you the summer of harvest will come,
When sower and reaper their fruit will bring home.

May you then gather up all the sheaves you have bound—
Reap the fruit of the seed you've dropped on the ground—
Show the sweat on your brow, and the marks on your hands,
Made by the sun and the thorns 'neath the bands.
May you with your partner have stamped on your breast
The marks of your toiling when you go to rest;
And then the Inspector of souls won't "forget"
To mark, and to crown you with love's coronet'

----------•----------

ILLS AND AIDS.

TEMPORAL ills need temporal aids:
    But if we cannot them procure,
There is a pow'r which earth pervades,
    By which we may those ills endure.

If any should desponding say,
"There is, in life's uneven way,
A place where thorns infest the ground;
Nor flow'r nor fruit has yet been found;"

We would to such, advice bestow,
And bid them onward, upward go;
'Tis not their duty or their lot,
To dwell in such a gloomy spot.

Now, listen to the Master's call:—
The invitation is to all,—
To every one by sin oppress'd,—
"Come unto me, I'll give you rest."

WHEN Jesus left Judea's land to go to Galilee,
He must go through Samaria and Sychar, by the way:
    And hungry, tired and thirsty, thus He sat upon the
        well,—
    Which Jacob unto Joseph gave, near where they used
        to dwell.

His disciples to the city had gone to buy some meat,
While there He sat beside the well, to rest His weary feet:—
A woman of Samaria,—as she approached its brink,—
Saw Jesus sitting, resting there: who said, "Give me to
        drink."

The woman was astonished when she saw He was a Jew,
(For Jews with the Samaritans have not a thing to do)
And said to Him, "How is it, sir, thou askest drink of me—
A woman of Samaria?—a thing so strange to see!"

"If thou hadst known the gift of God," He said, "or
        hadst known me,
Thou would'st have living-water asked, and I would'st give
        to thee."
She did not understand His words, and neither could she
        tell
From whence the living-water was, or how drawn from
        the well.

And then she said unto Him—when no bucket there she
        saw—
"The well is very deep, sir, and you've not a thing to draw,—
Art thou greater than our father, who gave it ere he died,
Drank of it, and his children, and his children were
        supplied?"

" Whoso drinketh of this water shall thirst again," said He,
" But the water I shall give him, a well of life shall be;
It shall spring up forevermore, and they who drink shall
          live;
And unto all who ask of me, this water I will give."

" Sir, give me of this water pure, that I thirst not, nor come
As I so oft have heretofore,—to draw and bear it home:
This water is so hard to draw, so far from where we live;
Sir, I will thank thee greatly for the water thou wilt give."

" Go call thy husband, and return," then Jesus said to her:
She, in reply, said unto Him, " I have no husband, sir."
" Thou hast well said; thou hast had five; he who now lives
          with you,
Is not thy husband, and in that thou saidst very true."

" Thou art a prophet, I perceive," she said, (for all she did,
Both good and bad, she plainly saw, from Him could not
          be hid).
" Our fathers worshipped in this mount; Jerusalem ye say,
Is were the worshippers should go, when'er they praise or
          pray."

" Believe me, woman," then He said, " the hour now is
          come,
When worshippers may worship God in every heart and
          home:
Ye need not to Jerusalem go to meet with Him in pray'r;
For they who worship God in truth, may find Him every-
          where.

God is a Spirit; and all they who would His presence prove,
May find Him, if they truly seek; and find that Spirit love.
He seeks the true, where'er they be—in all the land abroad;
And sinners, too, who Him receive, become the sons of
          God."

"I know Messias cometh, who will tell us all,' said she:
Then Jesus answered plainly, "I that speak to thee am
    He."—
With joy she left her water-pot, and to the city fled,
And cried, "Come see! Is this not Christ?—such won-
    drous things He said!

He told me of a well so pure, whose waters never dry;
And they who drink shall thirst no more, and never, never
    die!
O, how my bosom throbbed with joy, while list'ning to
    His word,
Which fell so sweetly on my ear! This must be Christ
    the Lord!"

Yes, it was Christ the Lord, who spoke, and to her did reveal
The truth she felt within her heart—which yours and
    mine may feel.
The water which He said He'd give, she would with thanks
    receive;
And all who drink of it may live, if they, like her, believe.

This water flows for you and me;—so freely flows for all.
"The Spirit and the bride say, Come!" O! don't you hear
    them call?
"O, whosoever will may come; and Him that heareth say,
Come, take and drink;"—it is so free that none need stay
    away.

It gushes from the hill-tops high; it sparkles in the vales,—
Runs down the smiling valleys low, flows on, and never
    fails!
It widens as it lengthens; and it deepens as it flows;
It will satisfy your longings, and wash away your woes!

It winds around the tree of life,—refreshing all its root;
It makes its blossoms fragrant, and its boughs to bend
     with fruit!—
Its branches strong and spreading, its foliage rich and
     thick;—
A shelter for the weary souls, and leaves to heal the sick.

It is lessened not in flowing, nor lost in Jordan's tide;
But helps to swell the sea of life upon the other side:
'Twill there spring up forevermore,—forever rise and
     swell;—
The very self-same water Jesus spoke of at the well.

He'll not be tired and weary there, resting beside its brink;
Nor wait till any come to draw, to ask of them a " drink; "
But drawing living water fresh, from God's eternal well,
Within the holy city where the happy angels dwell!

And He, with His disciples, when the ev'ning shades appear,
Will no more leave the city, for the mountain, lone and
     drear;
But with those who entertained Him so kindly in the town,
He'll dwell in that bright city, where the sun will ne'er
     go down.

And they who drink this water in the valley here below,
May trace it to the mountain, where it ceases not to flow;—
Their hearts will beat with gladness as they never beat
     before,
When they the crystal fountain see, with water gushing e'er!

They will not have to carry, neither draw the water up;
But each one from the fountain pure, may take a golden
     cup;—
Which hangs so brightly burnish'd, with inscriptions rich
     and rare:—
Their eyes will look with gladness on the names engraven
     there!

And then with untold rapture to each other they will say,
" This is the self-same water that we drank of on the way;
But we its fulness never knew; but now 'tis true we know,
What Jesus used to tell us when we supped with Him
     below !

And His beloved disciples,—those who went to buy the
     meat,—
Will never thirst or hunger more, or pay for bread to eat:
For bending o'er the fountain pure, the tree of life shall be;
And Christ will take its precious fruit and give it to them
     free!

And then they'll know what Jesus had when they return'd
     with meat;
And will not ask if "any one hath brought Him aught to
     eat,"
But " hidden manna," they'll behold, all white on Zion's
     hill,
And know 'tis meat and drink, indeed, to do the Father's
     will !

The people of the city, where the woman ran with speed,
Shall for themselves behold; and know that this is Christ,
     indeed;
And on Him they will not believe, just for the woman's
     word,
But will receive such precious truths as mortals never
     heard !

The woman of Samaria—who saw no bucket near—
Shall know from whence the water was, and drink it pure
     and clear:—
Shall see the bucket rising, and the water running o'er !
She then will understand His words, and doubt Him
     never more,

This well, it will be deeper than the well of long ago,
Where th' children used to draw and drink, and cattle
    come and low:
And He who draws the water, 'twill be very plain to tell—
Will be "greater than" their "father," who gave to them
    the well.

The Master's drawing water now—so fresh! and full! and
    free!—
Inviting "whosoever will:"—including you and me:
And bands of blessed angels the glad chorus loudly swell —
"O, come! O, come to Jesus now! He's waiting at the
    well!"

He's waiting, as He calls to you, with bucket running o'er;
To quench your thirst and cool your brow, and feet, so
    tired and sore!
He's felt the thorns, the heat, the thirst,—drank of the cup
    of woe,
And knows how blest it is to rest where living waters flow!

LET IN THE LIGHT.

THE flow'rs in shaded wood or vale,
May long for light,—with faces pale;
But if we cut away the brush,
They'll show their thanks in beauty's blush.

So, often if the darken'd heart,
Will push the boughs of doubt apart,
The waiting sun's refulgent rays,
Will turn the sighing into praise.

THE OLD SCHOOL HOUSE.

———

First Public School of Washington, D. C.; organized in 1804: Thos.
Jefferson, President of School Board. The other Trustees were Robert
Brent, S. H. Smith, Thos. Monroe, William Cranch, William Brent,
John Demphies, Nicholas King, Gab. Duvall and Geo. Blagdin.

The house is now (1884) occupied as a carpenter's shop, by Notley
Anderson.

———

THE suns of forty winters cold,
  And forty summers warm,
And many a calm and pleasant day,
  And many a beating storm,
Have fallen on the old school house,
  Since first I ope'd its door,
And from the teacher to my seat
  I trod the foot-worn floor;

Since first against the whitewash'd wall
  I hung my coat and hat,
And at the rough, inked, knife-notch'd desk,
  On backless bench I sat.
And there we spelled, read, wrote and talked,
  With one eye on our book,
And with the other, now and then,
  We'd at the teacher look:—

Who sometimes came and stung our ears
  With a small cowhide's heart,
Or drew our pants tight 'round our calves,
  And how he'd make them smart!
Which we then thought was very hard,—
  At least, not very kind,
And sometimes may have said, within,
  " I'll fix you,—never mind ! "

But now I venerate that hand,
  Which gently bore the rod,
And that kind heart, and lips which led
  My feet in paths they've trod;—
For if on any heart or hand
  With gratitude we look,
It is the one whose pages bright,
  First wrote in memory's book.—

I'd been away for thirty years,
  And, much to my surprise,
When I returned, the old school house,
  Still standing, met my eyes.
I trod upon the foot-worn sill,
  With rev'rent step, and slow,—
Much slower than I used to tread
  In days of long ago;—

Passed down to where I used to sit,
  With arms on desk, and bent,
(Just here I scarce could check the tears,
  Through which my heart sought vent.)
Saw Comly's spelling book, as then,
  All worn, and yellow bound,
And of the spelling, now as then,
  Could almost hear the sound;—

"Abandon—to give up; forsake.
  Abase—is to bring low.
Abash—to make ashamed; confuse;
  Abate—to lessen." So
Over the pages oft we went,
  And o'er and o'er again;
And sometimes not so much to learn
  As not to be kept in.

Two boys, before and after noon,
　　In turn and turn about,
Brought 'round the large tin water pot,
　　And all drank from the spout.
On Fridays we'd hold up our hands
　　To get to sweep the room,
That we on Monday eve might go,
　　Two hours earlier home;

When oft with baskets we would go
　　About two miles from town,
And blackberries and cherries get
　　From farmer Jesse Brown;
Apples and pears from John A. Smith's—
　　Where now the Soldiers' Home
Is built—and home with happy hearts,
　　And baskets filled, we'd come.

We read of Jackson's cotton forts,
　　On Mississppi's shore,
So we, with snow-balls and snow forts,
　　Would fight his battles o'er.
The forts we built just o'er the way:—
　　Near the old Foundry wall;—
And how we'd run, and cheer, and charge!
　　When we would see them fall.

The name of Henshaw still is fresh:
　　(This was the teacher's name.)
I see the picture now as then,
　　As in the door he came,—
Took off his hat, and took his seat,
　　Or by his desk would stand,
And wave his hand, or bow his head,
　　Attention to command:—

Then slowly from the good, old Book,
  A chapter he would read,
And would explain it, here and there,
  As onward he'd proceed—
Perhaps about the "needle's eye,"
  "Old bottles" and "new wine,"
Or of the "fishes" and the "loaves,"
  Or "demons" 'mong the "swine."

The lessons which I learned of him,
  I never have forgot,
Although the pages of my life
  Are stained with many a blot:
Yet back of all, and through them all,
  I see the lessons taught,
And know that through the years long past,
  Much good for me they've wrought.

The pictures made on minds when young,
  Like those on canvass bare,
Will often come before our eyes,
  And seem more clear and fair,
Than those the hand of time may paint,
  O'er pictures ready made;
Though time may paint with colors strong,—
  Of deepest hue and shade.

Of all the scholars of that school,
  I used to know so well,
I know but two; the most are gone,
  But where I cannot tell.
Some in the city still may be,—
  May pass it every day;
While some have died, and others live
  Perhaps long miles away.

But still there stands the old school house,
 Just where it stood of yore:
The same old walls, the same old roof,
 The same old swinging door;
Behind which stood the axe and broom,
 Where oft we hid our bats,
And just above them hung our skates
 And balls 'neath coats and hats.—

The same old tree, though taller now,
 (I think it is the same,) ·
'Neath which we used to eat our lunch,—
 Play many a youthful game
Of marbles, tops, and quoits, and ball,
 Or resting, oft would sit
Upon the log where many a turn
 Of kindling-wood we split.

The commons where we used to play
 Steal-clothes and pris'ner's base,
Are no more green, but houses thick
 Now occupy the place.
The school house, in a few more years,
 Will go and be forgot;
The hand of time from every mind
 Its memories will blot.

In forty years to come, or less,
 The school house will be gone,
And all of those who filled its seats
 In life's bright sunny morn;
And other structures take its place,
 Which other eyes shall see,
But nevermore the old school house,
 On Fourteenth street and G.

Of all the public schools of which
   Our city now may boast,
This was the first, and may be call'd
   The mother of the host
Of eight and twenty thousand strong,
   And schools at least six score,—
Whose birth and lineage may date
   From eighteen hundred—four.

Five hundred teachers and three score,
   At work on human minds,
In years to come, what they now write,
   May read in living lines.
Their work will last when they are gone;
   When marble shaft and bust
Shall fade, and, like the fallen leaves,
   Shall mingle with the dust.

Then, as you write, or carve, or cast,
   Let it be well and true;
For though the book of time be clos'd,
   You still your work may view,
Writ in a book unbound, unclos'd;
   Or on the endless scroll,
Which wraps eternal pillars 'round,
   And ever shall unroll!

THANKSGIVING DAY.

Written just after the close of the Civil War.

TO Thee, this day, O Lord, we raise
A song of thankfulness and praise:
For Thou hast all things made; and we
For this should render praise to Thee!

Thy fingers have the heavens span'd,
The mighty deep is in Thy hand,
And all that live in air or earth,
It was Thy hand that gave them birth:

And by Thy hand they all are blest;
And live and move at Thy behest:
And none but Thee shall ever claim
The praise and honor due Thy name.

For life we thank Thee; and we praise
Thee for the joys that crowns our days.
Yes, for the richest blessings Thou
Hast given us, and give'st us now.

We thank Thee for the sun's warm rays;
And for the rain we give Thee praise;
Thanks, for the bright and sunny hours;
Thanks, for the gentle vernal show'rs:—

They cause the seed to germinate,
And bring forth early fruit and late;
Which satisfies our wants, and fills
The cattle of a thousand hills.

'Tis from Thy hand the babbling brook
Comes forth and waters every nook:
And 'tis Thy hand (though oft unseen)
That spreads the fields in living green.

And when the sun's warm rays have fled,
And winter comes with all its dread;
Thou o'er the fields the snow dost cast,
To hide them from the wintry blast.

We thank Thee for the bread which we
Each day receive, O Lord, from Thee;
And for the fruits, the birds, the flow'rs,
Which comfort us in pensive hours.

And when from heat or toil we thirst,
From earth refreshing waters burst;
Which we may freely drink, and live;
For this, O Lord, our thanks we give.

We thank Thee that when tempests beat,
We have a place of safe retreat;
And fuel, too, to keep us warm,
When fiercely howls the wintry storm.

Thy hand, Lord, Thou dost open wide,
And dost for all that live provide.
Then we'll adore and praise that love
That sends these blessings from above.

We thank Thee that war's deadly hand,
No more is felt in all our land;
And pray Thee that the crimson gore
Shall flood and stain our soil no more.

For all these blessings Thee we praise,
And honor all Thy works and ways;
And thank Thee still that oft our eyes
Behold Thy blessings in disguise.

We thank Thee that our Nation's Head,
A day of thanks to Thee hath made.
May all within his wide domain,
From guilt in deed or thought refrain.

May all forsake our evil ways;
Make this a *Day* of *Prayer* and *Praise.*
And know our lives—our joys—depend
On Thee, our Father, and our Friend.

We thank Thee that when we had trod
The road that led from Thee—our God;
Thy blessed Son endur'd the pain,
To bring us back to Thee again.

We thank Thee, Lord, that when this life
Shall end, with all its toil and strive,
There is a life which Thou wilt give.
And all may come to Thee, and live.

And while we thank Thee for the past,
O, may Thy favors to us last;
And may we worthy of them prove,
By works of gratitude and love.

For all these things, and more we'll give
Our thanks to Thee while here we live;
And when to worlds on high we soar,
We'll THANK—we'll PRAISE Thee evermore!

FROM THE WINDOW OF MY ROOM.

During an absence, of some weeks, from home, I occupied a room at
Queenstown, Md., from the window of which I had a beautiful view of
Chester river; and while confined to the room by sickness, the following
verses were witten.

WAY out upon the river,
   From the window of my room,
I look upon the water
   Which divides me from my home:
The boats are lightly sailing
   O'er the water—dashing high,
As sunshine follows shadow,
   As the clouds are passing by.

I wonder if the lov'd ones
   Know—the lov'd ones of my home—
My eyes are turned toward them,
   From the window of my room;—
That I am looking, watching,
   As each coming boat I see,
And wish the lov'd and absent
   Ones were coming unto me.

I look, and half imagine,
   Far distant from the land,
I see a signal waving
   From a kind familiar hand;
Or see still nearer coming,
   In a little light canoe,
Familiar forms and faces
   Coming plainly into view.

And as I look intently,
  As they near and nearer come,
I wave my hand in answer,
  From the window of my room.
I almost hear their voices,—
  Which I've heard so oft before,—
And leave my window quickly,
  To go meet them on the shore.

I rise to leave the window,
  But behold! it is a dream:—
I am here, and they are far
  Beyond the swelling stream;
And yet, it seems so real—
  As bright visions often seem—
Which proves to us so plainly,
  That our life is oft a dream.

Yet oft our thoughts may traverse
  O'er the waters, deep and wide,
And bind the hearts together,
  Which are sever'd by the tide—
Though billows may divide us,
  And we many miles apart—
Still we can see each other,
  Through the window of the heart.

And soon the smoking steamer,
  Will come puffing through the tide,
And then with joy and gladness,
  I shall o'er the waters glide:—
No longer look in visions,
  From the window of my room,
But feel the happy kisses,
  Which await me at my home.

WATCH AND PRAY.

WATCH and pray when in temptation;
  Watch when snares your pathway throng;
Pray when you feel sin's invasion;
  Watch and pray, and you'll grow strong.

Watch and pray;—there may be danger;—
  Watch and pray; and do not fear:
And if Christ to you's a stranger,
  Watch and pray, and He'll come near.

Watch, e'en should your eyes be weary;
  Watch until the night is o'er;
Watch while on the shore you tarry,
  Watch till you need watch no more.

Pray until your bosom burneth;—
  See the "Man of sorrow" bow!—
When from praying He returneth,
  He may tell you, "Sleep on now."

Pray when strength you most are needing;
  Pray when God seems far away;—
He will listen to your pleading;—
  He will hear you when you pray.

Watch and pray in hours of trouble;
  Watch and pray in hours of peace;
Pray the more as sorrows double:
  Watch and pray, and never cease.

*A LESSON OF THE DYING YEAR.—*1884.

Written on returning from Watch-meeting at the Foundry Church, Washington, D. C., forty years after the time the writer used to play ball on the lot where the Church now stands, and from which he had been absent for thirty years.

’TIS night;—one o’clock,—and the Old Year is gone!
  An hour ago, and its last moments fled.
    We look where it linger’d;—we look and look on:—
      It moves not; it breathes not.   The Old Year is dead!

The huge wheels of time, as they swiftly move on,
  Will never more wake it, or e’er cause to throb
The pulses which throbb’d when to us it was born.
  Its grave is now seal’d, and no hand can it rob.

The booming of cannon o’er fields red with gore,
  The earthquake, the thunders which roll thro’ the skies,
The mad ocean waves, as they beat ’gainst the shore,
  Will wake it no more from the grave where it lies.

The winds they may whistle through cavern and cave,—
  May howl through the forest and sweep the broad plain,
But cannot disturb the Old Year; in its grave,
  Or wake into new life one moment again.

The bright sun, above, and volcanos beneath,
  The rains, and the snows, may together unite,—
The lightnings the heav’ns and the earth may enwreath,
  But they can’t wake the Year from its long, endless night!

  Though ages, long ages, roll on, and increase,
    Till Time is all hoary, the Year which has died,
  Will never again from its long sleep of peace
    Awake, or unite in Old Time’s onward stride.

Yet often will come in the lone quiet hour,
  Its deeds, good or bad—like the blossoms of spring,
Or like the chill frost, or the winter's cold show'r,—
  Which good, ill, or gladness, or sorrow will bring.

The steps are all trodden, the foot-prints are plain,
  And though we behold them, we cannot retrace,
Or tread the same hill-side or valley again,
  Nor marks we have made 'long the by-way erase.

It is dead! It is dead! The Old Year is dead!
  We will not forget it, but keep it in view.
With lessons, wise lessons, we gently will tread
  From the foot of the Old to the head of the New.

That when the New Year, in its march, shall grow old,
  And it, like the Old Year, shall from us depart,
We'll gather the fruitage, more precious than gold,
  And garner it safe in the mind,—in the heart.

Yes, forty long years have all taken their flight,
  And millions have borne on their wings to their rest,
Since first I bow'd down where I worshipp'd to-night;
  So we shall be borne when the Ruler sees best.

And this is the lesson the hour imparts;—
  As we step o'er the line 'tween the Old and the New,
To see that no stain from our feet, hands or hearts
  Be made by the way, which our eyes would *not* veiw.

"*THE STILL, SMALL VOICE.*"

IT is not in the tempest loud,
Nor in the busy, bustling crowd,
  God whispers in our ear:
 'Tis not in gay and giddy hours,—
When pleasure's cup o'erflows with show'rs,
  His sweetest words we hear.

'Tis oft at evening's curtain-fall,
We hear the voice, so still and small,
  Which falls, and on us rests:
'Tis when the King of day gives place
To night's fair Queen,—with placid face,
  And all her nightly guests.

Oftimes at midnight's silent hour,
That voice I've heard—felt most its power—
  When none but God was near;
Then oft I've heard the sweetest note
Of music—softest music—float
  So gently to my ear.

The words are not of oral sound,
Yet make love's tender chords rebound,
  Like sun-beams on the sea:
They warm the air, they melt the ice,
Turn darkness into paradise,—
  Thus God oft speaks to me.

GOOD NIGHT, AND GOOD MORN

WHEN we have spent the day in peace,
    And evening hours are bright,
How sweetly sounds the parting words,—
    The happy words "GOOD NIGHT!"

When love with love is interchanged,
    And hearts are free and light,
And hand in friendly hand is clasp'd,
    How sweet the word, "GOOD NIGHT!"

How sweet when 'round the glowing hearth,
    We part, at morn to meet,
And wish a peaceful sleep to each,
    "GOOD NIGHT," oh, then how sweet!

Yet that sweet word will sometime cease,—
    When day shall be more bright,
When evening hours shall come no more,
    Then none shall say, "GOOD NIGHT."

But when no evening shadows fall,
    And all the nights have gone,
Then friend to friend a sweeter word
    Will speak, 'twill be "GOOD MORN!"

AWAY FROM HOME.

IT is Sunday, Sunday evening,
  One of Autumn's fairest days;
The soft, balmy winds are lulling,
  And the birds half-hushed their lays.

Brown October leaves are falling,—
  Slowly falling, one by one;
They their evening kiss have taken
  From the day's retiring sun,

Whose strong arms have been embracing
  All day long the graceful trees,
And his hands have now at eve'ing
  Rocked to sleep the resting breeze.

His warm lips have kissed the roses,—
  Each now bows its bashful head,
As he changes his day raiment—
  Hangs gold curtains 'round his bed.

I am sitting, this calm evening,—
  A few sweeter have I known—
In my room I'm sitting thinking,
  Sitting, thinking, all alone.

I am thinking of the lov'd ones,—
  As their pictures plainly come,—
Thinking of the distant lov'd ones,
  Of the loved ones at my home.

I am sitting in life's evening,—
  While they'r treading up its morn,—
Thinking, thinking, how to bless them,
  Ere I go, and when I've gone.

They are looking up life's pathway,
  Looking, hast'ning, to its noon,
While I've passed its shining summit,
  And will tread its valley soon.—

Still I hope, when in the valley,
  To pull flowers by the rills,
And to drink the gushing waters,
  Gushing, bounding, from the hills.

And I trust when near the river,—
  Near the river of life's shore,—
Some strong hand will still support me,
  Still support and take me o'er.—

I can only point, and tell them
  Of the fruitful, fertile side,
And to where the seeds have fallen,
  Fallen by life's way and died.—

Tell them of the thorns half-hidden
  'Neath the roses' blushing leaves,—
How to miss the fruit forbidden,
  And the flow'er which oft deceives.

I am thinking of the meeting,
  Happy meeting at the door!
And the greeting, joyful greeting!—
  Of the greetings heretofore.

How I love those happy meetings!
  How they make my bosom thrill!
And the greetings, joyful greetings;
  Though the vocal chords be still.

Now the tender chords are waiting,
  Waiting now, but soon will ring
With the gentle, soft vibrations
  Which another week will bring.

And my sprit feels the music,
   Music of the hidden chords,
Softly touched by angel fingers,
   Oh, what joy the sound affords!

Strains, sweet strains! no tongue of mortal
   E'er hath sung, or ear hath heard,—
Play'd by hands—by hands immortal,—
   Strains my soul have often stir'd.

Now the shadow's growing longer,
   Longer, longer, 'cross the floor,
And the sun-rays fainter, fainter,
   Fainter through the open door.

Now the sun has ceas'd its shining,
   Ceas'd its shining in my room;
And its light is fast declining;
   Now the twilight hour is come.

Night's arch'd brow will soon be spangl'd
   With rich jewels, pale and red;
And the moon—her crown of glory—
   Will rest softly on her head.

Her dark eyes with tears are swelling,—
   Of the beams of day bereft,—
And the tears will soon fall gently,
   On the flow'rs the sun has left.

These dark eyes, so mild and tender,—
   Weeping for the King of day,—
Glad will smile at break of morning,—
   For he'll kiss the tears away.

So, when life's short night here closes,
   And the falling tears are done;
We'll rejoice like the glad roses ,
   When they meet the rising sun.

As the bright cheeks of the roses,
  By the tears are made more bright,
So at morning we'll be gladder
  For the weeping of the night.

Let me bathe my happy bosom
  In the dews of grace, which fall,
As God's hand unrolls the curtain,
  Star-lit curtain,—over all.

Now the music, softer, sweeter,
  Sweeter, deeper, than before,
Thrills my heart with holy pathos!
  Is it music from yon shore?

Is the music—angel music—
  Just beyond that curtain bright,
Sweeter, sweeter, than the music
  Ringing in my soul to night?

If it is, what glory! glory!
  When we hear the joyful lay;
And the Master, blessed Master,
  There shall teach us all to play:—

Teach our white, angelic fingers
  How to touch each sacred chord,
In the music-hall of heaven,
  Gather'd 'round the Master, Lord!

May these blessed strains now falling
  On my heart this evening hour,
Reach the bosom of my loved ones:—
  May they feel its soothing power.

May it ring still sweeter, louder,
  As from height to height they rise:
May it cheer them 'long their pathway,
  Till they hear it in the skies.

May it make our hands still stronger,
  Stronger bind our hearts in love,
Till o'er hill and vale no longer
  We shall tread, but rest above.—

Rest above, in those bright mansions,
  Mansions large enough for all,
Where no cloud the day shall darken,
  And no evening shadows fall!

THE SHEPHERD'S VOICE.

O, HOW much we do rejoice!
When we hear the Shepherd's voice,
O'er the vales, and mountains steep,
Calling to His scatter'd sheep.
But our joy will greater be,
When the Shepherd's face we see,—
When our joyful eyes behold
Him, with all the gathered fold.

THE GLITTERING LINKS.

HOW oft we think,—" How strong each link
Of gold! (?)—How well they'll fit us!
But as we take those links, they break;
And ere we bind those links, we find
'All is not gold that glitters!'"

NEW YEAR:—EIGHTEEN HUNDRED AND EIGHTY-ONE.

ANOTHER fleeting year has gone,
Kind reader, since in cheering tone,
We greeted you with friendly hand;
And asked God's blessing on our land;
Since which, rude death his jaws has clos'd
On hundreds, who life's laws oppos'd;
While He who watches all our ways,
Has blest and lengthen'd out our days—
Has noticed ev'ry falling tear,
And brought us through another year.

The planets all, around the sun,
Do, in due time their courses run.—
First, Mercury,—in three months' time,
His bells ring out their New Year's chime:
Then Venus—with her silv'ry blaze,—
In seven months and fifteen days,
Through evening late, and early morn,
She makes her round,—her year is gone.
While Mars, with blush'd and fiery face,
Requires two years to run his race.
Then Jupiter—so great in size,—
In twelve years marches round the skies.
And Saturn, with his moons and rings,
Around his course so proudly swings;
Just nine and twenty years he takes,
Ere he his lengthy journey makes.
Uranus, with its ponderous wheels,
Rolls round the vast ether'al fields;
And just in four and eighty years,
It at its starting point appears.
Neptune, the last and most remote,
Launches upon time's sea, his boat,
And in one hundred and four score
Of years, he sails from shore to shore.

(We've led you off thus far, to show
That all above, around, below,—
Within the scope of human range,
Have periods,—their times to change.)
So we, upon our little sphere,
Have made our round in one short year:
And ere we reach life's distant shore,
Our bark upon time's sea we'll moor;
The mast make firm, the sails renew;
The dangers of the past review;
And we should also keep in sight
Our goodly gains, and prospects bright.

For some years past, our hoping eyes
Have looked upon the darkest skies;
And many a back has felt the smart,
And bent beneath the business mart.
But now the clouds have pass'd away;
Our eyes behold a brighter day;
Our ears hear ringing through the land,
The hammer in the forger's hand:
We hear the clicking of the mill,—
Supplied by rivulet and rill;
The roaring of the furnace blast,
As from its mouth, in tons are cast
The liquid metal, hot and red,
Which give to thousands work and bread.
The Iron horse, he swiftly goes;—
With heated breath, he puffs and blows;
With whistle shrill, and ruffled mane,
He draws the heavy lad'n train;—
Which bears rich products to the door
Of far and near, of rich and poor.
The ships across the ocean plough,—
All loaded full, from stern to prow:
And in return, to us they bear
The shining gold, or foreign ware.

The farmer need no more complain:
His fields were ripe with grass and grain:
The prices fair, the labor low;
And while he sleeps, his crops still grow.

The paper trash,—so long deplor'd,
Has gone: and coin'd cash has por'd
Into our pockets, hats and bags,
Until they're torn almost to rags.

Our counters, too, are breaking down,
And safes are sinking in the ground;
But this, perhaps, may make some grieve,—
Who would have "green-backs," just as leave.

Now, as the Old Year lingers—dies,—
We'll not forget the lessons wise,
It left behind: but will revere
Its memories, with a falling tear.
Tho' dead, its deeds will never die,
But speak to us, as time rolls by,
And as the past, again appears,
In pleasure's smile, or sorrow's tears.
And as we from its grave return,
Our hearts with deep emotion yearn
For much we lost; but might have won,
If we had all its teachings done.
And, as we turn to eastern skies,
And see the morning star arise;—
The golden sun, with gilded rays,
Which speak to us of brighter days,
We thank God for the year that's gone.
And hail, with joy, the NEW YEAR MORN!
And ask His blessing, and His care,
Upon the labors of the YEAR.

THE NATION'S VOICE

Memoriam of

PRESIDENT GARFIELD.

Written on returning from the memorial service.

O GOD of the universe !—holy and wise,
Whose foot-stool the earth is, whose throne is the skies;
Almighty ! Omniscient !—forever the same.—
With reverence profound we would utter Thy name;
Thou Being whom arch-angels fall down before,
And hosts of high heaven delight to adore;
Thou Maker, Preserver, and Sovereign of all,
In deepest contrition before Thee we fall!

O God of past nations !— that sleep in the dust!
Thou, God of the present, in whom we will trust;
Thou, God of the future,—to us yet unborn,—
We bow to Thy chast'ning, though deeply we mourn!
We bow before Thee, as the dark shadows fall,—
The land deeply draped in one funeral pall,
And the solemn bells toll,—each catching the sound,
A signal encircling the whole globe around.

Why we are thus stricken Thou knowest full well:
Thy hand could have held up our Leader who fell;
But in Thy great wisdom (too high for our sight),
Thou saw best to take him,—Thou canst but do right.
If right, then, O Father, submissively we
Would bend 'neath the rod if it bring us to Thee.—
" For unkindness too good—for error too wise; "—
The hand that chastiseth will wipe weeping eyes.

He " fell," we have said;—in his fall may we rise;
And he, too, we hope,—from the earth to the skies.—
While all of his labors have come to an end,
May we work the harder;—our ways to amend.
In falling he left us some lessons to learn,—
That we from the way of transgression should turn,
Deal justly, love mercy, be meek in God's sight,
That the nation's bright day be turned not to night.

O God of our nation! help us to beware
Of the path that leads to the pitfall and snare
Of sin in "high places," fraud, avarice, and pride.
(The nations that guarded not against them have died.)
We'll honor our country, be true to its cause;
Be just in the *ballot*—observing its laws.
In all our transactions, at home and abroad,
Our hands will deal justly; we'll trust in the Lord.

Our God, and our children,   by example may we
Incline their young hearts to trust firmly in Thee:—
By precept and practice, from day unto day,
Lead them to know Thee, as we walk in the way.
Thus instructed in youth, no violent hand
Shall be raised in rebellion in all our fair land.
And may they remember that righteousness will
Our nation exalt.—O, may this be Thy will!

This day, as our Chieftain is laid in the tomb,
A mother and widow, in garments of gloom,
With five weeping children around him appear,
As sob smothers sob, and tear chases tear!
The sobs and the tears, like the lake's circled wave,
Spread o'er the vast throng as he sinks in the grave.
These waves may flow low, yet they'll flow evermore
Till they reach 'cross life's sea, to eternity's shore.

No North and no South, and no East and no West:
But all are united—by sorrow depress'd:—
All discord and malice and envy have flown,
No more, as we trust, to return or be known.
Not alone in our home, but in foreign lands,
Are the Rulers and ruled extending their hands;
While 'neath the broad ocean the messages fly,
And anxious hearts wait for a speedy reply.

But, O Lord, Thy glory our sorrow outweighs!
A nation, a world, bow'd in prayer and in praise!
While round Thee, in rapture, the angels of light,
Strike their harps to Thy praise at the glorious sight!
O Lord, were more faces e'er turned unto Thee?
Were more sad suppliants e'er bending their knee?
Did the tolling of bells, with sad, solemn lay,
E'er come to Thy ear as it comes up to-day?

The good-will and kindness pervading all hearts;
The tokens of friendship that come from all parts;
Would then have been, and would our vows have been
And the pray'rs ascend, if our Ruler had stayed? [paid,
Affliction, sore, deep! often brings us to Thee,
And opens our eyes, our condition to see.
Lord, surely man's wrath to Thy praise shall be turn'd,
When Thy hand correcteth, Thy lessons be learn'd.

Our Ruler is dead,—which our hearts sorrow gives,—
But "Jehovah still reigns!—the nations still lives!"
Our flag, though in mourning, still floats to the breeze,
 Still waves o'er the land, and still sails o'er the seas.
Though the "stars" have been dimm'd and "stripes"
        have been stain'd,
Their brightness and pureness may soon be regained.
They'll never be riven, nor trail in the dust,
While true to our duty, and in God we trust.

O God of our fathers—who planted the seed
Of "LIBERTY'S TREE"—may we pluck every weed
The hand of corruption has scatter'd around,
As it swells in the bud, or springs from the ground;
Then the " tree " will grow strong, its green branches
    spread,
And millions find shelter beneath its broad shade.—
Its fruits will be pure and abundant its yield,
And nations afar by its leaves may be heal'd.

And now may God's blessing descend on the head
Of him who has taken the place of the dead,
And all those around him, that they may devise
In *justice* and *truth*, and in council be *wise:*—
The halls of our Congress with echoes resound
For *right*, till corruption no longer be found:
Then the " *stars* and the *stripes* " will continue to wave
" O'er the land of the FREE," and not *lie* on its *grave*.

* * *

A PRAYER.

TEACH me, O God!—Of Thee I'd learn:—
    Help me, O Lord, Thy will to do !
    May I from all that's evil turn,
    And virtue's holy paths pursue.

"The heavens declare the glory of God; and the firmament showeth His handywork."

A few years ago, during the absence of my family, except my youngest son, I was reading to him from Denison Olmstead's "Letters on Astronomy," in which we were both much interested. And in contemplating the greatness of God and His works, my mind was lifted above the terrestial, while my heart was bowed in profoundest humiliation. And after my son had retired for the night, the greater portion of this poem was written; and was read to him on the following morning.

OHOW I long to see the Lord!—
His dwelling place on high.—
The works His hands have spread abroad
Throngh all the spacious sky.

I do not think forever there,
To linger around the throne;
But may perhaps glad tidings bear
From world to world unknown.

The bliss of that pure world above,
Is not in idle rest:
But in the happy work of love,
The spirits there are blest.

We see God in all nature's book:
There's not a leaf we turn,—
There's not a line at which we look,
But more of Him we learn.

Though we may not read this book through,
Its index is so plain,
That if we but one line pursue,
A glimpse of God we gain.

A single dew-drop on a flow'r,—
  Of grass a single blade,
Tell of the wisdom, skill and pow'r
  Of Him who worlds has made.

Yes, every limpid stream that flows
  And every cloud that flies,
In language plain, to us disclose
  A God above the skies.

There's not a single star that shines,
  There's not a grain of sand,
But what in unmistaken signs,
  Reveals His mighty hand.

And if these A. B. C.'s fortell
  Of God—His pow'r and might,
What wonders all the letters spell,
  If we but read them right.

If pebbles on the ocean's shore,
  Speak facts too plain to miss,
What; when we ride its bosom o'er,
  And fathom its abyss?

The name of God is stamped in gold,
  On all His hands have wrought:
And all of nature's works unfold
  The truths that Jesus taught.

The sun's bright beams, which cheer our hearts;
  The gentle rains that fall,
Speak of the blessings God imparts;—
  In love imparts to all.

We see this love where'er we look;—
  In every breeze that blows;
In every dancing, purling brook;
  In every flow'r that grows.

We see it in each drop of rain;—
　In groves, and fields of green;
In ripen'd fruit and golden grain
　God's love is plainly seen.

We praise Him for His works untold;
　His love and pow'r adore:
And as His boundless works unfold,
　We'll praise Him more and more!

We have a glimpse of stars and suns:
　For these our God we praise:
But there are greater, brighter ones,
　Than those on which we gaze.

Yes, there are worlds we may not scan,
　And cannot from this sphere:—
When God conceiv'd creation's plan,
　His fingers plac'd them there.

He opened wide His compass bars,
　And struck their bounds in space:
He roll'd out there those suns and stars,
　Like steeds, to run a race.

He marked the orbits of their course,—
　The greatest and the least;—
And whirled them with Almighty force!—
　With speed that ne'er has ceas'd.

Through all the thousand ages back,
　Not one has miss'd its way,
Or got upon another's track;
　But each and all obey.

No dire collision, no discord,
　No, not the slightest clash;
But each upon its destin'd road,
　With lightning speed they dash.

And though they have no spur nor whip,
    To urge them on their round,
A million miles through space they leap;—
    A thousand at a bound.

God holds the reins as on they go
    Around their circles vast:
Not one has ever gone too slow;
    Not one has gone too fast.

I want to see that God whose might
    Thus whirls them through the sky!
My heart's desire, my soul's delight—
    To see God when I die!

I want to see that God of pow'r,—
    Of wisdom, love and grace;
We see His works each day, each hour,
    But, O, to see His face!

We've seen enough to praise Him here:—
    To praise Him while we live:
But when we leave this mortal sphere,
    Eternal praise we'll give.

Can we ascribe the honors due
    To authors on the earth,
Before their works we clearly view,
    And understand their work?

Oh, must we go to every world,
    As upward in our flight,
Before we reach those "gates of pearl,"
    That "land of pure delight?"

Are those swift turning orbs, the wheels,
    Or chariots of the sky,
That take us on to "Eden's fields,"
    Where "pleasures never die?"

Are those bright suns the steps of gold,
  By which we reach the throne?
And will each step new joys unfold,
  To mortal man unknown?

If so, then quickly come the hour,
  When I begin my flight;
Prepare me for that heav'nly tour,
  That leads to realms of light.

With gospel preparation shod,
  To those bright worlds on high,
Clothed with the panoply of God,
  On faith's strong wings I'd fly!

I'd go up to the King of day;
  This orb of light I'd view,—
'Tis ninety million miles away,—
  Eight hundred thousand through.

No mortal could its heat endure,
  Or look upon its blaze;
But yet immortal spirits pure,
  May at its glories gaze.

Then forty million miles or so,
  To Mercury I'd soar:
And then from there to Venus go,
  Near thirty millions more.—

This morning star and star of eve;
  Perhaps would seem so fair,
That new spectators might believe
  That God and heav'n are there.—

To the fair " Empress of the night,"
  As to a friend I'd soar:—
Familiar as the village light,
  That hangs beside our door.—

I'd like to shake her friendly hand,
  Whose face from night to night,
Sheds beams of gladness o'er our land;-
  Crown'd with a wreath of light.—

Then I would stop on my return,
  As on to Mars I fly,
That those who dwell on earth may learn
  The glories of the sky.

But if no trav'ler ere comes back
  To earth, the news to tell,
I'd like to linger near her track,
  And beckon, "All is well!"

But then the glories of the skies
  Cannot be known below;—
Cannot be seen by mortal eyes:—
  Those only spirits know.

Tho' angels long to bring to earth
  The news, their lips are seal'd,
'Tis only to immortal birth,
  These joys can be reveal'd.

Tho' seraphs stand with ready hands
  To part the vail in twain,
That they who dwell on mortal lands,
  A view of heav'n may gain;—

Tho' angels wait at heaven's gate,
  The glor'ous news to hear,
Man cannot know that heavenly state
  Until he enters there.—

I pass the earth, pursue my tour
  Toward the distant stars,
A hundred million miles or more,
  And now arrive at Mars.

I quickly scan those Asteroids,
　　With Jupiter in view,—
Four hundred million miles away,
　　Near ninety thousand through.

On this vast orb I'd rest my wings,
　　Before I take my flight
To Saturn, with its golden rings—
　　Its moons of silv'ry light.

Upon this orb a while I'd stay;—
　　The sun's peculiar pride;—
Nine hundred million miles away,
　　Near eighty thousand wide.

And then nine hundred millions more,
　　And twice that from the Sun,
Off to Uranus I would soar,
　　And yet I've scarce begun.

Then five and thirty thousand miles
　　Across its disk I'd fly,
And then away to Neptune's isles;—
　　Last in the Solar sky.

Twenty-eight hundred million miles!
　　And yet we've scarcely paid,
A visit to the vestibule
　　Of worlds, God's hands have made.

But spirits count not millions far:
　　They know no day nor night;
But on they go from star to star,
　　Like comets in their flight.

The Sun is lost!—The Moon gone out!
　　Their light no more we view;
Still we behold a shining host,
　　As we our flight pursue.

Still on we go; still up we go:
　And still new worlds appear !
Oh ! shall we ever feel or know
　That God and heaven are near ?

Is there no limit, end, or bound ?
　Oh ! how far still the road,
Before the gate of heav'n is found,—
　Before we see the Lord ?

We cannot tell; on God we'll wait,—
　Who hung those worlds in space—
His time is best, early or late
　When He'll unveil His face.

God knows all things, and when we know
　As by Him we are known,
Then we shall see Him as He is,
　And bow before His throne.

Oh ! this is worship pure and true:
　'Tis nothing false or vain;
'Tis not produc'd by fear of woe,
　Or hope of heav'n to gain.

Yes, this is worship of the heart;—
　In such my soul delights:
O, may this be my happy part !—
　Such worship God invites.

Then God to know, is God to love;
　His word His works declare;
He dwells on earth,—in heaven above,
　For God is everywhere.

Here we may see this God of love;—
　Meet Him in praise and pray'r:
But when we get to heav'n above,
　We'll see Him better there.

And if we walk with Christ below,
  We'll learn the heav'nly way;
And when to higher worlds we go,
  We cannot go astray.

From God He came—He went to God;
  He dwells with Him on high:
And if we tread the path He trod,
  We'll see God when we die.

I'd bear the toil He bore below:—
  Share every pang and sigh:
And much of earthly joy forego,
  To dwell with Him on high!

HOME. SWEET HOME.

Written in a village in Pennsylvania on Sunday night, after returning from church;—February, 1881.

AWAY from my wife and my children so dear,—
  Where loneliness gives to my pleasures alloy;—
The moments go slowly; the hours are so drear;—
  I look to my home with mix'd sadness and joy!
Home, home, sweet, sweet home! how I long to be
    there,
Its sorrows to soothe, and its pleasures to share!

The churches are out, and the people gone home;
  The jingling is hushed, and the sleighs have all past:
But old thoughts and new ones, how thickly they come,
  And paint as plain pictures as artists can cast.
Home, home, sweet, sweet home! how I long to be there,
Its sorrows to soothe, and its pleasures to share.

The clock has struck ten, and the fire has burn'd low:
  The house is so lonely;—they 've all gone to bed:
I sit, and I hope for the time I shall go
  To my home, and in gladness its threshold shall tread.
Home, home, sweet, sweet home! how I long to be there,
Its sorrows to soothe and its pleasures to share!

I think of my lov'd ones, and ne'er can forget:
  I know that they need me; I wish I were there:
O, may they remember my eyes are oft wet,
  As I see them in vision, and name them in pray'r.
Home, home, sweet, sweet home! how I long to be there,
Its sorrows to soothe, and its pleasures to share!

Though seasons of sorrow commingle with joy,
　Which mother and children at home have to bear,
(Which much of its pleasure and gladness destroy,)
　They might bear it better if "Father" were there.
Home, home, sweet, sweet home! how I long to be there,
Its sorrows to soothe, and its pleasures to share!

The little heart troubles, which no one else feels,
　They've no one to tell to; and no one to care.—
The little heart troubles,—which telling oft heals,—
　Which might be made lighter if "Father" were there.
Home, home, sweet, sweet home! how I long to be there,
Its sorrows to soothe, and its pleasures to share!

My journey I trace till I come to the door:—
　The steps, so familiar, which quickly I bound,
And enter with gladness, as often before;
　Or ring at the bell, should the night-latch be down.
Home, home, sweet, sweet home! how I long to be there,
Its sorrows to soothe, and its pleasures to share!

I now hear the footsteps come quick in the hall:
　I now see sweet faces—give each one a kiss,
As "Papa is come!" quick to Mamma they call: -
　I see them; I hear them; but can't tell the bliss!
Home, home, sweet, sweet home! how I long to be there,
Its sorrows to soothe, and its pleasures to share!

In our homes on the earth we meet and we part,
　With hearts full of gladness, or tears in our eyes:
But eyes will cease weeping, and joy fill the heart,
　When we meet (not to part) in our home in the skies!
Home, home, sweet, sweet home! may I meet you all there,
To rest in its mansions; its glories to share!

SOLITUDE.

———

Lines to a sister who was absent with my children, for whom she had been caring two years, after their mother's death. Written at a late hour of night, after the departure from my home of a few friends who had gathered in the evening.

———

OH, Solitude; how sweet thy charms!
How sweet to rest within thy arms,
  And think of those we love:
Earth hath no dearer charm than this;
No higher, holier, sweeter bliss
  Can angels know above!

No aspirations, no desires,
Breath'd forth by man, as he aspires
  To God, to heav'n, to bliss;
No theme on which I love to dwell,
Can thrill the heart, the bosom swell,
  As thrill'd, as swell'd by this!

Yet, I'd not dwell in solitude;
But, seek it in reflecting mood,
  To drink its truths,—to rest;
That to the world I may impart
The truths there stamp'd upon my heart,
  That others too be blest.

In solitude, but not alone!
But with a Friend to all unknown
  But they who with Him meet;
'Tis there He enters in my heart,
And gives the joys I would impart,
  And holds communion sweet!

'Tis there I love to kneel and pray:
'Tis there I see the heavenly way,
  And learn to walk therein:
And when the way seems rough and dark,
'Tis there God fans the heav'nly spark,
  And gives me light again.

'Tis there I hear my Saviour's voice;
'Tis there I make His paths my choice;
  And feast upon His love.
'Tis there I hear His Spirit say,
" Be faithful, strong, press on thy way,
  And lift thine eyes above."

Oh! Solitude is sad I know,
Without a friend above, below,
  And when within the breast,
Stern conscience, with its lash, lays bare
The weight of guilt it carries there;
  Then solitude's unrest.

There is no solitude to those
Who on the Master's breast repose,—
  Around the festive board,
On Patmas Isle, in prison cell,
Or anywhere God deigns to dwell,—
  Though by the world ignor'd.

We call it solitude, but lo!
'Tis where the angels come and go
  When darkness shrouds our way,
And takes us up to Pisgah's height,
Above the darkness of the night,
  And shows the rising day.

'Twas solitude where Jesus wept,
While those who tarried near Him slept,
    Yet He was not alone,
For God was near to hear His pray'r,
And give Him strength His grief to bear,
    And joy for every groan.

So in this still, belated hour,
I feel the presence of some pow'r,—
    Some gentle, loving Guest,
Which says that God in every place
Will dwell with those who seek His face:—
    And solitude make bless'd.

But when by conscience we're condemn'd—
By sinful sorrow overwhelm'd,
    Then dreary every spot,
When all alone—with no friend near,
Then solitude is sad and drear,
    In palace or in cot.

PERCEPTION, Reason, Memory,
Form in the mind a Trinity;
Each has its special work to do—
Depending on the other two.

Perception is the open door
Through which the mind receives its store,
Which Reason classifies, defines,
And to its place each fact assigns;

While Memory, with book and pen,
Takes an account of where, and when,
And how, each treasure rich is stor'd—
Nor is the least by her ignor'd.

When Reason would a truth reveal,
She must to Memory appeal,
Who quickly to the written page
Turns, then unlocks the vault of age.

And brings from some safe niche or nook
The fact recorded in the book;
She locks the door; the key she holds;
Her hand alone the vault unfolds.

Perception might all knowledge gain;
Reason to highest skill attain:
Yet all of no avail would be,
Should Memory misplace her key.

Without her care the open door
Would let depart the treasur'd store,
And Reason's work, so wisely plann'd,
Would vanish, but for Memory's hand.

PERCEPTION, in its upward flight,
May reach the spangl'd vault of night,
And mount, and ride each fiery steed
Around its course, with lightning speed:

REASON may in her balance weigh
The ponderous orbs of night and day;
Their sizes, qualites discern,—
Just when they'll go, just when return,—

How near approach, how far they'll go,
Just here how fast, just there how slow,
And as they near each other, tell
How much attract, how far repel.

But all the labor, time and cost
Of these, would be forever lost,
Should MEMORY not follow on,
And mark the track which they have gone,

And every flight and thought sublime,
Inscribe upon the page of time.
If MEMORY's vast written scroll
Should close, and never more unroll,

PERCEPTION not a step could trace
Of all her track through ether space,
And REASON not a thought retain
Of earth, or air, or heav'n's domain.

No one of these was e'er design'd
To reign as monarch of the mind;
In unison abide the three;—
PERCEPTION, REASON, MEMORY.

"*NOT DEAD, BUT SLEEPETH.*"

Lines on the decease of a young lady.

THE Maid is not dead; but sleeping she lies,
Till Jesus shall say to her, "Damsel, arise,"
To live with the blest on the immortal shore—
To equal the angels, and die never more."

For they who to life, from the dead shall obtain,
Shall equal the angels, and die not again:
For Jesus has said it: His words they are true;
And what He has promis'd He surely will do.

Then sleep, blessed Maiden:—thy sleep is not death,
Though cold be the blood,—still, the pulse and the breath,
Thy body is free from all sorrow and pain;—
The loss we have suffer'd, we bear;—'tis thy gain.

In Christ's blessed kingdom, no soul ever dies;
But only exchanges the earth for the skies;—
By way the blest Master triumphantly trod,
From earth, through the grave, to the kingdom of God!

Sleep on, blessed Maiden;—sleep on in thy rest:
We bid thee farewell, as no longer our guest;
But trust we will meet thee again in the skies,
When Jesus shall say to us also, "Arise."

TO THE BARTHOLDI STATUE OF LIBERTY.

On Bedloe's Island, New York Harbor.

ONG ago it was said, when the nations were dead.
  When life's lighted banner unfurl'd,—
  "Let your light burn and shine in its glory divine:
  Lo, ye are the light of the world."

So we say here to-day, as we stand by the Bay,
  And look to that hand lifted high,
"Let the light shine afar, as the night's guiding star,
  And gladden the mariner's eye."

May the ships of the wave as the billows they brave,
  And plough through the white briny foam,
Look with hope to thy light, as the trav'ler by night,
  Looks gladly when nearing his home.

As you stand at the gate of the Nation's great state,
  With light streaming bright from your hand,
May that gate open wide to commercial's great tide,
  Now spreading all over the land.

May its hinges keep bright, as to left and to right,
  They're swung by the strong arm of trade;
And thy eye quick discern, should the tide chance to turn,
  Or light for one moment should fade.

May the moon of thy skies cause the low tides to rise,
  And send up the bright spray of hope;
And the rays of thy day, fall soft on the spray,—
  The buds into bright blossoms ope.

While the throb of the heart of the nation's great mart.
  Sends life through the veins of the land,
May that life long endure—shine as bright and as pure
  As the light which emits from thy hand.

May hammer and forge from hill-top and gorge,,
  Ring out through the land of the free;
And the click of the mill, and the whistle's loud shrill,
  Be heard by the isles of the sea.

As the great iron steed, with his two-minute speed,
  Sweeps out with the long laden'd train,
With its swift turning wheels, thro' the vast western fields,
  And returns with its millions of grain,

May the owner and groom, each be blest in his home,—
  Receive each his share of the spoil;
And that money and mind thus together combin'd,
  Unite with the hard hand of toil.

May thy light, by its glow, cause the millions to know
  This truth—and may ev'ry eye see,
That in union of hands our liberty stands, -
  That binding is what makes us free.

As thy light mingles in with the shadows of sin,
  Which hang like a pall o'er the dead—
May the shadows grow bright, and the pall change to white,
  And sin be captivity led.

May the waves at your feet, as they come and retreat,
  Keep the ground ever pure where you stand;
And the sun and the rain keep your hands free from stain,
  While lighting the sea and the land.

May thy eye often glance o'er the waters to France,
  And look to our infantile days,
When she stretch'd forth her hand in defence of our land,
  Our sun half eclips'd by the maze;—

Now with muscles made strong by our conflict with wrong,
  Our hands by defence of the right,
And with no mist or maze to obstruct the bright rays
  Which stream from the star spangl'd height,

May the dove of good-will, as it holds in its bill
  The emblem of friendship and love,
With its gentle wings spread, overshadow thy head,—
  Remind us of help from above.

And though FREEDOM and RIGHT be our motto, (not might)
  And we from all bloodshed would cease,
Yet the power of the sword should not be ignored,
  Though sheath'd in the scabbard of peace.

Yet the pulpit and press are our strongest redress,—
  Their weapons most potent for good.
May they battle for right till no shadow or blight
  Shall fall on Columbia's sod.

May you stand in your pride till all nations decide
  The goddess of peace to adore,—
Till the lion, docil'd, shall be led by the child,
  And men shall learn war nevermore.

May you stand, firmly stand, with your high-lifted hand,
  With banner of light wide unfurl'd,
Till from earth's distant bound, one vast voice shall resound,
  " Lo, ye are the light of the world ! "

When thy locks shall grow gray as the years roll away—
  And fall on thy shoulders like snow,
And thy high-lifted bust shall lie low in the dust,
  May the light of the nation still glow:

May it still burn and blaze till a million bright rays
  Shall stream out from Liberty's tree:
May it burn in each breast till from strife all shall rest,
  Burn on till all nations are FREE.

THE God who made revolving worlds,
   Made, too, the lilies fair,
The beasts, the birds, the worm,—which crawls,
   And for them all doth care!

He clothes the grass, of but a day:
   He notes the sparrow's fall;
Gives to the flow'rs their rich array,
   And watches over all.

And if He cares for bird and beast,
   And fishes of the sea,
And flow'rs, and worms—of all things least—
   I know He cares for me.

Then why should I repine, or fear,
   Or doubt, or be dismay'd,
While God doth watch, in kindly care,
   O'er all His hands have made?

O, cease, sad tears! no longer flow:
   Be still, O troubled breast!—
God hears each sigh,—feels ev'ry woe;
   And He will do the best.

TO " *GOOD TEMPLARS.*"

"The following lines were addressed to "Redemption Lodge, ' No. 1,
Independent Order of Good Templars, at Keedysrville, Md., March 28th,
1866, by Prof. A. S. Boyd."—*Boonsboro' Odd Fellow*, April 19th, 1866.

THE Seed of Good Templars, so recently sown,
Has taken deep root; and its branches have grown,
  Till we, by the wayside, through forest and field,
  Behold the good fruits and bright flowers they yield.

The Star of Good Templars, oh! bright may it shine,
Till all who now worship at Bacchus' shrine,
Shall see by its light their delusion and sin—
And worship no more at a shrine so unclean.

The Flag of Good Templars, oh! long may it wave,
And cheer on its thousand of noble and brave.
Oh! keep it still floating, as onward you go;
Be true to its colors—you'll conquer the foe!

The Sword of Good Templars, oh! hard may it fight,
Till all who oppose it, acknowledge its right,
And lay down their weapons—their weapons of war—
And join in our army as onward we go.

The Ship of Good Templars, oh! fast may it sail:
Tho' often oppos'd by the tempest and gale—
'Twill still proudly beat o'er the ocean's broad breast,
And take many safe to the haven of rest.

The Lamp of Good Templars, oh! bright may it burn,
Till thousands who now walk in darkness may turn
From the path that's infested with many a snare,—
Which leads on to sorrow! remorse! and despair!

The Eye of Good Templars, oh! far may it see
To make the blind victim both happy and free!—
Behold the bright future, review the dark past,
And see, on the waters, the bread that's been cast.

The Arm of Good Templars, oh! hard may it work;
Till venom that now in the bottle doth lurk,
Shall lose all its poison, and die, like the tares
That grow to be burn'd when the harvest appears.

The Hand of Good Templars, oh! fast may it hold
All who may come for support to its fold,
And lead them on safely—though winds beat and blow—
To rivers and fountains where pure waters flow.

In FAITH, HOPE, CHARITY, may you extend
Your hand to the fallen—the drunkard befriend—
Be kind to his family, in deed and in work;—
"A cup of cold water" shall have its reward.

The Voice of Good Templars, oh! loud may it sound
Till echoes come pealing from earth's distant bound—
From North and from South, from East and from West,
That whiskey is banished, and mankind is blest;—

Till fathers, and mothers, and children, made free,
Shall shout the glad tidings from hill-top to sea,—
Till nations and kingdoms respond to the voice,
And multipli'd millions be made to rejoice.

The Heart of Good Templars, oh! much may it love—
Like "Templars" who dwell in that Temple above:
Who look with compassion, in sympathy yearn,
And sing "Hallelujah" when drunkards return.

The Head of Good Templars, oh! long may it wear
The laurel which none but the temp'rate can share—
The crown and the glory, now worn on this head,
Shall fade not, but shine when intemp'rance is dead.

Now firmly united in Heart, Head, and Hand,
The Arm and the Sword, with a Voice to command —
The Ship on the ocean, with Flag floating high,
The bright Star of hope, beaming down from the sky —

The Eye looking forward to guide us aright,
The Lamp ever burning to cheer through the night:
Then onward you'll go, in the pow'r of your strength,
And conquest and glory shall crown you at length.

May all who have promis'd, while God gives them breath,
To drink not the water of sorrow and death;
Be firm to that promise—be faithful and true,
And morning and ev'ning that promise renew.

May you, my young Brothers, you lambs of the fold,
Resist the temptation—be faithful and bold;
And you, my good Sisters, (inclined less to stray,)
Encourage these Brothers, and lead on the way.

At last, may Good Templars triumphantly rise,
To dwell in the Temple of God in the skies;
Where none shall be drunken, but where the "redeem'd"
Shall " walk in the light" which on us here has gleam'd —

Where heart-broken Mothers shall weep not, nor sigh,
Or Orphans, with hunger, no longer shall cry;
But where with the "ransom'd " with praise to the Giv'r,
We'll drink the sweet "waters " from life's flowing riv'r.

And now, in conclusion, I say once again,
From every beguiling temptation refrain;
Though often you've heard it, I say to you now,
Be true, firm, and faithful—"REMEMBER YOUR VOW ! "

MONUMENTAL LODGE OF GOOD TEMPLARS.

"The meeting of Monumental Lodge at Scottish Rite Hall, on
last Thursday evening, was such as that new and ambitious organiza-
tion can well be proud of; and to thoroughly delight the large number of
visitors who were present. The "Good of the Order" program was of
especial interest, and included contributions by the excellent talent of
the Lodge as well as by several visitors. During these excercises the following poem, dedicated to the Lodge by Prof. A. S. Boyd, was read by
the author."— *Washington Record*, September 25th, 1884.

BROTHERS and Sisters, in whose hearts
  Are warmest love and earnest zeal—
Who may have felt the poisonous darts,
  Or seen the woes which others feel:—
May the good work you've well begun,
  Go on till rum's strong chain is broke,
Till every father, every son,
  Be free from the intemp'rance yoke;—

Till ev'ry aching heart and head,
  And tear of sorrow, pain and grief,
And ev'ry pitious cry for bread,
  Which drink has caus'd, shall find relief;
Till every waiting, weeping wife,
  Vow'd to be lov'd by him she wed,
And ev'ry child's unhappy life
  Be blest with peace and joy instead.

Then, "Onward" let your motto be,
  And high the standard of your aim:
Work—yours shall be the victory;
  Work,—yours shall be an honor'd name.
An honor'd name is of more worth,
  (By men of wisdom we are told),
Than all the fleeting joys of earth,
  And more to be desir'd than gold.

Be free ! it is your right, be free !
  This right your God to you hath giv'n.
Arise ! assert your liberty !
  Aspire to right, to truth, to heav'n.
Be free from all that tends to wrong;
  Be watchful: keep your armor bright;
Then in the battle you'll be strong,
  And ever ready for the fight.

Be free from every gloomy doubt:
  Be free from every survile fear.
Unfurl your flag, for freedom shout,
  And ev'ry foe shall disappear.
Be to your God and conscience true;
  From ev'ry slavish sin refrain,
Put forth your strength, your duty do,
  And then your cause you shall maintain.

But if we do our duty not,
  And leave no blessing to our race,
Our name shall die, and be forgot,
  Or live, alas ! to our disgrace.
With "right" inscrib'd upon your brow,
  On every tempting evil frown,
Success shall be your portion now;
  Honor and joy your future crown !

And may the monument your rear
  Here, be on firm foundation built,
With tow'ring top, proportions fair,
  Stand long; nor time nor tempest tilt.
We trust the ground was well survey'd
  Before the noble work begun—
The corner-stone securely laid,
  And all the work will well be done.

As stone on stone you upward build,
  And raise your work in bold relief,
See that your hearts and hands are skill'd
  To follow Him—of chiefs the Chief.
See that no sand-stone takes the place
  Of marble, nor clay, of cement;
Else failure, shame and sad disgrace
  May follow when your toil is spent.

For if we build on clay or sand,
  Or wood, or stubble, 'twill decay:
E'en gold and silver will not stand,
  For time will sweep them, too, away.
For no foundation other than
  That which the Master-builder laid
Shall long endure; the work of man,
  If not on that, shall fall and fade.

May this fair monument rise high,
  Until its white, reflecting dome
Shall catch and hold the wand'rer's eye,
  And the lost prodigal draw home.
May sweet, refreshing waters fall
  From mountain-top, from hill side burst,
And e'er keep white, its tow'ring wall,
  And satisfy the souls that thirst.

May the warm sun's refulgent rays,
  Bright moon and stars which on it fall,
Light hundreds in their darken'd ways,
  And loose the chains which them enthrall.
Beneath the shadow of its length,
  May many weak and wand'ring come;
Within its walls the weak find strength,
  The wandering, a welcome home.

May thousands come and gladly sup
  From the pure fountain at its base;
To where it points, with hope look up,
  And reach at last that sacred place,
Where streams of living waters flow,
  And tables broad are richly spread,
Where widows, pale, no sigh shall know,
  And orphans cry no more for bread.

Let " Faith " be your foundation stone,
  And " Hope " the strong cement let be—
Which binds the many stones as one,—
  The crowning cap·stone, " Charity."
Throw love's broad mantle over all;
  Assist all who your help may need;
Stretch out your hand to those who fall,
  And God will bless you in your deed.

Remember the wise lessons taught
  Within these walls—where oft you meet;
The promises, forget them not,
  Which you from time to time repeat.
Your hands will gather up the flow'rs
  They're strewing 'long the pathway now;
They'll reap the fruit in golden hours:—
  Remember well your sacred " vow."

The memory of these bless'd deeds—
  Like the returning birds in spring—
Will come, when winter's blast receds,
  And in the soul with gladness sing:
They'll come when fields are gay and green,
  With sweetest song and richest plume;—
They'll come when skies are all serene,
  And fairest flow'rs forever bloom.

THE MAN WHO SOLD HIM THE RUM.

Verses suggested by a sad story told to the writer by one who had deeply felt its sadness'

HIS health and his life, they were passing away;—
　His money for whiskey all spent:
His dwelling had well nigh now gone to decay,
　The hearts of his household were rent.

In wand'ring one day,—he could hardly tell where,—
　He was hail'd by the voice of a friend;—
His clothes were all ragged, his feet were half bare,
　And money, he had none to spend;—

The voice that called to him, said, "Come with me, come:
　Come go to the temperance hall:
Leave off all your drinking—your whiskey and rum,
　Beer, brandy, rum, cider, and all."

He went, and he there to the pledge put his name;
　Resolv'd by the help of his God!
That to live a new life, henceforth he would aim,—
　Forsake the old paths he had trod.

In but a few months, the picture so sad!
　Was changed to a picture so fair:—
His wife and his children were all nicely clad:—
　His home show'd much neatness and care.

The hearts of his household were happy and light:
　At return of each Sabbath day,
With raiment all clean, and with faces all bright,
To church they all wended their way.

For months in this way he had liv'd, and was blest:
  But he who had robb'd him before,
Watch'd all of his steps, and it seem'd could not rest;—
  He saw he was now making more.

So one day when passing the old tavern door,
  The landlord invited him in;
He took him around, and he show'd him his store
  Of rum, whiskey, brandy and gin.

He pour'd out a glass, which he said was so mild,—
  Held it twixt finger and thumb:
Then the man lost his strength, (Like Eve when beguil'd)
  And drank down the whole glass of rum.

The day pass'd away, and the hours went so slow;-
  The table still sat in the floor;
And often the mother or children would go
  To look for papa at the door.

The mother and children got weary that night
  In waiting for father to come,
When the door flew open, and sad was the sight!—
  They saw he had been drinking rum!

Away ran the children with trembling and fear!
  The mother, with sorrow, struck dumb!
She dared not to speak, but she thought, with a tear—
  " I wonder who sold him the rum ? "

Oh! woe to the man who an evil eye keeps
  On him who his life would reform!
Oh! woe to the man who would put to his lips,
  The glass or the bottle of rum!

The deed, oh, how dark! and the heart, oh, how black!
  Of the man who for a small sum,
Would hinder the man, or to death bring him back,
  By selling or, giving him rum!

His gold may increase and his coffers o'erflow,
   Until he can scarce count the sum:
But so sure as it came, so sure will it go,
   If made selling poisonous rum.

His children may dazzle in silk and in gold;
   In coach they may go and may come;
But shame and disgrace when the story is told,
   "The price of their riches is rum!"

His wife she may sneer, and may look with disdain
   As she passes the once happy home;
But she'll not be able to wipe out the stain
   Made deep by the poisonous rum:

Oh! woe shall it be when he lies down to die.
   The ghosts of the drunkards may come,
And stand at his bed-side, and look in his eye,
   And say, " 'Twas you sold us the rum."

The man he has ruined;—his children and wife,
   Before him in phantoms may come—
Before him present all the woes of their life,
   And say, "Oh, you sold him the rum!"

A hundred souls, haggard, and crying for bread,
   Around him in visions may come,
With some on each side, at his feet, at his head,
   All saying, "You sold us the rum!"

"Who's that?" 'twill be asked, as the dead-cart goes by;
   No mourner, no sound of a drum:—
And some one will say, with a pitiful sigh,
   " 'Tis the man who died drinking rum!"

"Who's that?" 'twill be asked, as the landlord goes by,
   With friends to his long silent home,
And many will say, with a tear and sigh,
   " 'Tis the man who sold him the rum!"

His friends will regret it, in shame and in pain,
  As they go from the grave to their home;
In tears they will say, (but will say it in vain)
  " I wish he had never sold rum ! "

" Who's buried there, with a monument fair ? "
  'Twill be asked by many who come;
But they'll soon turn away, when they'll hear some one say,
  " The man who sold poisonous rum. "

The birds of the air, they will never go there,
  Their sweet songs to chant, or to hum:
But they'll all keep away, for something will say,
  " There's the man who sold him the rum ! "

The soft summur breeze, it will not fan the trees,
  Nor flowers of beauty there bloom;
The grass won't grow green, o'er the man that's so mean
  As t' poison his brother with rum.

And the stars of the skies will shut up their eyes,
  And the moon will put on a veil,
And the sun in its track, will wish to turn back;—
  The whole hosts of planets turn pale.

Thus heav'n, earth and air will unite and declare,
  That through all the ages to come,
They never will smile on the man that's so vile;—
  On the man who sold him the rum.

The angels,—tho' brave,—they will keep from his grave;
  Should he call, they'll appear to be dumb:
They'll fear to come near, but will far off appear
  To the man who sold him the rum.

When the trumtep shall sound to call up the dead,
  Even the poor drunkard shall come.
But this man, shall dread to lift up his head,
  For he'll know he sold him the rum.

And now let me say, while the morning is fair,
　　Before the dark evening shall come,
Put your name to the pledge;—in God's strength declare
　　That you'll never drink poisonous rum!

And you, my dear brother, O, let me implore!
　　In the name of our Father above,
If you've done as this man, O, do it no more,
　　I beg in the spirit of love!

THANKFUL FOR THE WEEPING.

WE are thankful for the weeping,—
　　The weeping of the night,
As well as for the dawning of
　　The day, with skies so bright.

We are thankful for the morning,
　　For we will prize it more,
Than if no tear had swell'd the eye,
　　Or dropp'd the night before.

And if the day was always bright
　　And sunny here below,
We'd seldom look to heav'n above,
　　From whence all blessings flow.

So when we hail the morn above,
　　With ever cloudless skies,
We'll prize it more than if no night
　　Of tears had swell'd our eyes.

NATURE AND ART.

Lines suggested by the question, "Are the works of Nature more pleasing to the eye than the works of Art?" Written in the author's youthful days, and read at a meeting of the Randallstown Literary Association.

THE works of Art in grandeur rise,
With pleasing aspect to our eyes:
But do they man's best thoughts command,
As those which rise from Nature's hand?

What works of Art to man can give
Such pleasure as he can receive,
When he, with elevated thought,
Beholds the works by Nature wrought.

When we behold, with wond'ring eyes,
The rolling orbs, the azure skies,
The roaring wave, the calm blue deep,
The broad spread plain, the mountain steep;—

The rising sun that lights the morn;
And in his glory marches on;—
Now beaming in the noon of day,
Now glist'ning in the rainbow's spray,—

Now with rich tints and hues of gold,
The beauties of the eve unfold;
He bids at Nature's high behest,
Adieu to all, and sinks to rest;—

Hangs richest curtains round his bed,
Which Nature's loom, each tinted thread
Has woven, looped and interlac'd,
As artist's hand ne'er yet has trac'd.

The moon now follows in the train,
Illuming valley, hill and plain,
And sheds its silv'ry rays of light,
To cheer and beautify the night.

The planets now, in bright array,
Come whirling 'neath the milky-way,—
Which spans the skies in one grand arch;
O'er which bright hosts by millions march.

Ten thousand burning lamps on high,
Hang out to light and please the eye,
And bid us Nature's works adore;—
Not Art the less, but Nature more.

We might name here earth's swelling veins,—
Which bring to man such goodly gains,—
The crystal streams, the shining ore
Of Nature's deep, exhaustless store!

List, as earth's throbbing pulses beat,
As swelling waves come and retreat,
And see her heaving breast, whose lungs.
Breathe heated air, whose fiery tongues

From hissing lips, reach to the sky,
And lick the clouds, as passing by,
And turn the azure sea to fire,
As these inflated lungs respire.

The dashing show'r, the snow's soft flakes,
The sunbeams, dancing on the lakes,
The cataract, whose waters gray,
Deep music make;—the rising spray

In softest notes, makes music such
As only wakes at Nature's touch:—
Which thrills the soul, the thoughts elate;—
Which Art would gladly imitate.

Who, with discerning eye and thought,
These wond'rous sights—by Nature wrought—
Can look upon, and then declare,
That Art with Nature can compare?

But we have only had a look
At pages few in Nature's book,
Leaf after leaf we might yet turn,
And still sublimer lessons learn:—

Which to the mind, the eye, the heart,
Must the undoubted truth impart,
That Art is but a stepping-stone,
By which we rise to Nature's throne.

Oh! tell me not that works of Art
Can please the eye, or charm the heart,
To that degree that Nature can,
When her works we rightly scan.

--- * ---

NEGLECT.

THE flowers would pine, with their heads bended low,
  With no kindly show'rs of dew;—
If no gentle zephyrs upon them should blow,
  And th' rays of the sun prove untrue.

So th' hearts of the lov'd ones, who live 'neath our smile,
  Would bow down in saddest dismay,
If other attractions our love should beguile,
  And turn our affections away.

LOVE;—WHEN MOST NEEDED.

WHEN all things are prosp'rous and riches are rife,
We then need but little to gladden our life:
But when want oppresses, and sorrows abound,
We then need love's warm hand to hold and surround.

When we on life's tide can pull strong at the oar,
Tho' unlov'd and friendless, we'll still reach the shore:
But when hands are feeble, and waves rolling high,
We then need love's strong hand our oars to ply.

When sails are all hoisted, and swell'd by the breeze,
Tho' love be not there we may glide o'er the seas:
But with sails all riven, and broken the mast,
'Tis then we need that love which loves to the last.

When skies are all bright, and the winds are all fair;
Tho' love may be absent, we need not despair:
But when our bark founders, and black grow the skies,
'Tis then we need that love that fades not, nor dies.

And when sad misfortunes fall thick on our head,
The love which was promis'd each other, when wed,
Should not be forgotten, but stronger unite
The hearts which were wedded when prospects were bright.

But if love lasts only while riches abide,
When they take their flight, we have little beside:
But if love,—as promis'd,—dies not, but lives on,
We still may be rich when our fortune is gone.

FAMILY PRAYER.

Family devotion is one of the most sacred and salutary of religious exercises and privileges. It gives strength to overcome the temptations of the world, and prepares us to perform, more faithfully, the duties of life—duties we owe to ourselves, to our fellows and to God. It teaches our children to look to a higher power than that of earth; instills into them feelings of thankfulness, forgiveness and forbearance, love for God and sacred things. And when they grow older, and become engaged in the sterner realities of life, what a barrier against vice and immorality is thrown around them, when they remember the days of their childhood, and see the form of that kind and consistent father, or that loving and indulgent mother, bending over them; and hear that voice in earnest prayer, invoking the blessing of Heaven upon their heads, saying, "Lead us not into temptation, but deliver us from evil." They will love that father; they will love that mother. Their thoughts and affections will lead them from the ways of sin to the fountain of life. Though the winds of adversity may blow, the storms of affliction beat, the brow become wrinkled by many cares, and all earthly treasures fail, they will still rejoice in hope of that inheritance incorruptible, undefiled, and that fadeth not away!

Then let not the Family Prayer be neglected: particularly in places where there is no Church or Sabbath-school; but let every fireside have its altar. The service should not be conducted as a task; nor be a cold formality. It should be considered a Christian help;—a holy privilege.

Some may live Christian lives without this help: once a week may do for others; but I need it every day. I have no more power *of myself* to resist temptation, to overcome evil, to live a Christian life, without going to the Father and asking "daily bread" than our Lord and Master had, when He prayed to His Father, saying, "I can do nothing of myself." This living bread which cometh down from Heaven and giveth life to the world, is so sweet, so nourishing, and so free that I want it every day. If we had it to buy, we might be compelled to do with less; but as it is without price, we may say: "Lord, evermore give us this bread."

How sweet at morn or eventide,
When father, mother, side by side,
And all the little children dear,
Together in one group appear!
And in the name of Him who said,
"Give us this day our daily bread."
Ask God our hungry souls to feed,—
Us not into temptation lead;
To give us strength to travel through
Life's journey, and our duty do;
And then at last in that sweet home,
To meet where sin shall never come.

IN MEMORIAM.

———

My twin daughter, Grace Irene, died May 19, 1872, aged thirteen months.

———

THE buds and the blossoms, which sweetest appear,
　Are often the first to decay:
So those who to us are most lovely and dear
　Are often first taken away.

But not like the flower, that withers and dies,—
　Are the dear little ones we love:—
It falls to the earth, where there lifeless it lies;—
　They live, and are carri'd above.

If God clothes the grass, which soon withers and dies,
　And flowers which fade and decay;
Much more will He clothe, and receive to the skies,
　Dear children much—better than they.

If falls not a sparrow unseen by God's eye,
　And hairs of our heads are all known:
These lov'd ones, His notice will never pass by;—
　He loves them, and claims them His own.

TEN YEARS.

———

Inscribed to Mrs. Hester M. ten years after first meeting her—then a happy school girl—who died about ten years after this was written, leaving a husband and several children.

———

TEN years and more have pass'd away,
Since first I saw thee at thy play;
   Happy and gay and wild.
I, too, was happy then, and blest
With a kind wife: who oft caress'd
   One interesting child.

But time has chang'd: I've children four.
This child a mother has no more;
   Nor I no more a wife!
We know not what a day may bring:
One summer, autumn, winter, spring,
   May greatly change our life.

Then little you or I believ'd,
When we next met I'd be bereav'd
   Of one to me so dear;—
That you would have a husband kind,
A child (in which much joy you find.)
   But such does now appear.

Ten years to come, and none can tell
With whom, and how, and where we'll dwell,
   But He who all things knows.
Perhaps your lot in life may be
A lot from care and sorrow free,
   Or one of ills and woes.

Ten years—and you may be bereft
Of husband, and with children left;—
  For whom you must provide;—
Or to an early grave consign'd,
And leave these little ones behind;—
  No one their feet to guide.

Or they, perhaps, may go before,
To dwell upon a happi'r shore,
  And leave you here alone.
Or you may both from them depart,
And leave them here with cheerless heart,
  To walk a path unknown.

For what has happen'd oft before,
May happen once, yes, oftimes more,—
  Yes, oft beneath the sun.
Then let us look to God each day,
And trust in Him, and ever say
  " Thy will not mine, be done."

Ten years;—yes, one short year may find
Your lot in life as chang'd as mine:
  (The future none can tell
But He guides us by His hand;—
By whom we fall, by whom we stand:
  Who doeth all things well.)

But still I hope this may not be:
But that a life of joy you'll see:
  And spend your days in peace:—
That heav'n may blessings on you pour,
And send these blessings more and more,
  As toils and cares increase.

May you, your husband, and your child,
Long live, nor be by sin beguil'd,
  Nor walk in evil ways;
But live a life both pure and true,
And wisdom's holy path pursue,
  And give to God the praise.

And when your race on earth is run,
You'll sink as sinks the setting sun;—
  Which sinks to rise again:
But rise upon a brighter shore,
Where sin and death shall be no more,
  Nor sigh, nor tear, nor pain.

Where peace and joy shall fill each heart;
Where they that meet, no more shall part;—
  No more shall say, "Farewell."
But where to God, in joyful lays,
We'll sing a song of ceaseless praise,
  And with our Saviour dwell!

TRUE LOVE.

THE love that grows stronger when friends are apart,
Is love that is pure, and is deep in the heart;
But love that grows weaker, and loses it pow'r,
Is not love of life-long, but love of an hour.

The love that grows weaker when friends are away,
Is not love undying, but love of a day.
True love is not passion, nor is passion love,
One is from beneath, and one is from above.

A QUESTION.

WHAT'S best to do,—I cannot guess,—
My children's and my life to bless.
It seems, somewhere along life's track,
I miss'd my way, now can't turn back,
And now 'tis very hard to tell,
If best go on, or here to dwell—
The course I'm in to still pursue,
Or undertake some project new.
There is a path I'd gladly tread,
In which I hop'd I would be led,—
O, once it seem'd to me so near!
But now too far to reach, I fear.

When I, with my departed wife,
First started on the road of life,
It seem'd so plain,—so clear the skies,—
We scarcely thought a cloud would rise.
Hope may have rais'd her wings too high;—
Her star, so bright, have dimm'd our eye,
That it could not the snares discern,
Which may have caus'd my feet to turn.
My wife departing from life's shore,
Left me behind with children four,—
Which for three years, and more, I've tried
Their steps in virtue's paths to guide.
Queer thoughts come oft, and long time dwell;
And yet they do not plainly tell
The things which I desire to know,—
As 'long the road of life I go;—
If it is best to get a wife,
Or as I am, to spend my life;—

And if a wife I chance to get,
Would she be mild, or grieve and fret;
And would my words and actions fret her;
And would that make us worse or better.
Of all I know—there's no dispute—
But few in ev'rything would suit.
And how can I the wrong detect,
That I the right one may select?
(Ere I'd unhappy make the lot
Of any one, I'd choose some spot,
To all but solitude unknown;
There I would live and die alone.)
Some are too young, and some too old;
Some are too timid, some too bold;
While some could not the children rule,
Or try their youthful minds to school,
Or train them up as they should go;
But caring nothing what they do,
Whether they're in or out of place,
With uncomb'd hair, or unwash'd face;
Thinking, perhaps, 'twould nothing hurt,
To let them run in rags and dirt.
Some to dress and go, would take
As much, or more than I could make;
While some would be too close to spend
A cent, to entertain a friend.
And some might keep me in a stew —
Forever wanting something new:
While others would be just as bad,—
Caring but little what they had —
Shoes, new or old, upon their feet,
Or whether things were clean and neat;
Or whether when we come to eat,
What sort of butter, bread or meat.
Some would not take a moment's ease;
Or if you did, your life they'd tease
And vex, till almost out of breath,
For fear that they would starve to death.

And still I think 'twould set me crazy,
T' see one slovenly and lazy.
But least of all could I endure,
A wife with lips and heart impure;—
Who would by art and act deceive—
Things, false as true, would make believe.

Now all the faults of which I tell,
I hope in any do not dwell,
But one who is from them all free,
Is what we do not often see.
I know that faults belong to me,
Which others can more plainly see.
Free from faults there are not any:
Some have few and some have many.
If there be one without a fault,
Let him with stone, guilt first assault.

Could I some gentle maiden find,
With comely form and prudent mind;
Of pious heart, and temper sweet,
And in her ways both clean and neat,—
'Twould matter not how rich or poor;
I'd love her none the less or more;
If only she her duty knew,
And to her duty would be true:—
With her I gladly would unite,
And seek to make her burden light.
(It does our burdens lighter make
When we each other's burdens take)—
I'd labor hard to make her blest:—
Such labor brings the labor'r rest.

Though much of this may seem in fun,
Of all these traits there is not one,
But what would either make us glad,
Or sorrow to our lot would add.
And there's no bitter'r lot in life,

Than discord 'twixt a man and wife!
But who their happiness can tell!
When they in love and concord dwell?
And oh, how often do we see
Those who appear to well agree,
And to the world make a fair show,
When in their hearts reign grief and woe.
And on the other hand, we find
Oft those of loving heart and mind;
Who care and want seem to annoy,
When in their hearts dwell peace and joy.
So then it is not outward show
That gives us happiness or woe:
'Tis that which dwells within the breast
Which makes us miserable or blest.
Oft in the palace is the lot
As hard as in the humble cot.
And always does grief's galling chain
Bind most where sin and folly reign.
Then if in life, we would be blest,
And while we labor, still have rest,
Let us resolve to learn, and do
That which is *noble, pure* and *true.*

As best I can I will proceed:
Perhaps some kindly hand will lead
My feet, in plainer paths and straight.—
I'll work; I'll trust; I'll watch; I'll wait;
I'll ask God—if His will it be—
To give me light my way to see.
Some guiding star may yet arise,
To light my way 'neath clearer skies.

———

Oftimes, perhaps, we look too high;
  And ask for what we do not merit.
And thus may seek through life, and die.
  And ne'er the prize we seek inherit.

So after all it must be best,
  To be contented with our lot;—
Look up—go on, and we'll be blest,
  And happy now, with what we've got.

------•------

WORK WHILE IT IS DAY.

OH, why will you loiter and doubt in the morn?
The day passeth quickly;—the night cometh on,
  When darkness shall reign in the place of the light:
  And none shall be able to work in the night.

Then work while 'tis day: in the night none can see:
The morrow, perhaps, shall ne'er come unto thee.
The time is fast flying:—thou hast but *to-day*—
Then, O, do not trifle, and throw it away.

I know that our pathway with troubles is rife:
And trials assail on the journey of life:
And know that the blessings in life we obtain,
Would not be so valu'd if not bought with pain.

Then speed on life's voyage; pull hard at each oar;—
The clouds may then blacken,—the foaming waves roar;—
Confide in thy Father; dispel ev'ry fear;
Be true to thy duty, and He will keep near.

When storms are done beating, and tempests are past,
The crew with the Captain, shall harbor at last,
In th' haven of rest, with a calm, sunny shore;
Exposed to the storms and the tempests no more!

Where oft they will wander in sweet, shady bow'rs,
And gather rich fruits, and behold the bright flow'rs,—
To drink the pure water from life's flowing riv'er;—
There rest, and there worship forever and ever.

THE LIGHT OF LIFE DIVINE.

THE Heav'ns above; oh, how sublime!
Unfaded by the lapse of time.—
The sun by day; the moon by night:—
The stars, with their inferior light:

These rolling orbs, with brilliant rays,
All call for songs of sacred praise!
Who can behold, and not exclaim,
"O, praise; O, praise the Maker's name!

But all these wonders we behold,
As doth a garment, shall wax old,
And as a vesture shall decay,
And as a scroll shall pass away.

But there's a Light, more brilliant far,
Than sun, and moon, and every star
That in the firmament doth roll,
And shed their rays from pole to pole.—

A light which none can see but they
Who walk in virtue's paths by day,—
In righteousness and truth delight,
And heav'nly wisdom seek by night:—

Who God, and His commands obey;
And shun the vile and vicious way,
Which stains our life; polutes our breath,
And leads to wretchedness and death.

This Light descends from heav'n above,
And fills the soul with joy and love.
It eminates around the throne
Of God, the great and holy One!

When its bright rays upon us fall,
We see that God is good to all;
And so we love all men in part;
And love the Lord with all our heart.

This Light, all brilliant!—all serene!—
No cloud shall ever pass between;
Nor mist obscure one shining ray
Which guides us to the perfect day.

This is the Light of life divine:
We trust it ne'er shall cease to shine,
Till all for whom this Light doth burn,
Shall by it, unto God return!

CONCLUDING HYMN OF A SUNDAY SCHOOL ANNIVERSARY.

KIND Friends, this scene is o'er:
  Our thanks you are receiving:
We hope, if here we meet no more,
  We'll meet you all in heaven.

Now, let us look above,—
  From whence all good is given—
And trust in Him who died to lead
  Our wand'ring feet to heaven;

Where we shall bathe at last,
  In love's unbounded river:
And all unite in praising God,
  Forever and forever!

WHY SHOULD I MURMUR, OR COMPLAIN?

WHY should I murmur, or complain,
　Or deem my light afflictions great;—
Count life and labor, hard and vain,—
　Its cares and turmoils deprecate?

Why should I deem my lot so hard,
　Though oft my bosom heaves with sighs,
And though my joy by grief is marr'd,
　And tears of sorrow swell my eyes?—

The tears that solitude beholds;
　The sighs no words have e'er express'd;
The grief that in deep current rolls
　Beneath the surface of my breast!

With all these ills there's much to swell
　My heart with gratitude and praise
To Him who doeth all things well;—
　Though hid from mortal eye His ways.

Should I complain, though all around
　I see the honor'd, rich and great,
While I, unhonor'd, unrenown'd,
　Dwell humbly in my low estate?

Though oft in eloquence, I hear
　Fall from wise lips, in words of fire,
The truths my soul within me stir,
　And with new life my thoughts inspire.—

Though I cannot these truths impart
　In living words, nor sway the throng;
Though burns the fire within my heart,
　To teach the right—restrain the wrong.

Oh! much above me do I see;—
  So much to which my soul aspires:
My cag'd up spirit would be free
  To soar, and grasp my life's desires!

But when I look beneath the plain
  On which I live,—which God hath blest,—
And see the sorrow, want and pain
  Which ne'er have roll'd across my breast,

Ah! then my lips well may I close,
  My murmurs cease, suppress my sighs,
And count but light my fleeting woes,
  And dry the fountain of mine eyes.

While I have raiment, food and health,
  How many destitute there be,
Who'd count my fortune joy and wealth,—
  Give thanks for half the good I see.

How many now on beds of pain,
  With anguish toss'd, with dread disease,
Would count it joy my ills to gain,
  And call my deepest trouble ease.

I'm shelter'd from the raging storm
  That beats upon the homeless head,
While many have no fire to warm
  Their trembling limbs; nor crust of bread.

While I have children in whose hearts
  The springs of deep affections flow,
I think of those in which sin's darts
  Have pierc'd, and show the marks of woe!

Of those who born of wicked birth,
  And rear'd beneath the vip'rous tongue,
Who know not right, nor virtues worth,
  Because their infant hearts were stung.—

Or may be those, whose infant ears
  The voice of loving parents heard,
But now bereft, and in their tears,
  No helping hand, or kindly word,

While I have parents kind and true,—
  In virtue's ways my feet have led,
Who've watched me all my journey through,
  And pray'd God's blessings on my head.

While I have reason, faith and hope,
  And look for bliss beyond the grave—
No longer in the darkness grope,
  But trust in Him who died to save.

The rattling chain, the shriek, the groan,
  I hear within the mad-house cell,
And see the desolated throne,
  From which the monarch, reason fell.

And now in view of all these woes,
  Should I not still my murm'ring breast,
And ev'ry rising sigh oppose,
  When God my life so much has blest?

But if my eyes should swell with tears,
  And if my heart should beat with grief,
Oh, let it be for woes and fears
  I see, but cannot give relief.

Our precious life we should not spend
  In vain regrets;—there's work to do,
And if we can't to heights ascend,
  Then we can work among the low.

But more than all, my God I'll praise
  For hope when all life's ills are o'er;
We'll understand His hidden ways,
  Nor sigh, nor suffer ever more.

Yes, for the hope that sighs shall cease,
   And grief and want and ev'ry woe;—
That joy and gratitude and peace
   Shall reign, and tears shall cease to flow.

HEAVENLY TREASURES.

OH, let us lay our treasures up,
   Where thieves will not steal them away.
Where moth and rust do not corrupt,
   But where they'll richest int'rest pay

For all on earth is fading fast;
   This life below is one short day;
Its pleasures but a moment last;
   These transient scenes will soon decay.

But there are riches bright and pure,
   Which time nor change can ne'er destroy,
Which brighter grow as they endure,
   And pleasures give without alloy.

Before we reach that world on high,
   Its glory here our pathway cheers;
It checks the murmur—quells the sigh,
   While trav'ling through this vale of tears.

It warms our love, dispels our fears;
   Yes, even in a world like this,
What vice will make a "vale of tears"
   Virtue makes a vale of bliss.

HOW sad was the message, when Adam and Eve
Were told that fair Eden they'd now have to leave!
So sad that its message they scarce could believe:—
    Could scarcely believe it was true!
They look'd at the sorrow on each other's face!
They felt the remorse, and the shame, and disgrace;
Then took their last look at the beautiful place,
    To which they must now bid adieu!

O, how each one heav'd with a solemn, sad sigh!
As from Eden they turn'd, with sorrowful eye,
And bid it forever, forever good-bye!
    No more to behold it again.
How slowly they walked! and how heavy they trod!
With naught to support them;—no staff, and no rod;
No friend to assist them:—forsaken by God.
    What sorrow! What anguish! What pain!

Now see them while hopelessly wending their way!
Each feeling the guilt;—scarce a word do they say;
With no one to look to, and none to whom pray·
    For God they've betray'd, in their trust!
And now by exper'ence the lesson they learn,
That by toil and by sweat their bread they must earn,
Till unto the ground they in sorrow return—
    In sorrow return to the dust!

They wept, when they thought of that once happy place,
Where they with pure hearts did each other embrace,
And heard God's sweet voice, and beheld His bright face;
    But now they could see Him no more.
And, oh, how they thought of those bright, happy hours!
When t'gether they roam'd in those sweet shady bow'rs,
And with hands unstain'd, pluck'd the choicest of flow'rs.
    In th' air which the sweet fragrance bore.

Afar from the gate, through the wilderness wild
To live with the serpent, which first them beguil'd,—
More frightful than when in the garden he smil'd
    They now make their lonely abode.
No sweet plumag'd songsters to cheer them at morn:
No soft angel voices, when day-light is gone:
How sad their condition! How sad and forlorn!
    O Sin, Sin, how heavy thy load!

So heavy, they scarce on their journey can keep:—
Now see them again as they sit down and weep,
As night overtakes them,—with no place to sleep
    But near where the serpent has coil'd:—
No faint star of hope do they see in the skies,
And no light below, but the glare of the eyes
Of the serpent—half clos'd, his form to disguise—
    As when Eden's beauty he spoil'd.

Says Eve unto Edam, "At morn let us trace
Our steps back to God, from this horrible place!
Perhaps He will look with a merciful face,
    And take us to Eden again."
"Oh, if I could think we could ever retrieve,
How glad would I be! but I cannot believe
The least of God's favor we'll ever receive,
    Or ever more Eden regain."

" You think if we go back and stand at the gate,
And all of our sorrow and anguish relate,
It will not His anger towards us abate ? "
    Said Eve in a half-hoping tone.
" No, Eve," he replied, " it will all be in vain;
God never will list to our pleading again;
Forever we must from His presence remain;
    He never again us will own ! "

But will God's all merciful eye never look
With pity again ?—Will He blot from His book
Their names;—though His law they so early forsook,—
    Regard not the penitent tear ?
Will God's holy image—which on man He plac'd—
Which now seems so faint, and so badly defac'd—
Be hidden forever, forever eras'd;—
    No more on his heart to appear ?

Or will God's eye—sleepless—that image still view;
His strong arm protect it, the wilderness through,
The pure blood of Jesus, its brightness renew,
    As first in fair Eden it shone ?
And like the " refiner," will Jesus not blow
The breath of His love, till the image will show,
And skim off the dross till its brightness will glow—
    Until it reflects back His own ?

Will not happy angels from Eden's gate go
Swift down the pathway where man went so slow,—
With strong hands, the work of the serpent o'erthrow,
    And pull up the thorns he has sown,
And roll back the stone from the world's darken'd tomb,
And light up its pathway—dispelling the gloom,
That man may return to a far brighter home
    Than ever in Eden was known ! ?

S there any heaven other
  Than the land beyond the grave?
Hast thou ever felt, dear brother,
  Any pow'r in this to save?
Hast thou ever felt the Spirit
  Bearing witness in thy breast?
Didst thy bosom e'er inherit
  Any thing like heav'nly rest?

There has oft to me been given
  · Greatest joy when most depress'd;
When from dearest idol riven,
  God has reigned within my breast.
When, like Peter, I've been sifted,
  Till the chaff had left the wheat;
Then, like Paul, my soul uplifted
  In Christ, to a heav'nly seat!

I have oft in deepest sadness,
  Felt the joy akin to bliss;—
Drank the streams of life and gladness,
  Flowing from that world to this.
Why, then, should we thirst or hunger,
  While the living waters flow?
Why for heav'nly bread wait longer,
  While so bountiful below?

Is it not on sacred pages
  Writ with inspiration's pen,—
"God shall in the future ages,—
  Come and dwell on earth with men?"
Did not Jesus, in His teaching,
  Tell us of the heav'nly birth,—
Say, while up to heav'n we're reaching,
  God would send it down to earth?

Did not Christ say, "I stand knocking,
  And from hence will ne'er depart
While the key of love's unlocking
  The guest-chamber of the heart;—
I'll come in and sup at even'—
  Break at morn, the living bread . "
What can it be if not heav'n,
  When with Jesus' hands we're fed?

Did not God say, "I will feea thee
  Till thy soul shall want no more,
And to living fountains lead thee,—
  Fountains full and running o'er?"
He the heav'nly bread will leaven
  With His ever flowing grace:
What can it be, if not heaven,
  When God's presence fills the place?

Though with richest mansion, furnish'd,
  Golden streets and precious stones,
Diamond crowns, all brightly burnish'd,
  Whited robes and gilded thrones;—
Though to me a place be given
  In those mansions bright and fair,
Yet to me 'twould not be heaven
  If God's presence were not there.—

Though our state be lone and lowly,
  Though our comforts small and few,
If with aspirations holy,—
  If with purpose pure and true,—
If God's smile and approbation
  On our earnest efforts rest,—
We'll be happy in our station;—
  Heav'n will dwell within our breast?

Faith, and hope, and love is heaven;
  Heav'n, from sin and death to rise;—
Where'er the grace of God is giv'n,
  If on earth or in the skies.
Though our hearts be wrung with sorrow;
  Though our lashes wet to-day;—
Heav'n to know that in the morrow
  God will wipe all tears away.

It is heav'n to trust God's promise;
  It is heav'n to look on high,—
Feel the good He now keeps from us,
  Will be given by and by.
It is heav'n the sorrow-stricken
  To relieve, to aid the poor;—
Ev'ry deed of love will quicken
  Us in life and heav'n the more.

It is heav'n, I know 'tis heaven,
  When my heart with joy o'erflows
With the blessings God hath given;—
  When it rests in calm repose;
When my soul with deepest praises,
  Hope, thanksgiving, faith and love,
With my tongue—though feeble—raises
  Up to God, in heav'n above!

What can it be, if not heaven,
  When I hear the wooing dove
Whisper,—"All thy sins forgiven,
  And thy name is writ above:
Though such joys are not here given
  As await you by and by,
All the way from earth to heaven,
  God will guide you with His eye."

Tell me not that man—though mortal—
  Must the joys of heav'n await
Till he enters death's cold portal:
  He may enter here the gate
Which white angel hands are holding
  Open wide, and bidding come,
While the glories are unfolding
  More and more as nearing home!

Though a curtain now dividing
  Us from that pure world on high,
And its greatest joys half hiding
  From the view of mortal eye,
Yet, as soft love-laden zephyrs
  Gently fan those curtain folds,
O, what bliss the prospect offers!—
  Bliss my eye now half beholds!—

Half beholds the Father gracious;
  Half beholds those mansions fair;—
Mansions rich! eternal! spacious!
  Jesus said He would "prepare."
Heavenly joys with earth are blending,
  As the angels come and go;
Blessed angels now descending,
  Bringing heaven down below!

Blow ye zephyrs! cease not blowing;
  Bring us gladness from above!
Heav'nly Dove, cease not thy wooing;
  Fan us with thy wings of love:
Blessed Spirit, cease not flowing
  From that heav'n above to this,
Till our faith be chang'd to knowing'—
  Hope and trust, to sight and bliss!

May our faith grow brighter, stronger;—
  Broader, deeper, grow our love,
Till we walk by faith no longer,—
  Till we reach that heav'n above!
Till our hearts from sin be sifted;
  Till the pow'r of death shall fail·
Till the curtain shall be lifted
  Till we see beyond the veil!

Until then we'll cease not toiling;
  Until then we'll watch and pray,—
Till life, victor—death despoiling—
  Reigns in one eternal day;—
Until all earth's wrongs are righted;
  Until ev'ry storm subsides;
Until heav'n on earth's, united
  With the heav'n where God abides.

MOTHER.

—

Written for, and read to my mother, on the Eightieth Anniversary
of her birth-day, January 12th, 1881.

—

JUST Eighty years ago to-day,
A Child was born, whose tender form
A happy mother loved and watch'd,
As only mothers love and watch.
And as this Babe to childhood grew,
That mother held her little hands,
And taught her tiny feet to walk,
And said for her the good-night prayer.
And through the happy, sunny morn
Of golden-hair and girlhood days,
That mother, with more anxious care,
Watch'd all her playful, childish ways.
And when the morning hours had wan'd,
And she to womanhood had grown,
That mother's heart—more anxious still—
Pray'd that the lessons taught in youth,
Might guide her feet in virtue's ways,
And guard her head and hands from ill.

With skies all bright and hope aglow;
Her heart and hand she gave to him
Who with her on the road of life
For many years has work'd and walk'd.
But ere she reached the noon of life
That mother's eyes that watched in hope,
In quiet sleep of death were clos'd,—
Committing t' Him who never sleeps,
The treasure to her heart so dear;
And for whose good her life was spent.
That tender babe of early morn—

That hoping girl of matin mirth,—
That woman of the sunny noon—
In lengthened days and ripened years,
Still lives, and looks with faith serene,
Upon the evening star of life.
She lives; but not for self alone;
With heart and head and hands she lives:
Not idly sits and breathes and waits;—
As life's last taper flickers low,—
Watching the dying embers fade,
As one by one their light goes out,—
Impatient for her change to come.
But with a patient, kindly look,
And cheery words and deeds of love,
And hands of charity she lives.
With heart of hope and ceaseless pray'r,
And thankful praise, she lives—still lives.—
Not to herself, but unto Him
Who only life and peace can give;—
For those her life may cheer and bless.—
For him with whom for fifty years*
And more she's walk'd and sought to bless.
Who helpless lies, and long has lain
Beneath the twilight's lingering rays,
And who with glad and list'ning ear,
Catches the sound of her unweary,
Hasty tread, as near his couch she comes;
Dispensing that which comfort gives,
And keeps the night of death away:
Or bending aside the foliage of doubt,
That hope's fair, but declining star,
May shed some shining. cheering ray
Upon his worn and weary feet,
And vision faint and dim'd by time.

-----

*Since writing the above, my father—for whom mother had been so
tenderly and patiently caring—passed away, while she still remains with
us;—now five years after the above was written.

A dozen children she has borne,
And lov'd, and nurs'd, and wisely taught,
And counsel and example giv'n.
Some of tender years, whose feet had
Not yet learn'd life's rough road to walk:
While others of maturer years,
On whom she look'd with hopeful pride,
Have by the hand of death been led
Where suns set not, and no night comes:
But where the lov'd and lab'ring meet,
And for the gleaners watch and wait,
To bear the scatter'd golden sheaves
They've gathered from the field of time.
The little feet that never walked
The hot and bri'ry fields below,
May lead the way to silv'ry streams,
Where purest waters gush and flow.
The little hands that never pluck'd
The smallest flow'r, or sow'd, or reap'd,
May bathe the hard and aching heart,
Or wash away the marks of tears
The tir'd and weary reapers wept.

For four score years, through heat and cold,
Through beating storm and calm, 'neath clear,
And cloudy skies, early and late,
With trusting heart, and faithful hands,
Our Mother toil'd, and murmur'd not.
Nor will she murmur, when at eve
The Master of the vineyard comes,
And justly compensates her toil;—
With lib'ral hand, gives of his own,
To those who labor'd but one hour,
And less of heat and burden bore.

Though frail from toil and length of days,
Her usefulness she's not outliv'd: —
Not yet; or will it ever be.
Each child, grand-child and great-grand-child,
In her declining years, will love
And look to her for good advice—
For counsel and encouragement.
Her presence will maternal joy
And love, and peace, and hope impart.

May her life be yet prolonged;
And may each returning birth-day
Bring greater joy, like each step of
The worn and homeward trav'ler,
Until he sees the cheering "Light,"
And hears the familiar voices
Of his wife and loved ones, and feels
The warm and welcome embraces, and
The happy kisses that tell their
Joy with tears of love and gladness.

May her evening be serene and
Peaceful; and when her sun sinks low,
And darkness o'er the twilight steals,
And her last farewell is said, may
Her departure be triumphant.—
Not dead, but living in our hearts.
May her memory be long lov'd,
Her precepts honor'd and obey'd,
Her example priz'd and followed;
Her children venerate her name,
And proud and happy ever be,
To own and call her "Mother."

MY DAUGHTER.

To Mary Virginia, my eldest daughter, on the Twenty-fifth Anniversary of her birth-day.

'TWAS early in spring time, the Twenth-first day
Of the month of the flowers ;—bright, balmy May,
When sweet birds were singing in tree-top and lawn ;
When Nature was putting her spring garments on ;—
When the fields and the forests in green were array'd,
Inviting the weary to rest in their shade :—
When the hills, plains and valleys no longer ice-clad,
And all things in nature seemed happy and glad.
'Twas in this bright season, when all nature smil'd,
I looked with delight on my second-born child :—
My second-born child, as she opened her eyes
To th' light which beam'd from spring morning skies.
'Twas "Mary Virginia," we gave for the name
Of the babe that as a sweet spring-present came.
Just a quarter of a century to-day,
Since babe and its mother so lovingly lay ;
Babe that then knew not life's pleasures or woes ;
Now a mother who sorrow and pleasure both knows.
The mother, who unto this daughter gave birth,
Now peacefully rests in the bosom of earth.
While the babe, as a mother, now fills up her place,
Is passing the milestones on lifes flecting race.

And as she from milestone to milestone goes on,
O, may she learn lessons from miles she has gone.
And as from each milestone the past she reviews,
Pick up the rich treasures she never shall lose.
And as from the end she looks back on the road,
On flowers and fruits from the seed which she sow'd,
May no sigh of sorrow, or anguish of breast,
Disturb her sweet peace, as she lies down to rest.
And may her dear daughter, as she follows on,
Pick up the sweet flowers her mother has strewn,—
With hands full and arms full, and wreaths on her brow,
Present the rich treasures that she's sowing now;
And when the race ends, and her journey's complete,
Throw down the rich treasures with joy at her feet,
Of sweet flowers many, and thorns very few,—
Say, "Mother, these flowers were planted by you."
So let us be careful in sowing our seeds;
That from them we gather no thorns and no weeds;
But gather sweet flowers through time to the tomb;
And which in the future forever shall bloom.

LIFE IS THE TIME.

LIFE time is the time to work;
    And not the time for sighing:
And if our work be all well done,
    We need not grieve at dying

And if faithful watch we keep
    While sailing o'er the ocean,
We not fear the port beyond,
    Or think with sad emotion.

ET me follow Thee, O Lord:—
  Though no place to lay Thy head;—
Feast upon Thy precious word,
  With Thy promise for my bed.

Let me see Thee feed the throng,—
  Fainting for the want of bread—
Make the faint and feeble strong,
  Heal the sick and raise the dead.

Let me see Thee in that hour
  When the tempter came to Thee,—
Said I'll give Thee wealth and power,
  If Thou wilt but worship me.—

Oh! how quick the tempter fled,
  When inform'd by Thee, my Lord,—
" Man can't live alone by bread,
  But by ev'ry word of God."—

Let me see Thee at the grave,
  Where Thy tender soul didst weep;—
See Thy love, Thy pow'r to save,—
  Calling Laz'rus from his sleep.

Keep me near Thy feet, O Lord!
  Let me see Thy bleeding side;—
Feel the precious blood that pour'd:—
  Wash me in its crimson tide.

Let me kneel where Thou hast knelt,
  In the dark Gethsemane:
Let me feel what Thou hast felt,
  Let me see what Thou didst see.

Let me stand and hear Thee pray,
　(All forsaken; all alone,)
" Father take this cup away !
　Yet Thy holy will be done.''

Let me see those drops of sweat,
　Like blood bursting through Thy face;
While Thine eyes with tears are wet,
　For a lost and ruin'd race.

Let me stand at Pilate's bar;—
　Own Thee as my Lord and King;—
Feel the thorns that press'd Thy brow;
　While Thy foes false charges bring.

Let me help to bear Thy cross,
　Up on rugged Calvary;—
All things else I'll count but dross,
　If I can but follow Thee.

Let me see Thee on the tree;
　Let me hear that dying groan,
" Why, O God ! forsakest me ?—
　I for all mankind atone!''

Let me see Thee bow Thy head;—
　Hear Thee for Thy murderers pray,—
" While they live, O God, they're dead !
　Father, take their sins away!''

Let me taste the bitter gall,
　Given, my dear Lord, to Thee;—
Hear Thee say, " 'Tis finished all!
　Man may live, and live in me.''

Let me ere the break of day,
　Meet Thee, Jesus, at the grave;—
See the stone there roll'd away;—
　Feel Thy life,—Thy pow'r to save !

Let me feel Thy hands, Thy feet,—
  Prints, the rugged nails have made.
How dear, Lord! to me how sweet!—
  Oh! my unbelief upbraid!

Let me follow at Thy feet,
  Till to earth I bid farewell:
Then, dear Lord, grant me a seat,
  With Thee evermore to dwell!

———————•———————

WE, TOO, SHOULD LABOR IN LOVE.

JESUS in love His work begins
  On earth: In love His labors close:—
In life oft weeping with His friends,
And when His life of labor ends,
  He prays—dies praying—for His foes.

We, too, should labor, love, and pray,
  If we His crown of glory share—
Should love His law, His word obey;—
Should keep the straight and narrow way:—
  We, too, the crown of thorns should bear.

FAREWELL TO A FRIEND.

FAREWELL, dear friend: and is it true
That I, alas! must part with you?
    And must this tie now sever?
Oh! can we break this sacred tie,
That seem'd so strong twixt you and I!
    Oh! must it break forever?

This hand no more shall take thy hand:
These eyes which oft thy features scann'd,
    Shall look in other ways:
But yet this heart will doubtless yearn;
And oft to thee in mem'ry turn
    And think of by-gone days.

These feet no more with thee shall walk;
These lips no more to thee shall talk;
    No more we side by side,
Around the table of our Lord,
Shall we our love for Him record—
    For Him who for us died!

I'll see, perhaps, thy face no more,
As oft I saw in days of yore;
    Nor hear again thy voice.
And yet, no doubt, that voice so sweet,
In dreams my ears shall often greet;
    And make this heart rejoice.

And as from you I now depart,
I lay my hand upon this heart—
    This heart so warm and true—
And say, " 'Tis not my will to go
A way that I am yet to know,—
    A way unknown to you."

Our parting is no fault of mine;
Nor yet of yours:—we both resign
    By mutual consent;
Though in all things we well agree;
Yet are convinc'd 'twill better be
    To part, and be content.

And yet we now must say Farewell!
And break, or try to break the spell
    Which like a golden chain,
Binds soul to soul, and heart to heart—
Should not be rudely snapp'd apart:—
    It may be bound again.

A FIRM RESOLVE.

THE way which seems most straight and true,
With all my strength I will pursue.
With God,—with conscience for my friend,
I'll boldly press unto the end.
Though lions roar, and quicksands shake,
And threaten every step I take;
Though storms may beat, and tempest blast,
And darkness o'er my vision cast;
Though prowling wolves lurk in my way,
And seek—without reserve—their prey;
And vultures, soaring in the skies,
Unite to watch with envi'us eyes:
And should my friends unite with foes,
And ev'ry step I take oppose,—
With faith in God, and in His strength,
I'll press unto my journey's length;
And though my feeble body fail,
My spirit shall at last prevail;
And in the end obtain the prize,
If not on earth, beyond the skies.

THE DURABLE.

THAT which we write on sand or clay,
The early rains will wash away;
And if on iron, wood or brass,
It, too, from mortal view shall pass;
And if on silver or on gold,
The web of time shall it enfold;—
On granite shaft or marble bust,
It, too, shall mingle with the dust:—
On adament, or mountains gray,
Time still will wear the work away.
But what you write on human souls,
Will last while age on age unfolds.
Then as you write, see that your pen
Makes no line, you'd erase again;
Or chisel make a single groove,
Eternal years will not approve.
'Tis not the pencil, paint, or board,
That through eternal years is stor'd:
It is the thought, the word, the deed,
We through eternal years shall read.
What Pilate wrote o'er Jesus' head,
A million million eyes have read:
Millions of millions read it now,—
Not on the cross but on His brow.
Now Pilate's bar,—the thorny crown,
The heavy cross which bore "Him" down,
The nails, the spear the soldiers' used,
The gall and wormwood "He" refus'd,—
Now all are gone:—but still remains
The star that shone on Bethleh'm's plains,
Around the cross,—illum'd the grave;
And still shines on a world to save.

INDICISION.

BLEST with success he'll ever be
Whose thoughts and actions all agree;—
Not given to procrastinate;
But onward walks, both smooth and straight,—
Who stops not where two ways may meet,
And undecided takes a seat,
And looks ahead, and then looks back,
And says, " I must be off the track."—
But drives ahead with might and main,
The road that seems to him most plain.
He stops not at the river's brink,
And sits for hours and hours to think
Whether a boat would swim or sink,—
When all that he wants is a drink,—
Nor asks each traveler to tell
How far before he'll reach a well;
Which, when he finds, he'll stop and dwell,
And wonder how he best can tell
Whether 'tis best to draw, or bring
The water from some distant spring.
And when he lets the bucket down,
He hesitates, and looks around,
And empty draws the bucket up,
And to the spring starts with a cup:
And when he gets about half way
He'll stop, and to himself will say,
" I'll drink when I get farther on;
For now the day is almost gone."
Not he who travels in this way,
Shall travel far, though long his day:
Though he may often count the cost,
The time of counting will be lost.
But he who goes with all his strength,
Shall go the journey to its length.
He'll count the cost,—while counting gain,
And in the end the prize obtain.

THERE IS A HAPPY LAND.

THERE is a happy land,
  Not far away;
I see the golden strand,
  Wash'd by the spray;—
I see the gates unfold,—
Pearly gates, and streets of gold,
Of which the prophets told,
  Not far away.

There is a happy land,
  'Tis very near,
Where the kind Father's hand
  Dries ev'ry tear.
I feel that soft hand now
Resting gently on my brow,
Soothing—I can't tell how—
  Sorrow and care.

There is a happy land;
  'Tis very near;
Songs from the joyful band
  Fall on my ear;
List, as the angels cry,
" Holy is the Lord on high,"
Ring through the arched sky;—
  'Tis very near.

From that bright, happy land,
  Oft, oft I feel
Some gentle, loving hand
  Over me steal;—
Oft hear the cooing dove,—
Breathing messages of love,
Wooing to things above,—
  Sweet words reveal.

That land of joy untold,
  'Tis, 'tis so near:
Its blessings half unfold
  E'en to us here;
So near its gentle show'rs,
Falling on this land of ours,—
Make glad the smiling flow'rs,
  'Tis, 'tis so near.

Only a narrow bay
  Running between,
Keeps us from it away,—
  Half hides the scene;
Just back of which there rolls,
Swelling streams for thirsty souls
Hid by the hanging folds,
  Of living green.

Only a time we wait—
  Wait by the shore,
Until life's storms abate,
  Then we'll pass o'er,
Then our enraptur'd sight
There will see the glories bright,
And loosen'd tongues unite,
  God to adore.

Often across the bay
  Sweet music floats
From tongues not far away,
  In sweetest notes.—
List, as the notes vibrate,
Through the ever open gate,
Where beck'ning angels wait,
  Wait for the boats.

There is a happy land,
  With mansions fair,
Which the kind Saviour's hand,
  Now doth prepare.
That land is every place
God pours out His boundless grace
When we His truth embrace,
  Both here and there.

————•————

THE HEAVENLY MORN.

THAT bright and all glorious morn!
  No sin and no death shall be there;
There mortal shall put immortality on,
And we who the image of earthy have born,
  The heavenly image shall bear.

There angels shall welcome us home,—
  With gladness shall bid us come in:
And o'er those bright plains we forever shall roam,
There sickness, nor sorrow, nor death can e'er come;
  There all shall be sav'd from their sin.

————•————

TO AN ESTEEMED FRIEND.

IT is no other worth of thine;—
  No other worth but what thou art,
That draws, that holds this heart of mine;
  This loving, hoping, happy heart.

NOW with our hungry spirits fed
  With fruits that grow on Eden's shore,
And water from the fountain head
  We've drunk:—nor thirst nor hunger more;—

We'll take each wand'rer by the hand,
  And with him to the fountain go:
We'll lead them to that peaceful land,
  Where fruits on trees immortal grow.

This duty should be our delight,
  For what our Lord has done for us
In leading us from dark to light;—
  From sorrow's paths to paths of peace.

Such is the duty that we owe
  To Jesus for His matchless love,
In leading us from death and woe,
  To life and happiness above.

For said our Master—kind and true—
  Ye should your love to others give,
For freely I have given you,
  That love by which the soul doth live.

By this shall all men know thy love:—
  Shall know that ye are born of me;—
The love that came from heav'n above;—
  The love that sets thy spirit free.

UPON Blue Ridge's western slope,
  And near to Pen-Mar's rocky peak,
A spacious house is built for those
  Who rural rest and pleasure seek.
Its length three hundred feet and more,
  It rises full four stories high,
And, like a light-house on the shore,
  It catches many a distant eye.

Two hundred light and airy rooms,
  All nicely fit, with whited walls,
Where all its guests may find repose,
  Or walk its long and spacious halls.
To heat the building through and through,
  Facilities are well applied;
And through it, water fresh and pure,
  Comes gushing from the mountain side.

In standing at this Mountain House,—
  Which faces to the western sky—
What thrilling rapture fills the heart!
  What wond'rous beauty meets the eye!
Ten thousand acres reaching out
  To Alleghany's western base,
And to the right and left afar!
  Oh! can there be a grander place?

The mountain peak, just in the rear,
  Which rises up a thousand feet,
Is gray with rocks and green with trees!
  Oh! can there be a scene more sweet?
The sun steals o'er the mountain top,
  To kiss the flow'rs beneath its shade,—
Which all night long the dew have sipp'd
  Until their blushing heads are weigh'd.

So let us look which way we will,
  And beauty meets us everywhere;—
Here are rich fields of golden grain,
  Neat rural homesteads over there;—
Bright sunny slopes and shady nooks,
  And waving grass and fruitful trees,
All interspers'd with groves and lawns,
  Fann'd by the gentle mountain breeze!

The Iron horse around the curve
  Comes neighing with the laden'd train;
And speeds away, with unslack'd nerve,
  With echoes o'er the distant plain.
As beauteous sun-sets here I've seen
  As pen or pencil e'er portray'd,—
Bright golden beams with clouds between;—
  Sweet blending of the light and shade!

From this veranda, 'round the house,
  Hid from the noon-day's solar blaze,
Many an eye will look with joy
  At evening's mild departing rays:
Many a thought shall here inspire
  The poet's heart and guide his pen,
And strain of music float on air,
  And echo o'er hill, rock and glen.

Here lasting friendships shall be made,
  And too, perhaps, some sacred vows,
Which oft in mem'ry shall return,
  And linger 'round Blue Mountain House.
Who would not wish to spend a month
  From sultry city, toil and heat,
In such a lovely place as this;—
  In such a quiet, grand retreat!

We all may count the few short months
  Since here this structure was design'd—
Since axe and spade their work began,
  And art with nature here combin'd.
But who can count the lengthen'd years,
  Or span old Time's unmeasur'd bridge,
Since God its deep foundation laid,
  And rear'd in air, this mountain-ridge?

O! who can look on these grand hills,
  And beauties in the vale below,
And feel no better by the sight;
  Or feel not inspiration's glow?
O, tow'ring hills! O, lengthen'd vales!
  As I upon thy grandeur gaze,
My eye with rapture swells;—my soul
  Rises above thy heights, in praise!

THE VOICE OF NATURE.

Written at Blue Mountain House.

O YE hills! ye everlasting hills!
Who laid thy rocky depths, that they be
Not moved, and raised thy summits to the
Clouds?   Who at thy feet the verdure green
Did spread, and girded thee about with
Oaks, with walnuts, chesnuts and with
Pines, and vines and flowery wreaths?   Who hung
The azure veil around thy brow, and
Crowned thy lifted head with coronets
Of ivy, of myrtle and of moss?
Thy beauty, thy sublimity, thy
Grandeur answer—" God ! "

Who shaped thy dizzy heights and dug
Thy rocky caverns, where the eagles
Build their nests, and the foxes make their
Home.   Who from thy side,—though solid rock, --
The limped waters forc'd, and sent in
Sweet profusion through the vale beneath?
Who did the panorama of a
Million acres broad unfold and paint
With richest hues of blended light and shade?
The hills, the rocks, the valleys, the trees
And flow'rs and bounding brooks and beast
And bird—with one distinct, united voice
All answer, God !   And as with ear intent,
We do for other answer list, naught
Do we hear but, " God ! "

And as the husbandman with taught and
Tir'd hand prepares the fertile beds, in
Rich designs, and borders them about
With shrub and box and tree and vine, and
Sows—in hope, the choice and treasur'd seed,
So Thy hand, O God! unhid, untaught
And untir'd, spread this beauteous vale—
Reaching out till the admiring and
Wond'ring eye is by the beauty,
The distance, and the glory, dimmed;—
So Thy hand in beauteous designs,
Hath richly decked the valley, hill and plain,
With fruitful trees and shady bowers,
And flower and vine and winding wreath;
So Thy wise hand, at early dawn, hath
Sown the seed which bloom in beauty now.
And as at early morn, the plowman
With sturdy hand, turns up the furrow,
And in ridges lays the loamy soil,
So in the morn of time Thy mighty
Hand scoop'd out these depths and turned up these
Mountain heights. And as the mountain is
Greater than the plowman's ridge, and the
Valleys deeper than the furrow, so,
O God! is Thy power and Thy works
Greater than those of man; and Thy ways
And wisdom deeper! For Thy wisdom
And Thy power, the grandeur and the
Beauty, may our adoration—our
Rev'rence and our praise be deeper
Than the valleys, broader than the plains
And higher than the hills, O God!

To the thoughtless mind—the faithless heart—
The undiscerning eye, nought but hills
And rocks and trees and plains and chasms deep
Appear. But he of faithful heart, who
Thinks and sees with deeper thought and sight,

In rocks Thy name can read. and hear Thy
Voice in breezes soft, and by the trees
May know that Thou wast, and yet dost live!

O, hills! O, rocks! O, trees, and valleys
Broad, and dancing brooks, and running streams!
Let thy voice in plainest speech be heard,
That man may surely know thou art the
Handywork of God!

------•------

AN ACROSTIC.

Written in 1870,

TO-DAY, O how I miss you, dear!
O what a joy to have you here!

My spirit is by thine made bright.
Your love shall make my burden light.

At loving words our hearts rebound;—
But harsh expressions crush them down.
So, may our love forever blend,
Each loving each unto the end.
Nor trouble, pain, nor toil, nor care,
Too great for souls that love, to bear.

When soon we meet, O, then 'twill be
Indeed, a joy to you and me;
For love's strong chords, too strong to break,
Enchanting melody shall make.

THE STAR OF HOPE.

O STAR of Hope, let thy bright beams
  Inspire our hearts to onward press:
Though almost lost, O, let thy gleams
  Conduct us through this wilderness.

Although the night is dark and chill,
  O, may our hearts new courage take:
As thou hast led us, lead us still,
  Until the morning light shall break.

Shine on bright star; on thee we'll gaze
  Until our journey is complete;—
Till every murmur turns to praise;—
  Till every bitter turns to sweet !—

Till faith shall vanish, and our eyes
  Behold the sight they long have sought;—
Until our hands shall grasp the prize
  For which they hard and long have wrought.

Tho' deep the valley, high the hill,
  And tho' the way be rough and long,
O, may thy brightness guide us still:
O, may it make our weakness strong.

If not the brightest of thy beams,
  Grant us, at least, some friendly ray,—
Let us behold thee in our dreams,
  If not thy face in brightest day.

The roughest of the road we've past:—
  We'll quickly tread; no longer grope:
We've felt the hardest of the blast.—
  Shine on; Shine on ! bright Star of Hope.

O, may our eyes of scales be shorn:
    May they to visions brighter ope:
The hardest of the load we've borne.—
    Shine on! Shine on! bright Star of Hope.

May gladness make our bosoms beat;—
    Give to our faith a larger scope:
We've borne the hottest of the heat;
    Shine on! Shine on! bright Star of Hope.

We've crossed the deepest of the sea:
    Thine anchor with its golden rope,
Shall bind us firmly unto thee.
    Shine on! Shine on! bright Star of Hope.

The hardest of the fight, we've fought,
    And yet we feel we cannot cope
With snares the ills of life have wrought,
    Without thy aid, bright Star of Hope.

As we descend each valley deep;
    As we ascend each gentle slope,
Our eye on thee we'll firmly keep.—
    Shine on! Shine on! bright Star of Hope.

The night is nearly past; behold!
    The tokens of a brighter morn:
See in the east those beams of gold.—
    Bright Star of Hope! Shine on! Shine on!

"THE WATCHMAN SAID, THE MORNING COMETH."

THE daylight is dawning, and soon we'll behold
The light of the morning all tinted with gold.
The sun is now rising and we very soon
Shall see all the brightness and glory of noon.

The clouds which have cover'd and darken'd our sky,
Are fleeing like shadows which quickly pass by.—
The gay sparkling dew-drops which dance on the flow'rs,
Bespeak to us plainly the bright sunny hours.

The trees they are budding, the blossoms appear,
Which say to us plainly the summer is near,
When fruits shall be gather'd and groves o'erflow,
And fields shall be fairer and whiter than snow.

The nations are shaking:—how blest it will be
When all from " gross darkness " in Christ shall be free;
When light of the gospel shall open our eyes,
And they who now sleep in their graves shall arise.

Glad tidings ring out, with the rays of the morn;
Be wafted to millions from darkness unborn.
Ye harp strings resound in melodious lays,
Till all are enchanted, and join in God's praise!

May light, truth and knowledge continue to spread,
Like wings of the morning all tinted with red —
Which fly through the noon-day, and stop not to rest,
Till folded at eve in the far distant west.

O, watchman, O, watchman, we list for thy voice,
Which tells of the morning, and bids us rejoice!
We list as it echoes the flight of the night—
The coming of morning, when all will be light!

MY ABSENT SON.

———

To my eldest son, who left home for Kansas, April 3, 1871.

———

TEN years ago, this very day,
   For the far west my son left home:
Five years, he said, he meant to stay:
   Twice five have passed:—he has not come.

My first born child, (a household joy,
   Which as an angel guest appears)—
A modest, truthful, honest boy;—
   A comfort to declining years.

Oh, what is there in western wilds,
   That can present such scenes of joy?
What can it be that so beguiles,
   And keeps from home my missing boy?

Has he a father's love forgot?
   That love that often flows in tears:—
That secret love that sleepeth not;
   Still never to the world appears.—

Or did he ever know that love
   That guarded him in infant days;
Before his feet had learn'd to rove,
   Or ere he knew the world's rough ways?—

That love that held his little hand,
   When first his tottering steps he took—
That love that smiled to see him stand,
   And brightness saw in every look.

Has he forgot his sisters, dear?
   The sisters whom he oft caress'd,
And who oft drop a longing tear,
   To clasp that brother to their breast.

Has he forgot his brother kind—
  Who looked to him with hope and pride,
And thought in him a friend to find,
  To help and cheer him at his side?

It cannot be he has forgot,
  That love that binds two hearts as one:
It cannot be that he feels not
  The tender love of brother—son.

It cannot be he never meant
  To see us more when home he left,
And to a land of strangers went;—
  Of ev'ry joy of home bereft.

I know my boy has not forgot:
  There must be reasons for his stay:
It cannot be he has forgot,
  The reason he's so long away.

I know my boy will come one day:
  At morn, or noon, or eve he'll come.
It may be when the bird's are gay,
  Or when the autumn flowers bloom.

It may be when the reapers reap;
  Or when the hills with ice are clad;
It may be when we mourn and weep,
  Or when our hearts are light and glad.

But if his stay secures success,
  And heaven blessings on him pour,
The day he went and comes we'll bless,
  And love him as in days of yore!

He went for better or for worse;
  But which we cannot now discern.
He may come back with well fill'd purse,
  Or like the prodigal return.

But let him come when e'er he will,
  We will rejoice to see him come:
The fatted calf for him we'll kill,
  And welcome him again to home.

I see him as at three years old;
  His rosy cheeks with dimples fair;—
His mirthful forehead—broad and bold;
  His full bright eyes, and curly hair.

I see the place he used to play;—
  The little hat he used to wear;
The little coat and pants of gray;—
  The little shoes—a tiny pair.

Tho' all these things have chang'd or gone,
  Yet mem'ry holds them as of yore.
The darkest night, the brightest morn,
  Is treasured up in mem'ry's store.

That child has now to manhood grown;
  Has tasted some of manhood's care—
The care to sunny youth unknown,
  When hopes were bright, and skies were fair.

No, youth feels not the pangs nor bliss,
  That will in riper years appear:—
Knows not the meaning of a kiss,
  Nor half the sorrow of a tear.

Youth laughs, youth weeps;—no secret knows,
  Its greatest joy and pain reveals;
While manhood hides its deepest woes,
  And oft its greatest joy conceals.

Often when looking at the trees,
  (The trees he planted ere he went,
The boughs of which the summer breeze
  Or winter's blast has broke or bent,)

I wonder if the storms that blow
　And. beat upon this son's fair head,
And bend his boughs and branches low,
　Have broke, or caused them more to spread.

O, may the adverse winds that sweep
　Across the boughs make strong the root;
That it may grow both broad and deep,
　And in due season yield its fruit.

O, may the Lord his path direct,
　While wand'ring in a distant land;—
His head, his feet, his heart protect,
　That he against life's ills may stand.

The night I never will forget,
　When parting with him at the train !
Two bosoms clapsed: two faces wet—
　Not knowing if we'd meet again !

The promise I have not forgot,—
　The *promise* then and there he made;
Which if he keeps, I know he'll not
　Go wrong: and I'll not be afraid.

If God regards affection's tear,
　And answers when a father prays,
His skies shall yet grow bright and clear;—
　A joy to my declining days.

Go on, my son, in all thy strength:—
　The strength and light that God hath giv'n.
Sweet peace shall crown thy work at length,
　And gild thy pathway up to heav'n.

AS Nature's true hand, in the bright balmy May,
   Presents the sweet flowers of spring,
So may thy glad heart, as it looks up to-day,
   To God its best offerings bring.

As birds of the forest with plumage so fair,
   In spring-time return with their lays,
So may thy calm bosom forget every care,
   And send up its tribute of praise.

As clouds of the winter, which darken'd the skies,
   By sunbeams are now chas'd away,
So may the bright sun of thy life now arise,
   And shine through the noon of thy day.

The sun of the morning at each bright return,
   Gilds its path through the heav'ns with light; —
Though its face in the evening we may not discern,
   It shines through the eyes of the night.

And so may the light which thy life may emit,
   Make bright all thy path here below;
And when, in the ev'ning, thy sun shall have set,
   Its brightness may cease not to glow.

Though in the still ev'ning the shadows may fall,
   And dews on the flowers may lie,
The eye of the morning will smile upon all,—
   Its warmth all the dew-drops will dry.

The flowers would pine—with their heads bending low—
   Without the sure promise of day,—
If no gentle zephyrs upon them should blow,—
   The rays of the sun turn away.

The rain and the sunshine both sweeten the flow'rs;
  The storms they give strength to the wood;
So God sends us sorrow, and gladdens the hours,
  For, for us He sees they are good.

If no sigh of ours e'er came to His ear,—
  If no burden caus'd us to bow,
Perhaps we'd not know of His love and His care,
  Or feel His soft hand on our brow.

So God sends the Spring-time, the Summer and Fall,
  And winter, with storm and with sun;
May He, in His goodness, lead thee through them all,
  In peace, till thy winters are done!

CHANGE.

"AND I cannot but think it strange,
  How every thing in time will change."
  Thus said a friend, in whom time wrought
  A change of which he little thought.

  Exactly so I cannot say;
  For all things change from day to day,
    Except the great First—Cause:
  All else within thought's boundless range
  Must see—must feel—must know a change,
    For such are Nature's laws.

WHERE is my absent boy to-night?
  Where can, where can he be?
O Father, watch him with Thine eye,
  Thine eye that all doth see.
O, watch him till his gladden'd eye
  In love be turn'd to Thine,
And see the love which lights Thy face:—
  This absent boy of mine.

Where is my absent boy to-night?
  Where can, where can he be?
O Father, hold him with Thy hand,
  And turn his feet to Thee!
Hold him until his willing feet
  Shall gladly, quickly come—
Casting the worldly husks aside,
  And feast with us, at home!

Where is my absent boy to-night:—
  He's just as dear to me
As when I led him by the hand,
  Or held him on my knee;—
As dear as when his infant tongue
  First learn'd to lisp my name;
Or when, with mine, I press'd his lips:—
  To me he's just the same.

Where is my absent boy to-night?
  Where can he be? O, where?
O Father, strengthen him for good!
  O, hear for him my prayer!
O, let him feel Thy boundless grace—
  The wond'rous love of Thine:
O, keep him from the snares of sin;—
  This absent son of mine.

So plainly now I see the place,
  Where first we kneel'd to pray;
And with his little hand in mine,
  These words he learn'd to say,
"Lead us not to temptation, Lord:
  Deliver us from sin:
And thine the pow'r and glory be,
  For evermore.   Amen."

I know his feet would not depart
  From virtue's pleasant ways,
Or hands would do a thing that's wrong,
  Through all life's lengthen'd days.
But yet there are so many things
  In life's path all along,
To lure aside weak hands and feet,—
  Not only weak, but strong.

So strong are these temptations, Lord,
  So bright these lurements shine,
That none can pass them by but they
  Who have their hand in Thine.
Lord, hold the hand of my dear boy,
  That he may pass them by;—
That no remorse shall swell his heart,
  Nor sorrow's tear, his eye.

Where is my absent boy to-night ?
  May he be free from harm.
O Father, let him hear Thy voice—
  Feel Thy supporting arm.
I listen, as the hours go by,
  To hear him tread the stair,
And as I close my eyes in sleep,
  I trust him to Thy care.

TO MISS BELLE F., ON HER WEDDING DAY.

EAR Friend, as in faith, you now venture, untri'd,
Your bark on the sea—with an uncertain tide,
With hope in your heart, may your eye look above,
  As white sails are set for the zephyrs of love.

May faith, hope and charity strengthen your heart,
As you from the shore, with your partner depart:
May both, like the compass, be true to the star,
Which guides and protects o'er the billows afar.

The treasures with which your fair vessel is deck'd,
Are too rare to founder, too rich to be wreck'd:
May they, with the weight of your heart's treasure keep,
As ballast, your bark, as it sails o'er the deep.

No doubt, you will find, as you sail the sea o'er,
Some waves to be rougher than those at the shore;
Some clouds may be cast o'er the blue of your skies;—
The bright star of hope be half-hid from your eyes.

Should tempests arise, and the dark waters roll,
Cast forth the strong anchor—" the hope of the soul "—
Till tempests be still, and the rough waters rest:—
They even obey at the Master's behest.

With trouble and fear should your heart be dismay'd,
Then call on the Master, and be not afraid;
He'll wipe off the tears--from your eyes should they roll --
And calm your rough brow, and speak peace to your soul.

Forget not the scene on Tiberias' deep,
When quickly they ran to the Master—asleep —
Cried, save; or we perish! when quickly he woke,
And peace to the waves and the rough tempest, spoke.

I hope, on your voyage, no storm may arise;
And no cloud of sorrow may darken your skies;
But working together at helm and at prow;
The rainbow of promise may bend o'er your brow.

Should one turn the rudder—the other the sail,
In different directions, your voyage may fail:
But banded together by love's endless chain,
Your way will be smooth, and the goal be your gain.

May no word of discord your peace ever break,
Or act, in each other, your confidence shake:
But should trouble come, let it stronger entwine
Each heart around each, like the olive and vine.

The Pilot of pilots in safety will guide
Your bark, with its treasure, o'er life's ruffled tide;
In moments of danger, or sorrow, or fear,
He'll kindly watch o'er you, and keep very near.

In lonely night watches, when sleep folds its arm
Around you, He'll watch you, and shield you from harm:
The oil of peace pour on the sea's troubled breast,
And take you at last to the haven of rest:—

To the haven of rest on the ever bright shore,
Where turmoil and tempest shall come never more;—
Where friends who've passed over await on the strand;—
There waiting and watching, with outreaching hand,

To take you, and lead you where pure waters flow,—
To clothe you with raiment far whiter than snow;—
Then up to the Father, the golden streets tread,
Who th' bright crown of glory shall place on your head.

Where millions of millions, redeemed by His grace,
Shall look, with thanksgiving, upon His bright face:
Where treasures more precious than rubies or gold,
Through ages eternal in beauty unfold.

Among these rich treasures, may yours, too, be found;—
Not sordid, or rusted, or in napkin bound,
But greatly increased since the Master and Lord
Bestow'd them;—and now your eternal reward.

"As thou hast been faithful in that which is least,
Now thou shalt have rule o'er thy treasures increas'd;"—
Rich treasurers locked up in the mansions above,
Which thou canst unlock with the key of God's love.

Again let me say as your bark is unmoor'd.
With treasures on deck, and in cabin are stor'd,—
As love's gentle zephyr now swells the spread sails,—
To trust in the Pilot whose skill never fails.

He's taken ten thousands life's troubled sea o'er;
And He is still able to take thousands more;
And all those who follow, He safely will lead.
And now, with kind wishes, I bid you God-speed.

DEDICATION HYMN.

ITHIN these walls with willing feet
And thankful hearts, O Lord, we meet;
And trust Thy spirit oft shall come,
And dwell in this Thy earthly home.

Our willing hearts and hands have wrought,
And rear'd the house we long have sought;
Where oft we hope in joy and praise,
To Thee our hearts and voices raise.

Tho' darkness seem'd to hang like shrouds,
And mountains almost pierc'd the clouds,
The clouds have flown—the mountains high
Are gone, and left a cloudless sky.

We dedicate to Thee, O Lord,
This house, and here our vows record;
Oft here we'll come to praise and pray,—
Our vows to make, our vows to pay.

Tho' not in temples made with hands,
Art Thou confined; nor tribes nor lands
Exhaust Thy love—which ever flows
In ceaseless streams, for friends and foes:

Yet Thou wilt come in every place,
And dwell with those who seek Thy face;
Or hear the faintest, weakest cry,
And answer from Thy home on high.

And now, O Lord, accept, we pray,
The offering we bring to-day:
It is not from our hands alone,
Our hearts rise with it, to Thy throne!

DEPARTED TREASURES.

Written for a widow lady, who had lost her wealth, her only daughter and granddaughter.

THE world here, O, what are its pleasures to me;
   Since all that is nearest and dearest are gone?
  Its beauties may charm us, but how soon they flee,
   Like sunbeams which dance on the wings of the morn

Ah! once I was blest with earth's brightest gem,
  Then hope mingled sweetly with pleasure and pride;
But shadows of darkness were spread o'er my realm,
  When pride, hope and pleasure were made to divide.

They parted, and never more met in embrace,
  Nor clasp'd the soft hands that for each other's weal,
Would wipe off the tear-drops, which moisten'd the face,
  And lighten the burdens each other might feel.

I know that bright visions should strengthen our heart,
  And make us from sighing and weeping refrain;
For tho' here the nearest and dearest must part,
  We trust they will meet where they'll part not again.

The bright flowers fade; and their fragrance alone
  Perfume the lone bush of their beauty and bloom:
We linger with mem'ries where brightly they shone,
  And weep when we think they are hid in the tomb.

In the tomb? No, not in the tomb,—in the sky —
  It is but the shed leaves which lie resting there;
The germ, with new beauty, is blooming on high;
  By kinder hands tended,—in gardens more fair,

Here flowers soon wither;—their beauties soon fade,
  And snow-drifts may cover the spot where they grew:—
There frosts blighteth never, and storms ne'er invade;
  But heaven's rich virtues forever renew.

No rask, ruthless hand in that garden on high,
  Will pluck the fair flowers that blossom and bloom;
No shadow of darkness, nor death shall pass by,
  Nor half open'd flower shall fade in the tomb.

We cannot help weeping:—our Lord groan'd and wept,
  As Bethany's Daughters, with grief swollen eyes,
There stood 'round the loved one,—who three days had
      slept—
  Tho' they knew the dead at His call would arise.

My heart is not here, for my treasures are hid
  Where the dim eye of mortal cannot see their worth:
But we shall behold them when thither we'er bid.—
  Far greater than those which we lost on the earth.

Though earth hath no luring attractions for me,
  I'll work and I'll wait till the Master sees best—
Will hope, when from toiling and sorrow I'm free,
  To be with the lov'd ones forever at rest.

EXTRACT FROM A LETTER.

Written to a friend, from Harrisburg, Pa., May, 1865.

"We had a delightful walk yesterday to the cemetery; and a most enchanting view of the surrounding country.   I can think of no spot, if I were an artist, from which I would more delight to take a sketch.   The setting sun just peeping through, and partly dropping behind a waving cloud, tinted with many colors; the distant mountains, raising their lofty peaks, as if to meet the lowering and distilling clouds;—the tall and stately trees, pointing to a land where "fruits immortal grow:" while those of smaller size, are bending their boughs to the gentle breeze.   The one seeming to say, "Look up to God in faith and hope!" The other,— "Bow to Him with gratitude and praise!"

To the right,—the green fields,—which betoken an abundant harvest, —spread out in their verdant beauty:—the well set orchard, through which the whited domicile seem to say, "Here is the home of industry:— Here is the dwelling of contentment!" To the left, is Harrisburg in full view; while around thickly stands the monuments of memory to the dead:

> And here and there, in beauty grow
> The sweetest flow'rs, of richest hue,
> Which with their fragrance fill the air,—
> Say, "All is beautiful and fair."
>
> And over head some little bird
> Can in its softest notes be heard,
> (While warbling there its sweetest songs)
> Say "Unto God the praise belongs,—
> Without His notice none can fall:
> He rules and watches over all."

And even the little insects, that swarm the air, seem to say, "Thou openest Thy hand, and satisfiest the desire of every living thing." And under foot, we seem to hear, "As for man, his days are as grass, or a flower of the field, so he flourisheth. For the wind passeth over it, and it is gone, and the place thereof shall know it no more." And the voice of the Lily is, "Even Solomon in all his glory was not arrayed like one of these." And all things conspire to raise our thoughts above, and lead us to say, "Without Him was not any thing made that was made."

> Is there a brighter world than this?—
> A world more sweet and fair?
> If so, God's praise,—if so, our bliss
> Will be still greater there!

THE SORROWS OF MEMORY.

OW sad it will be to look back
  On the heart, with its sin color'd stain!
How gloomy the picture! how black!
  Which before our eyes shall remain.

How sad it will be to behold
  The hungry, we've turn'd from our door;
The friendless left out in the cold,
  While our table was full—running o'er.

How sad to remember the words
  In anger and malice we've spoke,—
The ill-gotten gains we have stor'd,
  And the weak, bleeding hearts we have broke.

Oh, how we will long to return,
  To undo the wrongs we have done:
In anguish the bosom may burn,
The race we have lost, to re-run.

How glad would we be to paint o'er,
  Dark picture, which may not depart;
But hang on the wall evermore;—
  E'ermore on the wall of the heart!

THE PLEASURES OF MEMORY.

OW sweet it will be to review,
　All the past from that glorifi'd shore;
(When our work has been noble and true,)
　Where the storms never beat any more.

CHORUS.

" In that sweet by and by,"
　We'll remember the deeds we have done by and by,
" In that sweet by and by " we'll remember the deeds
　we have done.

How sweet to remember the hour
　When at first we heard Jesus' soft voice,
And felt His warm love and its power,
　When we made His bright precept our choice.

We'll remember the roses we've spread
　In the paths of the weary and worn;
And the pillow placed under their head,
　And the burdens for them we have borne.

We'll remember the hungry we've fed;
　And their tears, and their anguish, and sighs;
And the souls to the fountain we've led,
　And the tears we have wip'd from their eyes.

We'll remember the orphan—bereft
　Of a father and mother to love;
To our pity and sympathy left,
　Or left friendless in sorrow to rove.

We'll remember the kind words we spake;
  And the souls we've made happy and glad,
When the heart was all ready to break,—
  And the shivering limbs we have clad.

We'll remember the words of our Lord,
  "If you give with a heart warm and free,
In no wise you will lose your reward,
  For this kindness is done unto me."

We'll remember the feet we have led
  To the "Rock that is higher than I,"
And the path where the virtuous tread,
  And that leads to that "Sweet by and by."

We'll remember the songs; and we'll wait
  Till we catch the sweet notes from on high.
And, then, when we are nearing the gate,
  We will know it's the "Sweet by and by."

We will know by the loved ones we meet,
  By the lips we have press'd here below,
By the hands that have toiled in the heat,
  And which are now far whiter than snow.

We will know by the angels in white,
  By their harps, and the crowns that they wear,
By the faces of Seraphs so bright;
  And we'll *know* when we see *Jesus* there.

We'll remember, remember all this,
  And much more, when we meet Him on high.
And oh! then what comfort and bliss,
  When we meet in that "Sweet by and by,

OF the bright Christian graces three,
Faith, Hope and love – or Charity—
The greatest of the three,—the last;
And when the lesser gifts have past
She will abide, and never fail,
But over all at last prevail.
She hath some good, for all in store,—
Holds out her hand to rich and poor.

Though I with angel tongues may speak,
And tongues of men (less wise, more weak,)
And have the gift of prophecy,
And understand all mystery;
And though unbounded faith I have,
So that I mountains could remove,
Yet without modest Charity,
I with them all would nothing be.

Though should I of my temporal store,
Give all my goods to feed the poor,
Yet without love, or Charity,
With all these works I'd nothing be.
Charity she suffers long,
Is gentle, kind, and does no wrong,
Is not puffed up, she vaunteth not,
And is content with what she's got.—

Doth not unseemingly behave,
Nor goods of others doth she crave;
Not easily provoked is she,
Nor glories in iniquity;
No evil thinks, seeks not her own,
Nor careth for herself alone:
She beareth all, believeth all,
She hopeth all, endureth all.

When prophecies shall pass away,
And tongues shall cease her words to say,
And knowledge vanish, like a tale,
Bless'd Charity shall never fail.
Faith and Hope go hand in hand,
While Charity makes strong the band:
And now abide these graces three;
The greatest of them—Charity.

------------•------------

FAITH, HOPE AND CHARITY.

WHILE Faith may tread the troubled wave;—
May see some ready hand to save,
And Hope may see through darkest night,
The golden beams of morning light;
Fair Charity she seeks to save
The soul half hidden by the wave;—
Brings near the light which Hope afar,
Sees in the distant morning star.

Hope springs within the human breast,
And gives to its possessor rest:
Faith, all our fears and doubtings quells,—
Blesses the heart in which it dwells;
While Charity finds sweet employ
In bringing others peace and joy;—
Seeks not her own, but would bless all,
When Faith is weak, and Hope is small.

I CANNOT TELL HOW.

O SPIRIT, blest Spirit! come down from above,
And dwell in my bosom, blest Spirit of love;
I need Thee; I need Thee; I need Thee just now;
So oft hast Thou blest me; I cannot tell how!

When dwelling on earth, in the form of the Son,
Of all who besought Thee, Thou turn'st away none:
With hands ever ready the needy to bless;
The sick were made whole at the touch of Thy dress.

And now with the Father, blest Spirit of love!
Thou still canst descend from those mansions above:
And Thy robe of whiteness o'ershadow my heart,
And cause the new life in my bosom to start!

In humble contrition, O Father! I plead,
And look up to Thee, in this moment of need;
And ask but a touch of Thy garment divine;
And light, life, and love in my bosom shall shine!

I now feel its touch—just the touch of the fold,
Encircling the arm which I long to take hold;—
How precious the virtue! how soothing the touch!—
Imparting the life I am needing so much.

Though hidden the hand, and the arm be not bare,
In faith I will cling to the garment they wear,
With outreaching hand, and with uplifted brow;—
Faith springs into life; but I cannot how.

We feel the soft zephyr, as gently it blows;
Know not whence it cometh, or whither it goes:
We see the small grass and the forest oak bow,
And know the wind passeth, but cannot tell how.

So, Father, I feel, in this lone, quiet hour,
The flow of Thy spirit,—its life-giving pow'r,—
Speak peace to my bosom, and calm my rough brow:
It cometh, it cometh,—I cannot tell how!

When life is so languid, and sin reigns instead;
My spirit so weak, or in trespasses dead,
Then Christ gives the new life, which dwells in me now;
He giveth, He giveth,—I cannot tell how!

When my soul is cast down, and dark waters rise,
And tears of deep sorrow fall fast from mine eyes,
I feel some soft hand wipe the tears from my brow,
And grief from my bosom;—I cannot tell how!

With pathway so rugged, and burden so great,
And with steps so feeble, I bend 'neath its weight,
I feel some blest power, as 'neath it I bow,
Give strength to my feet; but I cannot tell how!

When this earthy house shall lie low in the grave,
Thou'lt roll back the stone, by Thy power to save,
And this mortal soul with Thy life wilt endow,
And raise it to heaven;—I cannot tell how!

Will raise it to heaven, where spirits shall know
The things which are hid from their eyes here below!
Where millions of millions are praising Thee now; [how
And we, too, shall praise Thee;—Thou, Lord, knowest

O, Spirit, blest Spirit, abide in my breast,
For while Thou art with me my soul is at rest!
I need Thee each moment, my Saviour, for Thou
Dost grief turn to gladness;—I cannot tell how!

We need not know how, if we only know this;—
That Jesus can turn all our sorrow to bliss;
And if we will trust Him, He'll bless us just now,
And bless us forever;—we need not know how.

But when from this body of death we are free,
And "through a glass darkly" no longer we see,
But see face to face, as the Father sees now,
If He shall so will it, we then shall know how!

IMPROMPTU:

At the close of a letter to my daughter, in 1874.

WHEN " days and nights shall pass " away,
We hope to see one endless day,
  Whose sun shall ne'er go down:
Where skies shall be forever clear;
And hope shall banish every fear;
  And sorrow be unknown.—

Where those who meet shall never part:—
Where love shall gladden every heart;
  And all shall be delight:
Where none shall hear the dying knell;
Where none shall ever say Farewell;
  Or ever say "Good Night!"

For in that land " there is no night:"
For God himself will be the light
  Of that unending day.
Here night and death and sorrow reign;
Here sickness, fear and grief and pain;
  There these shall pass away.

No angry word shall there molest;
No malice reign in any breast,
  To mar that heav'nly peace.
There pomp and pride shall have no place:
But meekness rest on ev'ry face;
  And love and joy increase.

That land with sweetest praise abounds,
But not a note of self-praise sounds,
  In all that vast domain:
But unto Him, shall praise ascend,
Who bore the burden to the end,
  And sin and death o'ercame.

Then as we journey here below,
And oft with heavy burden go;
  The " veil " aside we'll cast;
That we, with vision bright and clear,
May bring that land of glory near:
  And share its joys at last!

TO MY DAUGHTER, MARTHA, ON HER BIRTHDAY.

September 25, 1885.

THE Sun, which warms and lights the day,
Is many million miles away;
  Yet like a chain of gold,
With links unbroken,—always bright—
Its shining beams dispel the night,
  And drive away the cold.

So, mountains gray and forests green,
And waters blue may stretch between,
  And miles may us divide,
Yet cannot break the links, so bright,
Which heart to heart in love unite
  As strong as side by side.

Sometimes a dark'ning cloud may rise,
And cast a shadow o'er the skies,
　Or moon may roll between,
Yet beams the sun with light and heat;
And when the clouds and moon retreat,
　Its glory still is seen.

So, space may eye from eye eclipse—
Keep hand from hand and lips from lips,
　And drown the voices dear,
Yet cannot quell the life and heat
Which cause the loving hearts to beat
With hope to soon draw near.

And as the sun from day to day,
Sips dew-drops from the flow'rs away,
　As o'er the mountain peaks
He reaches to the lowest vale,
To blushing rose and lily pale—
　Kisses their fragrant cheeks;

So, as each birthday bell may chime,
May joy steal down the hills of time,
　(Tho' cheeks be pale or red)
And kiss the tear-drops all away,
And happy make each natal-day—
　Send blessings on your head.

THE HOPEWELL DROUGHT

AND

THE STEWARTSTOWN STORM.

IN the Township of Hopewell, the County of York;
Both the townsmen and countymen oft meet to talk
Of the news of the day, of the prices of grain,
　Of the prospects of crops, and the heat and the rain.

"It is so dry," says one, "that I'm greatly afraid
Quite a short crop of hay and of grain will be made.
The clover and timothy are all turning red,
And the wheat, rye and oats will be light in the head."

Says another, "The weevil, the rust and the fly
Are now thick in the wheat; and half of it will die;
The straw be very short,—not a half crop of grain,
And potatoes be scarce, if there don't come a rain."

Says another, "On 'count of the winter and drought,
I'm afraid that the fruit crop will be very short;
The pears, apples and peaches, the few that remain,
Will dry and drop off if there don't soon come a rain."

Says another, "The cut-worms are killing the corn;—
There will soon be a famine, as sure as you're born!
There's my crop of tobacco, I counted great gain;
But I can't plant it out if there don't come a rain."

Says another, "The pastures are burnt by the sun;
And the streams are so low that the mills can't half run;
They can scarcely saw timber, or grind any grain.
O, what will we do if there don't soon come a rain?"

Fair matrons and maidens close their windows and doors:
If a moment left open, the dust through them pours;
"All our sweeping and dusting and scrubbing is vain,"
They say, "and things ruined if there don't come a rain."

And the lass and her lover, (don't say it too loud,)
They, half stiffled with dust, and annoy'd by the crowd,
Turn aside from the highway and stroll down the lane,
When they little else talk of and think of but rain.

The rosy cheek maiden, as she stands at the gate,
Says, "I know rain is needed, but hope it will wait,
(So shine on bright moon) till he meets me again;
And then I don't care much how soon it will rain."

And the fancy young man, with his "two-forty" horse,—
With the dust on his buggy—eclipsing the gloss,—
Along the road dashes, with might and with main,
Regardless of heat, or of dust, or of rain.

He dashes ahead—sends the dust in the air,
Which covers him thickly, both him and his fair:
But doubtless some thoughts have invaded their brain,
Which make them forget both the dust and the rain.

But when they return, with the dust covered thick,—
The heat so intense that their clothes to them stick,
Veil, dress, gloves and bonnet no more fit to wear, [hair;
While dust, like small snow-flakes, roll down from their

His white stiffen'd collar and smooth-iron'd vest,
So cover'd you scarcely can see how he's dress'd;
They both firmly vow they will not go again;
But stay home forever if there don't come a rain.

Those dreading the turnpike, and trav'ling by rail,
Propound the same question, and tell the same tale,—
Say to the conductor, as he goes through the train,
"How are things up the road? Have they had any rain?"

Men meet you at church, and with hearts of dismay;
They bid you " good morning," or time of the day,—
And then, as in sadness, or sorrow, or pain,
Say, "Another week's gone, and yet we've no rain!"

The preacher exhorts them in God to confide,—
"He feedeth the ravens; for you He'll provide;
The lilies He clothes; not a sparrow can fall
Unseen by the Great Eye that watches o'er all.

Thus somewhat consol'd, now their hearts grow more light;
Their heads get more heavy, and dimmer their sight:
They soon commence nodding,—so dull is their brain,
Made by the foul air and the absence of rain.

He speaks of God's judgments; they seem not to heed,—
"The Lord you thank not, and His poor you don't feed:
He has ever blest you in basket and store,
And yet you are fearing, and sighing for more."

He tells them to doubt not, but look to the skies;
They raise their heads slightly, with half open'd eyes,
As he points to the clouds, which he sees through the pane.
(Which the sexton keeps clos'd 'gainst the dust—not the
                                                      [rain.)
He cites then Elijah, the Tishbite of old,
Who prayed, and for three years the Lord did withhold
The rain from the earth; and he then pray'd again,
And the land was refreshed with abundance of rain.—

Refers to the message delivered to Lot;—
To the fire unquenched, where the worm dieth not;—
The unrighteous cities consumed in the plain,
By brimstone and fire, that descended like rain.

He even refers to the great judgment day;—
Their eyes are so heavy they still nod away:
E'en this seems to rouse not their heart or their brain:
Can sleep under this, if they only get rain.

They wish'd and they pray'd through the county and town.
The true prayed in faith, that the rain might come down:
The false and the faithless, to be true would feign,
In hopes the Great Ruler would send down the rain.

On the last day of May, Eighteen eighty-one,
Not a leaf seem'd to move, and hot beam'd the sun;
The air seem'd so sultry, that all felt the pain,
And said to each other, "No prospects of rain!"

The dust and the heat, how they rose from the road!
The horses would pant with a moderate load.
Of the many who met, not one could refrain
From saying, "O, my! if we could but get rain!"

———

PART II.

Ere th' Sun reached the zenith the sky chang'd its hue,
The mercury descended, the wind slightly blew;
Small cloud follow'd cloud, like a long ladened train,
Till the sky was all cover'd and all look'd for rain,
And said, as they looked up, "good surely will fall."
From th' hand that provides for, and rules over all.

And late in the eve, ere the sun went to rest,
From north and from south, from the east and the west,
The dense vapor gathered, and still denser grew,
Till blackness had hid every vestige of blue;
Which blackness hung low o'er the town, like a pall,
Held up by the strong hand that rules over all.

Now heaven's artillery roll'd fast through the skies!
Sound startling our ears, and the flashes our eyes;
Sharp lightning cross'd lightning, and flash follow'd flash,
Till heav'n and earth seemed to meet with a crash!
Stout hearts, for protection, now tremble and call
On th' God of the tempest, who rules over all.

Large drops now descend, as the thunders still roar !
The lightning still flashing; the torrents now pour;
The doors and the windows seem ready to break,
While houses from bottom to top seem to quake !
The faint and the faithful, secluded now fall,
And plead with the Sovereign who rules over all

The battle is ended, and hush'd is the sound;
Each star, like a sentinel, is still on its round;
The moon, with its white flag of truce, shows her face;
While earth's solid pillars stand firm in their place.
We felt 'mid the crash, that no evil could fall
From th' hand that deals justly, and rules over all.

And we thought we could see the just and wise hand
That marshall'd the forces, and gave the command:—
The hand that could crush out with one single blow,
All th' hosts of the heavens, and nations below;
And yet gives existence to great and to small,
Protects and provides for, and rules over all.

The earth is refreshed, and its wants all suppli'd,
The fields now look green, which were said to be dri'd,
The fruits and the flowers, the grass and the grain,
Now look up with joy, and give thanks for the rain.
The air is made pure, and the dust disappear'd,
And hope fills the heart that had doubted and fear'd.

The sweet songters of air are warbling His praise;
The brook through the meadows the soft music plays;
The cattle lie down in the shade by its brink,
Or wend their way slowly for evening's last drink.
They look to the cow-boy, and list to his call—
Whose heart is made glad by the Ruler of all.

My story is told of the drought and the rain:
Though long and amusing, 'twill not be in vain;
If you heed the moral I name and conclude:
'Tis simply to "Trust in the Lord and do good."
And then He will answer whenever you call
In faith on the Father *who rules over all.*

GOOD NIGHT,—WHEN ABSENT.

NOW here in solitude I lay me down to sleep;—
  In quiet solitude until the morning light.
And in my latest thoughts the happy hour I'll keep,
  When loving hearts and voices shall repeat "Good
    Night."

Until that happy hour no loving voice each night I'll hear,
  Nor feel the gentle, tender hands I oft have press'd;—
Unless in dreams it softly whispers in my ear,
  Or fingers touch the chords which vibrate in my breast.

"Good night," then I will say with heart, if not with tongue.
  " Good night," I say, as on my pillow now I rest.
Some kindred word to me in sleep perhaps may come,
  And softly, sweetly whisper "Good night," in my breast.

IMPROMPTU TO A FRIEND.

THE winter is dying, and spring-time is near.
The clouds disappear'd, left the skies bright and clear,
  And so from your mind may all sorrow depart;—
The sunshine of gladness spring up in your heart,
Through life may your pathway be light'd by hope;—
Each bud and each blossom to living fruit ope,
  Your wants to supply, and your garner o'erflow [sow.
With fruits which your hands in the spring-time may

MAN IS A FOOL.

IN his own eyes man's strong and wise;—
 His actions when they speak,
Say, "As a rule, man is a fool,
 Conceited, blind and weak."

With little cause, against God's laws
 He runs, and thinks it pays:—
Stops not to heed,—with hurried speed
 He runs in folly's ways.

Through life he toils to win its spoils,
 And lay up treasured gain;
But when he dies, how soon it flies!
 And all his toil is vain.

Though man was blest 'bove all the rest
 Of creatures here below,
Yet not content,—he quickly went
 From paradise to woe.

By party click, with artful trick,
 Is man used as a tool,
Like battered wedge, with heavy sledge:
 Then is he not a fool?

He goes to war—spreads woe and awe—
 Sends thousands to the grave
For fame or pay,—that men may say,
 "A patriot, true and brave!"

The world applauds!—man's heart accords,
 And loves its praises loud:
So, as a rule, man is a fool,
 And often fools the crowd.

God says He'll save beyond the grave,
  And here give joy and peace,
But men refuse these gifts to choose,
  And from their sins to cease.

Man wise would be if he could see
  Wherein true wisdom lies,
But as a rule, man is a fool,
  And cannot it disguise.

"*GO, AND DO THOU LIKEWISE.*"

ONCE from Jerusalem did go
A man down unto Jericho;
There met with thieves, who bruised his head,
And stripp'd, and left him there half dead.

While there he lay, a Priest pass'd by,
Looked on, and left him there to die:
When he had gone, a Levite came,
And passing by, he did the same.

After which there came that way,
A trav'ler from Samaria.
The last named person of the three,
Was neither Scribe nor Pharisee;

Nor did he like the two profess
To teach the way of righteousness,—
Who fill'd with selfish love and pride,
Pass'd by upon the other side.

He raised the man up off the ground,
Appli'd some oil, and dress'd his wound;
Then him upon his beast he laid,
And took him to an inn, and paid
Two pence; and said unto the host,
"Keep an account of all the cost;"
Be kind to him; of him take care;
And all of the expense I'll bear;
And on the morrow, when I come,
What e'er it be, I'll pay the sum."

Now, which, kind reader, can you tell,
Was neighbor to the man who fell
Among the theives? and which could claim,
More rightfully, the Christian name;
And in the eyes of Him above,
Fulfill'd the perfect "law of love?"

In this short lesson, we can find
A precept unto all mankind;
For it to us—to all applies,
And bids us "GO, AND DO LIKEWISE."

"*REPENT YE, FOR THE KINGEOM OF HEAVEN IS AT HAND.*"

REPENT ye, for the kingdom's come;
Repent ye, for the kingdom's come;
Repent ye, for the kingdom's come;—
  Happy, heavenly kingdom!

Forsake your sins and enter in;
Forsake your sins and enter in;
Forsake your sins and enter in;
  In the heavenly kingdom!

Oh, God the Lord is King; and we
His happy subjects e'er shall be:
We shall the King of Glory see,
  In the heavenly kingdom!

There will be gladness all the day;
For God shall wipe all tears away,
And we will His commands obey,
  In the heavenly kingdom!

There none shall hunger, thirst or sigh,
For God will be forever nigh,
And lead to streams that never dry,
  In the heavenly kingdom!

O, there shall be no rich and poor,
Nor bond, nor free, as heretofore,
But one in Christ forevermore,
  In the heavenly kingdom!

We will not need the moon by night,
For God Himself will be the light,
And make all things forever bright,
  In the heavenly kingdom!

The gates shall not be shut by day;
The holy angels guard the way,
And " we'll conduct you in," they say,—
   In the heavenly kingdom!

One half the glory is not told:—
The streets are pav'd with purest gold;
And every hour new joys unfold,
   In the heavenly kingdom!

We'll know no more of grief and pain;—
There sin nor death no more shall reign;
But endless life and love obtain,
   In the heavenly kingdom!

Life's river there forever flows:—
The tree of life beside it grows;
And none shall eat and drink but those
   In the heavenly kingdom!

We'll come, O Lord, with thanks to Thee,
For this great gift—so rich and free—
Which Prophets long desir'd to see,
   In the heavenly kingdom!

These things Thou hast hid from the eyes
Of men of old, " prudent and wise,"
But dost to babes in Christ devise,
   In the heavenly kingdom!

Our work below we need not leave
Before the blessings we receive;
But they will come when we believe
   In the heavenly kingdom!

THE TEST OF LOVE.

MY heart is full! it overflows
With love—which soothes my wounds and woes:
And as this love my heart expands,
To other's woes I stretch my hands,
To soothe my brother's heart—which sighs,—
To wipe the tears from other's eyes,—
To help when care and want oppress,—
To give relief when in distress.

And thus man's love to God we know,
When unto men that love we show
In acts of kindness unto those
God loves;—if blest, or mark'd with woes.
So he who says, "I love the Lord,"
Should prove it not alone by word,
But doing as the Master taught;—
Whose love was shown in works He wrought.

MAN'S NEEDS.

FOOD, rest and exercise and air,
Man needs; and none of these can spare.
Food rest and air and exercise,
Denied to man, and soon he dies.

So, in the spirit life man needs
All this;—denied, his life recedes.
So, he should eat life's bread, and breathe
The breath of heav'n—God sends beneath.

Love, faith and patience exercise:—
Dry sorrow's tear from weeping eyes;
And with long life you shall be blest,
And in your work find sweetest rest!

BIRTHDAY ACROSTIC.

To my Daughter.

MY heart, how it throbs with emotions unknown;
As I think of my daughter, so kind and so dear,—
Reviewing her steps,—as I sit here alone—
To the place where she started.—O ! why starts this
    tear ?—
How oft, when a babe, I so fondly caress'd,
A sweet little form to my bosom I press'd.

Very dear to me still; tho' no longer a child,
I look and I love with the same anxious care
As I did when she play'd, and so trustingly smil'd
Near my side, on my lap:—O, why falls this tear ?—
Nor can I forget how her tear-drops would start,
At one harsh expression to her tender heart.

Be hopeful, my daughter; O, be not dismayed:
O, look to your Saviour; His precepts obey.—
Your pathway, oft darken'd with shadow and shade,
Depicts in the future, a bright, better day.

WE'LL REAP WHAT WE SOW.

WE'LL surely reap whate'er we sow,
    If good or ill;—e'en here below,—
      Neglect, or hate, or love.
    And who can tell what joy—what bliss,
    When in a better world than this,
      We'll reap the fruits above !

AN ACROSTIC.

To a Niece.

VIRTUE, with modesty, candor and truth,
In woman excels all the beauties of youth.
As you pass on the journey of life, dear Niece,
Nothing will give you such pleasure and peace—
Nothing to you will such comfort impart
As faith in your Saviour and pureness of heart.

"Peace," says the Saviour, "in me you shall find;"—
In the world tribulation and trouble of mind:
Then go to Him early, in Him put your stay;   [way.
Take Him for your friend through all life's rugged
Seek first His favor; He will hear when you pray.

Forever then, Annie, in all that you do,
Incline to the right, to the pure and the true:
Take the yoke of the Master,—He says it is light;
Commit your cause to Him, and all will be right.
He'll love you, He'll bless you, and never forsake,
E'en death can't destroy, or His love ever break.
Tho' lashes be wet with sad tear-drops to-day,
There's a soft loving hand to wipe them away.

BLEST BY HOPE.

THROUGH tribulation, pain and sorrow,
  While cheering hope lights up the way,
We see new beauties in the morrow,
  Which lend to us their joys to-day.

And tho' the prize we ne'er obtain,
  While trav'ling through the clouded night,
Unending joys we hope to gain,
  When hope shall lead us into sight!

"BLESSED ARE THE PURE IN HEART, FOR THEY SHALL SEE GOD."

THE pure in heart shall see the Lord;—
  Shall feel His power and grace:
In calm and storm they hear His word;—
  His steps through darkness trace.

They see Him in the heav'ns above;
  In earth and rock and rill:
Where'er their feet or mind may rove,
  They see His matchless skill.

They see Him in the mighty deep,
  He holds within His hand,
And in the ice-capp'd mountain steep;
  And in the ocean strand.

They see Him in the sun's warm light,
  Which makes our hearts rejoice;
And in the watches of the night,
  They listen to His voice.

They see Him in the clouds that shed
  Their tears upon the earth,
And water all her parching bed,
  And give to beauty birth.

In flow'r and fruit and grass and tree,
  That deck the earth abroad,
The pure in heart can plainly see
  The ruling hand of God.

A million burning lamps of light,
  Shining through boundless space,
The vision of the pure invite,—
  Reflect God's smiling face.

The kingdoms great and empires vast,
  Which felt the chastening rod,
In present, and in ages past,
  Declare, " There is a God ! "

The City built on seven hills,
  That held Neroic rod,
To good and bad plainly reveals
  The truth—" There is a God."

The City of four million souls,
  With walls and bulwarks high;
Where now the owls and bats and moles,
  Salute the passer-by;—

Where palaces and streets so fair,
  And images of gold,
With hanging gardens, rich and rare,
  So wond'rous to behold !—

The hundred massive gates of brass,—
  The enemy defied;
And none through them unbid could pass:—
  So strong, and high, and wide !

For sixteen hundred years stood she,
  In pow'r, and pomp, and pride:
But in one hour of revelry,
  She lost her pow'r !—she died !

They trampled on God's holy law !
  The wine-cup passed:—they drank:
God's hand upon the wall they saw,
  They trembl'd, fear'd and shrank !

Wild beasts and reptiles now dwell there;
  And every unclean bird:
Their howls and cries that rend the air,
  In doleful dirge are heard.

The city where the Saviour taught,
  And pray'd, and wept, and died,
Could not see God in all He wrought,
  And scarce when crucified.

The vile may see God's ire and wrath;
  The " pure in heart" His grace,—
May walk a peaceful, happy path,
  And meet Him face to face.

O, SON OF MAN! O, LORD OF LORDS!

O SON of man! O, Lord of Lords!
  Help us to see Thee as thou art;—
As dwelling in the highest heav'n,
  And in the meekest, humblest heart!

O, Word of life! O, Prince of peace!
  In whom dwell glory, truth and grace!—
One hand with sceptre on the throne,
  And one beneath a sinful race!

O, Saviour! Prophet! Priest! and King!
  May I thy glory ever see!
And from a life of sin and death,
  Be lifted, Jesus, unto Thee!

TO MY DAUGHTER, GERTIE, ON THE FIFTEENTH ANNIVERSARY OF HER BIRTHDAY.

JUST Fifteen years ago to-day,
  With brow and features fair,
You and your sister Gracie lay,—
  A lovely, tiny pair!

A few months only pass'd away,
  When in your cradle-bed
You'd sit, and with each other play,—
  One at the foot; one – head.

We watched the winning smiles which used
  To play upon each face,
And all who came would be amus'd
  At cunning " Gert and Grace,"

When we would call each by her name,
  How she would smile and play.
But in one year the angels came,
  And bore sweet Grace away!

But God, who gives and takes away,
  Has left you in our care,
And bid us guard you day by day,
  From every evil snare.

Tho' pain has often racked your head,—
  Disturb'd your peace of mind;
Yet God's soft hand your way has led;
  He's been to you so kind.

And in the coming years, I pray,
  His grace may give you strength,
And lead you in life's peaceful way,
  Until you reach its length.

Sometimes, in life, we may suppose
  We know the safest road,
But always find before its close,
  'Tis best to trust in God.

Now, Gertie, from a father's heart,
  These words now come to you:—
I trust you'll choose the better part,
  And naught but good you'll do;—

That as your way through life you press
  You through the sunny hours,
Will sow the seeds of happiness,
  And reap the sweetest flow'rs;—

That health and strength and joy may chase
  All aches and pains away,
And reign triumphant in their place
  Through all life's lengthen'd day.

IMPROMPTU.

To a Friend, on the exchange of Photographs.

THOUGH you may closely scan this face;—
Its form, and every feature trace,
  Nought will find so much to prize
  As luster beaming from your eyes.—

Your dark, full eyes, which brightly shine,
(You may not see such worth in mine,)
And although silent, plainly tell
Of valu'd traits that in you dwell.

And all who can this language read,
And all who will this language heed,
Can plainly see in nature's book,
How much is spoken in a look.

THE HAPPY MEDIUM.

TOO much of wet, or too much dry,
Will cause the flow'rs to fade, or die;
While wet and dry will, both together,
Give life and growth, and healthy weather.
Too much quiet, or too much fun,
To one extreme, is apt to run;
While some of each will make our life,
With happiness and pleasure rife.
In fact, all blessings cease to bless,
When they are taken to excess.
Milk and meat are good, but never
Should we feed on either ever.
One is too weak, one is too strong;
Nor could we live on either long.
Too much of work, or too much play,
Will wear or rust our life away.
The happy medium is best,
And gives to life a relish'd zest.
Yet, he who'd rise, or lead, or rule,
Must labor hard his mind to school.

ACROSTIC.

EARTH has its sunshine and its shade;
Life has its joy and sorrow;—
Like flowers of spring, which bloom to fade,
And die upon the morrow.

RURAL BLISS.

YOU may talk of Long Branch, or noted Cape May,
And pleasant resorts on the banks of the Bay;
Of Atlantic City and White Sulphur Springs,
Massive "brown houses," or mansions of kings,
All furnished so richly, and everything gay,
And board of the best, at five dollars a day,—
The brine of the ocean, the foam of the sea;
But a low, shaded cot in the country for me!

Yes, a low, shaded cot:—I say what I know—
And write from the one I took ten days ago.
The locust and walnut hang low o'er the eaves;
The moss cover'd shingles are swept by the leaves;
The lilac and burdock grow thick by the door
Of the cottage I've slept in, for ten days or more.
O, dwellers in cities, who crave rural bliss,
Just come to the country and try such as this!

In front sweeps the soft balmy breeze o'er the lawn;
To th' back is the orchard and tall waving corn;
To th' left is the meadow, just mow'd to the ground,—
The brook's limpid waters flow, babble and bound.
To th' right are the cattle, all homeward inclin'd,
From th' green shady slope, which the sun sinks
    behind.—
The spring by the rock, which the willows bend o'er,
From which, in profusion, the clear waters pour!
O, dwellers of cities, who crave rural bliss,
Just come to the country and try such as this!

No yelling of ragmen, nor rumbling of cars,
From morning to midnight, to grate on your ears.
The song of the birds, with its sweet sounding notes,
Awakes with the morn, and on soft zephyrs floats,
Till the chirp of the cricket, as twilight draws nigh,
And th' curtain of evening is drawn o'er the sky;
When th' lamps are lit up in the vault overhead,
And th' dew-woven carpet, for night guests is spread,
Till night with its star-gilded banquet is past;
When again 'tis roll'd up, ('tis not tack'd very fast)
And like a rich garment again put away
From th' dust and the tramp and the travel of day;
Or hung to keep pure on the beams of the sun,
Till th' hosts of the skies have another round run—
When again they appear as guests, who unite,
To bathe in the courts of the empress of night

I now from the beauties of nature depart,
To speak for awhile of attractions of art:
And trust that " Dame Nature " will not blush for shame,
Should Art in its beauties excel its own fame.

My cot is of logs—about sixteen feet square,—
Has two broken windows—to let in the air—
One door in the front and one door in the back,
A large fire-place with a big iron rack;—
On which pots and kettles – a long time ago—
O'er a blazing wood-fire, were hung in a row.—
A loft overhead, where the rats and mice play,
And a cave underneath where ash-barrels lay.
O, dwellers in cities, who crave rural bliss,
Just come to the country and try such as this!

Sunk in the middle and much worn is the floor;
And thick cakes of whitewash hang loose from the door.
The hearth of rough stones,—about five feet by six,—
(Which doubtless was made long before they made
    bricks.)

Some up and some down, some square and some round;
Between every stone there's a big space of ground
O, dwellers in cities, who crave rural bliss,
Just come to country and try such as this!

From window to window, from front to back door,
Not one level spot can be found on the floor:
And everything sits on a kind of a lop,
Except where.I stuck in a chip as a prop.
All of its contents are sure proof against fire,
But th' bed and a bench, and a hand-and-face-drier.
O, dwellers in cities, who crave rural bliss,
Just come to the country and try such as this!

An old iron bedstead, about two feet wide,
Two blankets,—which let in the air at each side,—
A mattress and pillow;—and thus I have said
The whole sum composes my bedding and bed.—
An old rusty stove and a bench of six feet,
And lantern with candle are contents complete.
Stop! I have just seen—as I happen to move—
An old iron kettle, just back of the stove:
Now, I know I've named all, when here I throw in
A towel, pin box and a basin of tin.
I look all around me, but not a thing more,
Except bugs and millers I've knock'd to the floor.
And every few minutes I have to strike at
A wasp or a bee, or a small buzzing gnat.
And amid all of this, I think of my home,
And feel very thankful mosquitoes don't come.
O, dwellers in cities, who can't sleep at night,
What comfort to be where mosquitoes won't bite!

I sit on the bed,—on the stove put my light—
Which is so gloomy I scarcely can write;—
The bed on one side,—in the corner the stove,
They are too far apart, and too heavy to move.

So, near to the stove I just draw the pine box,
Ane fix up a seat with a board and some blocks,
Which in front of the door, I found on the ground,—
Which doubtless were put there to climb up and down.
And on this pine box I now have my paper,
Writing away by my dim tallow taper.
The ten-plate stove looks as if never been heated
Since Eighteen-fourteen—when the British retreated.
O, dwellers in cities, who crave rural bliss,
Just come to the country and try such as this!

The door locks outside, and the latch has no ketch,
The heavy oak bench each night I just fetch,
And turn upside down, with one end on the floor,
And the other end up, as a prop to the door.
O, dwellers in cities, who crave rural bliss,
Just come to the country and try such as this!

Just here I must stop! for I hear a great shaking
At window or door!—I can't be mistaken!
Yes, 'tis at the window! of that I am certain:
It sounds like a hand 'gainst the newspaper-curtain:—
Comes louder and louder! I ne'er heard its equal!
(What it turn'd out to be, I will give in the sequel.)
I feel greatly startled, though not badly frighten'd;
But, for the night, it has finished my writing.
O, dwellers in cities, who crave rural bliss,
Just come to the country and try such as this!

Two days have elaps'd since I spoke of the door,
Propp'd with the oak bench; with one end on the floor.
My candle expir'd —I remember full well—
And now I'll continue my story to tell.
The door with the steps I keep closed night and day,
That the five social dogs on my bed cannot lay;
The door at the back they can't get up or down,
As it is five feet from the sill to the ground

So it I keep open on all sunny days,
That the sun may brighten my room with its rays.
The fresh air keeps close to the bed where I lie:—
The ceiling's so low it can't get very high:—
Except what escapes through the chimney's broad head,
Which comes through the broken pane, over my bed.
O, dwellers in cities, how can you endure
The heat, and the dust, and the air so impure?

Of course I don't eat in the room where I sleep;
But out of the door with a bound and a leap,
And two hundred feet the tall grass I go through,—
All laden'd and dripping with fresh morning dew,—
To a little pine table, 'bout three feet by four,
Which sets 'gainst the wall, 'twixt the window and door;
By linen 'tis cover'd two-thirds of the way,
Just back of which twenty pine milk-covers lay.
O, dwellers in cities, who crave rural bliss,
Just come to the country and try such as this.

How pleasant to rise in the country at morn,
And sit at the table which colors adorn!—
Oft times, three or four, but at least always two,—
When "brown" breaks its harshness by mixing with
    "blue."

No growth-stunted tea-cups, which hold a 'bout a gill;
But yellow quart bowls to the top you can fill.—
Don't need any saucers;—don't have them about;—
Its gone out of fashion to pour coffee out.—
And no half-yard napkins around you to pin,
Or lay by your plate, or to hang 'neath your chin;
But a large family towel at pump, near the door,
Where we can go wash when the meal is all o'er.
O, dwellers in cities, who crave rural bliss,
Just come to the country and try such as this!

We're not very stylish; to be we don't try;
'Tis style very often makes boarding so high.
Some places you go to (so people tell me),
There is so much of style that you little else see.
Style is very good—we will not deny that—
But stuffing is better to make a man fat.
O, dwellers in cities, who're starving on style,
Just come to the country, try stuffing awhile.

I spoke 'while ago of the " brown and the "blue "—
The colors we have when we have only two,—
You will comprehend this full well when you come,
And see the "brown" bread and "blue" milk, free
    from skum.

From what I have said, you a lesson may learn:—
When spring-time is past, and the hot days return,
Don't go to Long Branch, or the Springs, or Cape May,
Or pleasure resorts on the banks of the Bay,
Or to Atlantic City—where prices are steep;
But come to the country where living is cheap.
But those who unable to come, but yet would,
E'en reading my story may do them some good.
But I must stop writing, unless I write wrong,
My candle is spent—which was six inches long—
By its last dying flicker, just let me say this,—
O, come to the country, and find rural bliss!

THE BIRD OF EVERMORE;

OR,

SEQUEL TO RURAL BLISS.

THE night I ever shall remember;
It was the first of mild September;
  When I, with not another member
    Of the entire human race,
  Was in a lonely cottage sitting,
  With a well-spent candle, flitting,
  Which—a gloomy light emitting—
    Dimly lighted up the place.

A story I had just been writing,
Of that lone cot—so uninvitiug,—
  Was to myself the lines reciting
    In subdu'd, or under-voice:
  And I was just about retiring,—
  Feeling quite tired, and sleep requiring,
  And my dim candle near expiring,
    When I heard a sudden noise,

Like something at the window scratching;
Or like the back door slow unlatching;
  When I my breath quite quickly catching!
    As one does at great surprise; —
  I turned my head around quite slily
  Toward the door, but very shily,
  And felt my heart was beating highly,
    While I looked with anxious eyes!

Heard something like hail 'gainst the windows:
Or more like sifting sand or cinders;
But could not tell if out, in doors:
  Look'd every way, but couldn't tell.
The cause, perhaps, of my not knowing,
Was that the wind was slightly blowing,
And back and forth the trees were going,—
  On the roof the branches fell.

This scratching sound kept on repeating,
And faster grew; and then came beating,
Like glass and gravel quickly meeting,
  When I rose up from my seat,
And softly crept toward the window,
Looked out, when all seem'd black as tinder,—
Which did my anxious vision hinder:
  While my heart still faster beat!

A single word it did not utter;
But I thought I heard the shutter
Open slow, and something mutter;—
  Look'd, but saw no shutter there.
Then I began my cogitation—
Wondering what in all creation,
It could be there! and in vexation,—
  Said, " It is some one to scare."—

"It may be some one dissipated,
Who is, perhaps, intoxicated,
And lost his way, and is belated,
  And has come to stay all night.
But then how came he from the highway,
To my lone cot, here on this by-way,
Unless he thought it was a nigh way;
  Or attracted by the light?"

But now the beating grew still louder;
I thought of pistol, ball and powder,
And some one there to rob or murder,—
  Shoot or strike a deadly blow !
If so, I thought, I'd be no coward,
And for the door I started forward;
But then I thought it would be horrid !
  If indeed this should be so.

No other house but one was near me,
And that so far no one could hear me;
And should the thing attack or scare me,
  What to do I did not know;
But this I knew,—Should there be battle
'Tween me and what had caus'd the rattle,
There would be no one but me at all
  To engage the midnight foe.

And as I was not used to fighting,—
Although the hour was quite exciting—
I did not feel like pitching right in-
  To a rough and tumble fight.
Besides, I'd nearly half undress'd me,
That I might go to bed and rest me,
When first this rapping did divest me
  Of the quiet of the night.

Continuing my cogitation,
I said, " Tis all imagination,
Wrought up by my lone situation;
  I will take my seat again:
It may be nothing but the bushes,
Mov'd by the wind—which 'gainst them rushes—
Which them against the window pushes
  To and fro across the pane.

Or it may be the bead or facing
Worked loose, and rattling 'gainst the casing,
Or the old window sash displacing
  In the place so wide between."
And there I sat in pensive pondering,
List'ning, looking, guessing, wondering,
While the thing continued thundering
  Like some battering machine!

I'd often heard of ghosts appearing,
With faces pale, and white sheets wearing,
And superstitious people scaring,
  When as phantoms they appear'd:
I'd heard of houses being haunted
By evil spirits, which had daunted
Brave men, who of their courage vaunted:—
  Men who said they nothing fear'd.

Somehow these spirits mostly happen
To come when one is 'bout half napping,
And ragged window curtains flapping,
  And the doors and windows loose;—
When we are in some lonely hovel,
Or reading some exciting novel;
Then we can plainly hear them grovel,
  As they creep around the house.

In all these things I'm no believer;
But like the shuttle of a weaver,
Worked by the hands of some deciever,
  Wove a web across my brain.—
In fact, this web was wove and tighten'd,
And its false colors greatly heighten'd.
When in childhood we were frighten'd!
  Now it only comes again.

But now the rapping came still faster,
At which I said, "There's some disaster;
And it or I will soon be master,
  Let the fate be what it will.
There must be something there; there must be!
And something not afraid to trust me;
And what it is I will and must see."
  When each nerve I felt to thrill!

And so I thought I'd be a hero;
So to the window went still nearer,
That what it was I might see clearer:
  It I could no longer stand.
(Out doors still seemed as black as tinder,
And not a great deal lighter in door.)
I went right close up to the window
  With the candle in my hand:—

I saw a head toward me heading;
Two wings across the window spreading,
And two feet on the sill quick treading,
  And a bill against the pane:
The wings against the window flapping,
The bill in quick succession rapping,
And with the feet kept quite a tapping,
  All at work with might and main.

Though not a single word it utter'd,
I knew by how it flapp'd and flutter'd,
And by the way it tapp'd and tatoo'd,
  In the house it wished to come.
And when I saw its sad dilemma,
I knew the only speedy reme-
Dy, was to let it quickly emi-
  Grate, by window to my room.

But ere I got the window lifted,
It near a hundred times had shifted,
And from my sight entirely drifted;
  No more, perhaps, to come again.
I for a moment stood and wonder'd
If this strange bird had only blunder'd;
And other thoughts, perhaps a hundred,
  Fill'd the chamber of my brain:—

Some I tried to put on paper,
But found my little tallow taper
Had vaporated into vapor,
  When I open'd wide the door;—
Thinking the bird might still be waiting
In tree or bush—anticipating
Entrance—his thoughts, like mine, vibrating,—
  But I never saw him more.

My mind partook somewhat of sorrow,
Both for the bird, and that the morrow
My thoughts would go: so tri'd to borrow
  From my brain a page to write
Them down.—All night my mind kept tracing
Thought after thought, and each on placing
Upon the page, ere their erasing
  From my mind ere morning light.

Perhaps I'll never know the reason
This bird should come so out of season, —
The time when birds are roosting trees on,
  Or in barrack, barn or hay;—
Why he my window pane should fly at,
At that late hour, when all was quiet:
Whether by chance, or choice, or fiat,
  Or how he there found the way.

Perhaps some savage bird had fac'd him,
And from his quiet rest displac'd him,
Aud to my window fiercely chas'd him;—
  Chas'd to take him for his prey;
And he to me came for protection,—
Not knowing I was in reflection,—
Asking, if I had no objection,
  T' drive the savage bird away.

It may have often been there peeping
In the room where I'd been sleeping;
Wondering if its company keeping
  Would afford me much delight,
And thought, perhaps, I would not censure,
If in the room this night he'd venture,
And say, "For good I have been sent here;
  And will stay with you all night."

I'd read the story of the "tapping"
By bird, which came so "gently rapping"
At "chamber door" of one half "napping;"—
  Came from night's Plutonian shore;
A bird that only one word utter'd,
When in the room he flew and flutter'd:—
Yes, only one sad word he utter'd;
  That sad word was, "NEVERMORE!"

I'd often heard, in youthful chidings,
Of little birds which carry tidings,
Birds which reveal our secret hidings;
  Making all our secrets plain:
But never read, in all my reading
Of bird in such strange way proceeding;
Rapping so loud, so strongly pleading—
  Rapping at a window pane!

Perhaps had this bird been admitted
Into the room where I was seated,
He'd have some sweeter word repeated
   Than the sad word—"NEVERMORE!"
Perhaps had I asked, "Will there ever
Be lone abodes beyond the river?"
He would have answered, "Never, never
   Friends shall part on that bright shore!"

Should I have asked, "Will there be pining,
Or burning tears, or love declining,
Or will the sun e'er cease its shining,
   On that far and unknown shore?"
He may have answered, "Never! Never!
But joy, and light, and love forever,
Shall live and last beyond the river;
   Live and last FOREVERMORE!"

Perhaps had I asked, "If the treasure
Which we've lost here, and much sought pleasure
Will there be granted without measure:
   Or with measure running o'er?"
He'd said, "The good we've wished or wanted;
And all for which the heart has panted:—
The loved, and last, shall there be granted;
   Granted on that happy shore!—

"And will the friends we love here dearly,—
Visions bright—we've seen so clearly—
Come, abide, and bless us really,
   Where our hopeful spirits soar?"
"Lov'd ones there shall never leave you,
And no vision bright deceive you,
And no ill shall ever grieve you:—
   Joy shall bless you EVERMORE!"

This bird sits at my heart, still beating,
And these sweet, happy words repeating,—
" There 'll be no parting at that meeting, -
   At the meeting on that shore!
No burning tears, nor love declining,
Nor aching heart, nor pain, nor pining;
But peace and joy forever shining!
   Shining there FOREVERMORE! ''

Kind bird, if you should come in future,
You need not be afraid I'll hurt you;
But in my room I will invite you:—
   You will meet with no chagrin:
If I to be asleep should happen,
Rap on the pane, and keep on rapping
Until you wake me from my napping;
   I will rise and let you in.

Now, here's the lesson we may borrow:
The things which give us fear and sorrow,
We oft find, in the happy morrow,
   Were no real cause of dread:
The blackest clouds may rise and gather,—
Betokening the foulest weather;
And winds may waft them like a feather,
   Leaving sunshine overhead!

OFT the vision seems the brightest
  In the darkest hour of all;
Like the Master's,—whose was lightest,
  When He drank the cup of gall.—

When He said, " 'Tis finish'd, finish'd ! "—
  Dying, yet His joy untold !
When the darkness all had vanish'd,
  And heav'n's eternal joy unroll'd !

Though He cried in deepest anguish,
  " Why hast Thou forsaken me ? "
Through the darkness, through the anguish,
  He could light and glory see !

'Tis because the loving Father
  Shows the brightness of His face,—
And illumes our darken'd bosom
  With the glory of His grace.

Now I see—through scenes of sorrow,
  And the darkness overhead—
Gladness in the coming morrow,
  'Neath the skies, with blue o'erspread.

Now my bosom burns with gladness,
  As I feel the morning rays,
Drive away all thoughts of sadness,—
  Turn each murmur into praise !

And the gladness will be gladder
  When the Lord and King of kings,
In the morning us shall gather
  'Neath the shadow of His wings !

THERE was a man—a Pharisee—
  And Nicodemus was his name:
A ruler of the Jews was he:
  By night he unto Jesus came,
And said to Him, " Rabbi, we know
  Thou art a teacher, come from God,
For none these miracles can do,
  Except accompani'd by the Lord."

And Jesus said unto him then,
  " Verily, I say unto thee,
Except a man be born again,
  God's kingdom he can never see."
When Christ these truths had plainly told,
  Said Nicodemus to the Lord,
"Can man be born when he is old?—
  I do not understand Thy word."

" That which is born of flesh," Christ said,
  " Is flesh, and only born to die:
That which of spirit born and bred,
  Is Spirit, and is born from high.—
No marvel that I said to thee,
  If unto heav'n man would attain,
And would the heav'nly kingdom see,
  Tho' born, he must be born again.

If I have told of things of earth,
  And yet you cannot them receive,
How can you then, the heav'nly birth
  Discern, and heav'nly things believe?
A master of the Jews, art thou,
  And an instructor long hast been?
We speak the things of which we know,
  And testify of what we've seen.

None hath ascended up to heav'n,
  Except he who from heav'n came down,—
The Son of man, to whom 'tis giv'n
  The heav'nly kingdom, for His own.
And as Moses lifted up the
  Brass serpent in the wilderness;
Just so the son of man must be:
  And they who look to Him, He'll bless.

For God, His only Son hath giv'n,
  That man forever shall not die;—
But rise from sin and death to heav'n,
  And ever live with God on high.
God sent His Son not to condemn
  The world; but that the world might live:
And all who will believe in Him,
  Eternal life to them He'll give.''

THE TEMPEST OF TIBERIAS.

Y faith is renew'd by the scene,
  When out on Tiberias' deep,
When all was so calm and serene,
  And wearied,—the Lord fell asleep;
When fiercely the tempest began;
  Which fill'd the disciples with dread;
When quickly to Jesus they ran;—
  "Lord, save, or we perish!" they said.

CHORUS.

The Pilot now is near;
And no storm I'll ever fear,
  Tho' the ocean's rough and wide!
And if I trust His skill,
He will every tempest still,
  And will take me safely to the other side.

How quickly the Master awoke:—
  "Ye fearful and faithless," said He:
Then peace to the tempest He spoke;
  And calm were the winds and the sea.
And so in each hour of distress,
  If we in the Master confide,
Our care and our sorrow He'll bless;
  Though rough be the winds and the tide.

The sails may be tatter'd and torn;
　The mast may be swept from the deck;
The keel by the shoals may be worn,
　The vessel be well nigh a wreck,—
The hull may asunder be riv'n;
　Not left with a beam or a board;
By faith I will still reach the hav'n;
　For Jesus the life-boat has lower'd.

I'll fear not the current,—so swift,
　Nor rock which are hid by the tide:
I know that I never shall drift,
　While Jesus is close by my side.
When winds of adversity sweep,
　And storms of calamity fall,
I'll think of Tiberias deep,
　And Jesus—who woke at the call.

ACROSTIC.

MORE to be desired than gold,—
And harder should we seek to find,—
The wealth that words have never told;—
The riches of the heart and mind.
In nothing else is perfect bliss:—
Earth hath no greater wealth than this.

Vain all our strivings after peace,
If we neglect the valued prize:—
A prize whose value will increase
'Neath bleeding heart, and weeping eyes.
Naught else on earth will give us rest,
And soothe the longing, aching breast.

THE MARRIAGE VOW.

WHILE standing together, and with solemn vow
  You promis'd each other in word and in bow
  Together thro' life's lengthen'd journey you'd go:—
  That love would continue through weal and through
     woe,

Not only in fortune did both then decide,
The bride to love groom, and the groom to love bride;
But through life's reverses, you still would be true,
And good for each other would not cease to do.

It was not, "Should you quite a large fortune make,
I'll help, and I'll cheer every step you may take;
But if the reverse, I will frown, and I'll fret;
And wish that together we never had met!"

It was not, "Should you gather by the road side,
A large pile of gold, I will love and confide;
But in this should you fail—though faithful you be—
From all of my promises, I will be free."

To render life's pathway more blessed and sweet,
Pull out the rough thorns, which are piercing the feet;
And plant some small flow'rs in the place where they grow:
And gladness will banish much sorrow and woe.

To wipe off the tear-drops from each other's eyes,
Will cure many sorrows, and quell many sighs.
And should worldly riches decrease, or recede,
'Tis then you the love of each other most need.

Fault-finding, contention, disputing, abuse,
Will lessen affections, and be of no use:
While a kind, loving word, or a smile, or a kiss,
Will gladden; and often turn sorrow to bliss.

And yet, in our life we should never expect
That each in each other no fault will detect:
And if we endeavor each other t' improve,
'Tis no mark of censure, or coldness of love.

* * *

THE TEMPERANCE SHIP.

BE free!   It is your right, be free!
    Your God has given you this right:
Arise—assert your liberty,
    And He will give you strength and might.

Be free from whiskey's galling chain:
    Be free from wine, from beer, from rum,
And then your freedom you'll maintain;
    And we will meet you as you come.

Though fetters strong may bind you now;
    Yet you have pow'r—you do not know,
Come make in God one solemn vow;
    And you can break them all like tow.

Accept no traitor's flag of truce:—
    Press forward from each point you gain:—
This flag is but a false excuse,
    To bind you with a stronger chain.

You now may feel too weak to start;
    Hundreds have felt as weak as you:
But O, what strength inspired the heart!
    When they resolv'd to rise and go.

Now come on board the gallant ship;
    Which never wrecked, or sprung a leak,
And never let a cable slip.—
    Your passage on this ship bespeak.

Her hull is sound; her beams are strong;
    And stiff and sound are all her masts;
Her deck is dry, and broad and long:
    Her sails have stood the hardest blasts.

See how she rides the dashing wave!
    See how her flag at mast-head flies.
Her crew is large and true and brave:
    Her officers are kind and wise.

She's rescued thousands from the wreck
    Of founder'd barks, and sinking boats;
With tens of thousands on her deck,
    She o'er the briny billows floats!

See! Now she stops to take you on:
    Come now, as she her life-boats lower:
A moment, and she may be gone
    To far to reach her from the shore.

She's never struck a bar or rock;
    Tho' tempests beat, and clouds may lower:
Her pilot's ever on the look;
    And knows the dangers 'long the shore.

O, noble ship, sail on! sail on!
    Touch every port on ocean's coast
Until you rescue every one:—
    Until you rescue all the lost.

THE POLITICIANS.

THE Politicians in our day,
Oft seek the office for the pay,
 And if emergencies require,
Will pull or push at either " wire."
And if they think 'twill break or bend,
They're apt to take the strongest end.
(We don't say all: there are a few
Firm, fair, and faithful, tried and true.)
How they hang around the " ring ! "
Some pull the wire, some tie the string;
And should the " ring," perchance divide,
They'll quickly grab the strongest side.
They go ahead, but do not lead—
Look back, and watch the party's speed;
And if they see it going back,
They flank it by the " inside track."
They keep it always in their sight,
And turn with it to left or right;
And if they see it forward go,
They keep ahead, and loudly crow.
They are curious men indeed;
And in such funny ways proceed.

The politician goes to church,
And in a forward seat will perch:
And when the services begin,
He puts on a sardonic grin;
With one eye on the parson's notes,
And with the other, counting votes.
And when the basket passes round,
He first looks up, and then looks down,
Until he catches every eye;
And then he holds a quarter high:

Lets drop – and thus lends to the Lord,
Expecting back a rich reward.
And when the church is deep in debt,
And must be sold, or money get,
And when the parson makes a call,
"Five dollars! " he will loudly bawl.
He wants his gift to be well known
Before he makes the Lord the loan;
So, puts it down in white and black,
For fear he'll never get it back:
And if he don't, you may be sure,
He'll never feel like giving more.

When the concluding hymn is read
And sung, and benediction said,
With fawning, sycophantic smile,
He'll stop, or pass along the aisle,
And shake the hands of all he meets,
As "How are you," he oft repeats,
" You're looking very well to-day."
But how he looks, I cannot say;
I know, but cannot well explain:
Not exactly, as if in pain,
Nor in great joy: but like, between
The two.   Well, you know what I mean;
Just like men you've often seen.
It is a very peculiar way:
Which says, or means, "Election day."

But should you ask him for the text;
Things being mix'd, and he perplex'd,—
He'd likely say, " November next;"
And in his flurry and his flare,
Would say, " I 'spose you'll all be there."
(The honest man we'd not reprove,
Who gives in charity and love;
But he who through the Christian name,
Aspires to wealth, or worldly fame.)

Before election day begins,
He meets you, and with smiles and grins,
Takes you by the hand and shakes,
Until your arm he almost breaks,—
Says, how's your health, your children, wife?
As if he knew you all your life.
He asks you all about your friends;
Pulls out his dollars, fives and tens;—
Says, " Come and take a social drink;
Come on my boys! I've got the chink! "
And as each one a ticket takes,
He says, " I think we'll sweep the stakes."

But when the ballots are all cast,
And the election day is past,
And you are out of work and bread,
And it should pop into your head,
To see your politician friend,
And ask him fifty cents to lend;
Perhaps he'll meet you at the door,
And say, "Have I met you before? "
And you'd think not, he seems so strange,
And is, of course, "just out of change."
He'll twist and turn;—the favor shirk,
And say, "I'm sorry you're out of work."
And as you from the door-way go,
He thinks, "Each man must *hoe* his row."

We do not say he should give all
Who on him for assistance call:
But should give half as much, we think,
For *bread* as what he gave for *drink*.

For " Uncle Sam " he now sets in,
And tries the game he thinks will win;
But if his basket he can fill
Without his *hoe*, he surely will.
In fact he'll seldom use the hoe

Except to reach his "Uncle's" row.—
Of course we do not say, he'll steal,
But only takes from Uncle's field,
What others might,—" 'Twill be no harm:
For he can " buy us all a farm;"
So says the song—it must be so;—
" I'm poor, and he's so rich, you know:
And if I take a little more,
He will not miss it from his store."
Uncle employs a lot of hands,
With "*wires*" and strings, in "*rings*" and bands
They work; and should the funds get low,
Why, he'll just raise the tax, you know.
Tax is the best crop Uncle sows;
Hot, cold, or wet, or dry, it grows:
Wheat, rye and oats, corn, hay and flax,
May fail, but there's no fail in tax.

See what the Politicians know
About the taxes,—how they grow.
" If taxes get too thin," they say,
" We sow a little more;—'twill pay—
And when the harvest comes, we then
Employ a few good extra men,
To do the work—we oversee;
They get one-fourth, and we get three.
We always lay a little by,
In case next year they don't grow high;
And things should take a turn about;—
Others get in and we get out."

When " Uncle " comes his part to get,—
Having to pay a heavy debt—
Across the fields, all brown and bare,
In crib and barn, and everywhere
He looks, and looks in sad despair!
And looks again; but no tax there!
And then he blows, and blows his horn,—

But men and tax and all are gone!
He blows again, but none appear.
(They've gone, no doubt, to 'lectioneer.)
With carpet-bags and empty sacks,
Then off to Washington he packs,
And there relates the solemn facts,
And says, "We'll have to raise more tax."
Year after year this crop they sow,
Because it never fails to grow.
Land high or low, or rich or poor,
They sow it o'er and o'er and o'er.
Are not the Politicians queer;
As they so many ways appear?

This may be but a tale of "tax:"
Yet fiction often shows up facts.
Of course, our tale will only hit
Those whom the shoe may chance to fit.

THE FOURTH OF JULY.

'TIS the Fourth of July! and we can see why
Its name should be honor'd, and not left to die:
  The bells we will ring; "We are free!" we will cry;
  And we'll hail the return of the Fourth of July.

The fact in the minds of our children we'll fix,
That in seventeen hundred seventy-six,
When money was low, and the taxes were high,
  In council we met on the Fourth of July;—

On the Fourth of July, our fore-fathers swore
They'd groan 'neath the chain of oppression no more:—
"Our honor, our fortunes we'll give: or we'll die
To be free," they declar'd, on the Fourth of July.

When we came from England, that we might be free.
The Englishmen follow'd us over the sea,
And laid heavy taxes on all we could make,
And threaten'd the most of our products to take.

We drew up a paper and each signed his name;
And then the next time when for taxes they came,
The shot and the powder,—which then made them fly,—
Was all they could get on the Fourth of July.

Again they came back with great ships and great guns,
To kill, or to take of America's sons:—
Their ships we knock'd low, and their guns we knock'd high;
We met not to play on the Fourth of July.

In " Fourteen " they came back to take Baltimore;
But found her brave sons, with their guns at the door:
And found we meant work, on the Fourth of July;
So hoisted their sails, and they bid us " good-bye."

For three hundred years, on Columbia's soil,
We plow'd and we sow'd, but we reap'd not the spoil;
For old " Johnny Bull," he would break in our field,
And eat up, or take of the best of the yield.

But now we can sing, for our country is free,
And fruit we can gather from Liberty's tree;
And all hostile feelings long 'go we let die;—
Now shake Johnny's hand on the Fourth of July.

We will not forget, but will ever rely
On Him who we trusted, the Fourth of July;
But 'neath this great tree—in its far-reaching shade,
We'll worship: and none shall e'er make us afraid !

BUNION'S PROGRESS; OR, A PLAY ON WORDS.

While words are not to play upon,
No harm to make a little fun,
If it will give to sadness joy,
And make a man feel like a boy.

DEAR E.:—As I O U A letter, and am confined to the house to-day, I will pay U what I O U, as U will C B-lo!

For more than a *week* past I have felt a *strong* interest in the *progress* of *bunion's pile-grim*, which has been my *joint* companion night and day; and which has attracted my *attention* to the detracting of its *tension*. I have *not* thoroughly *read* it, though it is thoroughly *red*, and often makes me feel *blue*, and *yell-"oh!"* and while it is *red*, it does not seem to be *read-y* to go *toward* a *heal* or *head*, but continues at the *foot*, though it is continually *rising*.

I am trying to-*ward* the *toe* by *salving* the *bunion*, with a view of *saving* the *toe*, by making a *heal* of the bunion, and the *toe*. But to *foot* it all *up*, bunion, in its *progress,* came *down upon* my *toe*, and by *perch*-ing *upon* my *foot* made it a *rude acher*, of a lower *section;* and though it is not a *furlong*, I *long for* its departure; and *for* that purpose would be willing to apply *long fur* or *short-fur*, to *fur*ther its *heal*-ing. I have been *pain*-ting the *toe* with great *pains*, *to heal*-the *pain* and *toe*.

The *progress* of this *pile-grim*, which is as unpleasant as a *pill-grim*—has *taught* me a *lesson* in regard to a *taut* *bunion*, which will be no *less on* until it begins to *heal* and *lessen;* and as it *lessens* and *heals* the *bliss increases*, while the *blis-ter decreases* more than when swollen *in-creases*. I have been advised to *apply*—to make it *pliable*—a little *costic*, with a *fine-stick*, of *course*, and not a *coarse stick*, as the *fine-stick* would be more *plastic*, and *elastic* than the *last stick*. I have not taken the advice of my *stick-ler*, for fear it would give the *corn* a *corn dough-mess-stick* appearance, and prove a *cheat*, and produce a *rye* face.

While this may appear to be a *play* on words, or display of *art* in *vain*, the *bunion* appears more like an *artery* than a *vein*, except at the *changes* of the *weather* when, it acts more like a *vane* on a *barn* or *barn*-acle; when it seems *vain* to try, and change its *course*.

Now, if you think I am trying to *soar* to the *head* of the *pun list* in a *pun upon* my *foot, upon* my *word*, if you *list* to me for a moment you will find you are *mistaking;* but the *corn* has not *missed aching* for a week, though it is *knot* now *a-king*, yet it is *aching* with a *crown*. I do not see how you can call me a *punster* when I can scarcely *stir* *upon* my foot, which is *corn*-tinually *stirring* my feelings, and making my foot feel as if it needed a *stirrup*, or *supporter*,—not that I wish to *sup porter*, though I am often *ail*-ing, and am badly *corned*, and am occasionally in a *rest-or-rant*, with a *tender raising*—a *rum-pus;* when, if you should *salute* me, you would likely *say-loon*.

But to stick to the *corn*, I would say I am not the *sower* of the *corn*, but the *corn* is its own *sore, rooted* and *grounded:* and while I neither *sowed, harrowed, stalked, bladed*, topped, nor in any way *cultivated* the *corn*, the *corn* has *sored*, and *harrowed* me, and prevented me from *stalking* the ground. So I suppose all that I can do is to *leave* the *corn*—though it is *ripe*, and in a *shooking* condition— and *cultivate* patience. And though it goes *against* the *grane*, I must corn-*cede* the *corn* to be a *cob*—produced by a *cobbler*,—and *proceed* on my *pile-grim-age* till it goes off, or *till* the *toe* is *healed*, but not *till* the *corn*.

Though I am not a *wag*, or a *wag-oner*, I will have to *way-on* with my *corn*. And though I am not a-*mill* with a *hopper*, yet I *am-ill* and am a *hopper* with *corn*.

A *toe* without a nail, may be *heeled* by a *sower*, who decreases the *ball* and makes *awl hole*.

Now, while I am not *paring* or *repairing* the *corn*, I am not *despairing*, but *comparing*, or *paraphrasing* a *pair* or two of *phrases;* or *elucidating* a subject which appears like a *tight date*, or a paradoxical—but not a *paradisical*—parable, the subject of which is *unparalleled* and *unparable*, being a papulous *bony-fied matter*, which often makes the "*shoe fly*," with *butt-on* the floor; which *discloses* and *closes* a *long string* and a *loose tongue*, though a quiet *sole*.—Call the *subject* a *spun* or a *bun-yarn*, which does not seem to be *subject* to any *rule;* while I am *subject* to the *foot* rule, which keeps me from the *yard*.

While *some* of the above composition is in apposition, and the *sum* of it is given in deposition, to get an exposition only requires a little transposition to the opposite position of its present position.   And while it may require a *translation*, I am not in a *trance* position;—that is, I do not *sit* in a *trance*, although I am anxious for the *transit* of the corn;—which may have been caused by *trans* gression; and causes me to *lay* my foot in a *prop*-position, which is hard to *stand:* there-*fore* I *lay* the *matter* before you in its present position and ask your attention *there-too*.

TO AN EXCESSIVE SMOKER.

———

Written by request to a minister—an excessive smoker—who acknowledged that he had become very nervous, and in other ways injured by the smoking habit; and would give a great deal if he could abandon it.

———

"The smoke of their torment ascendeth up forever and ever!"

———

DEAR FRIEND:—The object of this communication, as I hope you will readily see, and appreciate, is to reform the smoker, by showing the evil results growing out of the habit of excessive smoking; and condemning the smoke which has been ascending for a long time, and may ascend for a long time to come; if not forever and ever. And whether I should succeed or fail in my object, I hope you will receive what I may say in good will, and still regard me as your friend.

If there is any kind of smoke which ascends continually, or forever and ever, it seems to me it must be the smoke of tobacco. Whether the term, " forever and ever " means a limited, or an unlimited time, it is not my purpose to discuss. But if the smoke of tobacco extends only through time, it will be bad enough;—especially to the excessive smoker. The habit of excessive smoking would not appear so bad or influential if practised only in the lower walks of life, and by those whose minds have never been schooled and educated to look with sorrow and sympathy upon the untaught and unfortunate. For it is obvious that their example would not be so readily followed; and the condemnation not so great: for he that knoweth not his duty and doeth it not shall receive fewer stripes. But when we see one whose mind has been schooled and educated above the common mind,—one who has studied, and to a great extent, mastered the physical and mental laws,—who teaches morality and religion, economy and temperance, violate these laws and precepts, we cease to wonder that his influence for good is less than desired, and labored for, and are convinced that practice, or example is more powerful than precept. Thou that sayest, "Thou shalt not steal," dost thou steal? You, my friend, are a teacher;—one whose every act is watched; you have under your care and instruction young and tender hearts, which can easily be led for good or evil; and your example will leave lasting impressions upon them,—like the seal upon the placid wax. You are more than a teacher: you are a shepherd, whose work and office are to care for the sheep. It is said, "a good shepherd will lay down his life for the sheep." And if this is so, would it be too great a sacrifice for him to lay down his cigars for them, instead of sending up smoke to darken the sky of their sunny pastures,—throwing dark shadows between the trembling sheep and the blinded and nervous shepherd,—offering a good opportunity for the approach of the devouring wolf!

Doubtless, Paul, in his perils by land and by sea, in stocks and prisons, and in hungerings oft, had experienced the keenness of a starved appetite; and would heartily have relished a morsel of meat; but meat was an offense to some, and he, in a very self-denying spirit, said, "If I make my brother to offend, I will eat no meat while the world standeth." Perhaps he remembered the words of the great Teacher,—"Woe unto that man through whom offense cometh." Many have been taught—and that rightly—that excessive smoking is not only useless, but that it is injurious, expensive and offensive; and the voice of conscience is, " Woe! if I indulge."

While I believe every man should be free to smoke if he desires so to do, and it may not injure him when indulged in moderately; but I earnestly and honestly believe that without smoking, most men in every respect, would be better, that a preacher could preach better sermons, be less nervous and irritable, enjoy better health, have a greater and better influence, a clearer conscience, a keener perception; while many a one may say, or think of a preacher who smokes to excess. "He would be more consistent; he could live on much less; could do more good, by taking the money spent for cigars and buying and distributing tracts, administering to the poor and destitute, getting premiums and books for the Sabbath school, contributing to the church, clothing the naked, and he would hear the voice of approbation, in angelic tones, sweeter than the best cigar, sounding in his ears, 'Well done, thou good and faithful.'" But this is all in reference to the present life. I do not say, if we smoke out our days with nervous trembling, that we will be compelled to smoke through all eternity; yet the smoke of our torment may ascend up forever and ever: or, at least, for ages and ages.

The river which separates the seen from the unseen, must be broad and deep, and pure and unlimited in its efficacy, if it will wash away the smoke that has saturated our body, weakened and benumbed our brain, before we reach the other shore: and even if it does, the passage must be darkened, and the waters tinted—unlike the sight which John beheld when he was shown a "pure river of water." But if the smoker enters that land as he departs from this, the smoke of his torment must ascend.

I have spoken thus plainly to you as a brother, and as a friend, who sticketh closer than a brother: (unless the smoke prevents the sticking.) I have desired and endeavored to give you strong meat,—instead of strong smoke—as man's, and not children's food. I hope my words may be sharp enough to separate habit and conviction; and divide asunder smoke and brain. If I did not know you so well, I would not dare to use such plainness of speech, for fear of offending you; but as you are a reformer, and have passed the time to become offended at what is intended for good, I have thus plainly spoken,— knowing that you cannot but see this in its proper light when presented to the discerning eyes of your understanding. After all, I may have said nothing that you do not know, or that you could not have said much better yourself. But perhaps I have reminded you of what you knew before, and have brought your case before your eyes, as similar cases of others are seen by yourself. But, doubtless, you may think it is time I had come to the point, by giving some remedy, or showing some means by which the evil may be overcome. I do not know that I can give you an infallible remedy, but will make some suggestions which may help you.

In the first place I will say I do not much believe in substitutes:—that is such substitutes as are often resorted to. If a person is in the habit of stealing from another that which is valuable, I do not think it will help him, to allow him to steal things of less value, with a view of breaking him of stealing: or, if one is in the habit of gambling, to advise him to break it off by swearing, as it would be hard to quit both at once.

A man who is in the habit of gormandizing could not easily break himself of it by changing his diet only: and it would be hard for him to quit the practice all at once. But he could easier effect a cure by reducing the quantity of his food a little each day, without feeling much uneasiness by the change. So, if you smoke a cigar every hour, I would suggest—if you cannot do better—to reduce the number from fifteen to fourteen per day, and then to thirteen, and so on down to one, if you thought it necessary. I believe this could easily be done without experiencing any great self-denial. But there is a difference between the desire for food and that for cigars. One is a natural taste, or desire, while the other is acquired. I do not believe any one ever liked the taste of tobacco, before acquiring a taste by its use. Hence the desire for it is not natural, but acquired. Not so with most kinds of necessary food. It is natural for the child when first born to crave or desire nourishment.

As I am not a smoker myself, I can't say how hard it is for those who smoke to abandon it. Neither am I the one to say that every one should abandon it altogether: or that it has never benefitted any one. But when I see a person who smokes to excess, by which he is being injured, and is injuring others, and he knows and acknowledges it, I think I can safely say, if he had better not abandon it altogether, he had better continue it in moderation; and if he cannot do that he had better discontinue it altogether.

' When in conversation with some clergymen a few years ago, one of them, who was quite an advocate of temperance, said he was formerly a great chewer: but finding the practice was doing him great injury, resolved to quit it, which resolution he successfully carried out. But in walking along the street, in Baltimore, one day, he saw some tobacco in a window, and the sight of it so tempted him, that he went in and bought a piece, and has been using it moderately ever since. I said to him, suppose in your temperance work you should be the means of reforming some drinker; who should afterward be tempted by seeing some liquor in a saloon window, and should go in and take a drink; would the act be any worse than yours in giving away to temptation and buying the tobacco ? He could not but see and reply that there was not much difference in the two acts. So, while we are censuring and teaching others, we should not be so benevolent and so interested in others as to forget ourselves.

Now, dear sir, if you would take the advice you so earnestly give to others, you would say to whatever may offend,—" Get thee behind me Satan: thus far shalt thou go, and no further." And by a few repulses, and aggressive movements he will fall back, when you can advance, and take and hold every position he held; and he will finally retreat. Accept no flag of truce; but take every evacuated spot, and press on from rampart to rampart, and you will come off more than conqueror. If you give the enemy a chance to adjust and discharge his guns, he may give you a deadly shot, or bewilder you by blinding you with smoke; and then by flank movement, capture and carry off your forces.

Hoping that you may be victorious, and drive back the foe from whence he came,—even if the smoke of his wrath ascends up forever and ever—and that a pure atmosphere may ever surround your brow, and the bright sunlight of heaven may ever beam upon you,—cheering and strengthening you, and lighting your pathway, I remain,

VERY SINCERELY YOURS.

TO A ZEALOUS CHRISTIAN LADY.

DEAR Friend, it affords me much joy and delight
A few pleasant thoughts in your favor to write:
But you look so high, and the things above seek,
I'm afraid no thought I can write or can speak,
In your mental garden a lodgment will find,
Or welcome receive by your well tutored mind
Though with this opinion, I nevertheless,
These few broken thoughts hereby briefly express.

Our acquaintance is short, yet I can discern
That folly you shun, and for wisdom you yearn;—
In fact I discover, by words and by ways,
The much valued traits—which the world does not praise—
That strong love of nature, that ardent desire
Which burns in your soul, like a half smother'd fire,
By high walls of caution securely pent,—
Now warming and waiting, and seeking for vent;—

To pour out its heat, and to dry up the tears,
The dampness and doubts and the sorrows and fears;
To light up the skies and to drive back the clouds
Of sin—which so many in darkness enshrouds.
And yet you oft feel you but little can do
Without the approval of friends warm and true,
In whose love and friendship your love firmly rest,
And pours back the warm love which burns in your breast.

You seek not the giddy, nor follow the throng,
Yet love and devotion and friendship are strong;—
Are strong for the few; but not many you find
Who rise to your standard, accord with your mind.
Few know your rejoicing—and fewer your grief,
And none but these few can afford you relief,
Or share in the gladness hope brings to your soul,
As it raises its wings and points to the *goal.*

While drinking the waters from wisdom's deep spring,
You have not neglected the " one needful thing,"—
The stream of salvation, the fountain of grace,—
Refreshing the soul, giving strength for the race:
O, may their rich waters continually flow,
And keep your heart purer and whiter than snow,
And He who hath washed you, come often and sup,—
In seasons of sadness your spirit bear up!

Though young, you have found it is pleasant and good
To walk in the path the dear Saviour hath trod,—
To feel that His gentle hand leads you along
When you are so weak and temptation is strong.
O, what would you do, when affliction comes nigh,
And life seems so lonely, if He were not by?
Has He once denied you, or ever refus'd
To bind up the wounds when your heart has been bruised;

Or turn'd a deaf ear to your piteous cries,
When tears of deep sorrow fell fast from your eyes?
He knows well in sorrow what comfort is worth.
In th' garden when grief bore Him down to the earth;—
Deserted by all, in that dark, lonely place,
The blood-drops of sorrow rolled down from His face!
He then knew the comfort which comes from on high,
Though drank of the cup which He pray'd to pass by.

Full well do I know that sad seasons have come,
When you've half desired to depart and go home!—
Sad hours! when you felt that the trouble and care
Were greater than you, unsupported, could bear:
It may be these shadows now only pass by,
That you may prize higher, the bright and blue sky,
Which shall bend o'er your head—your pathway illume,
And banish forever all darkness and gloom.

Though cold days and cloudy may linger in spring,
The flowers will bloom and the birds they will sing,
The sunbeams will drive all the coldness away:
The forests will throw off their raiment of gray;
And nature's true hand—to enliven the scene—
Will cover the fields with its carpet of green;
And all will be beauty wherever we roam.
Yes, winter will pass, and the summer will come.

Then drive from your bosom whatever may blight
The hope of your heart—fairest prospects and bright;
Let darkness and doubt and despondency cease;
And hope will wave o'er you her banner of peace.
Be brave, true and trusting, but never despair:
The bread will be gathered, we scatter with prayer,
And none of our labor will e'er be in vain—
'Tis God gives the increase—the sun and the rain.

Tho' your feet may oft tire, and your hands may be sore,
The fruit will be sweet when the harvest is o'er!
Tho' riches may vanish—false friends may betray,
The true and the faithful will not turn away;
But the heart will respond, and its love you shall share:—
Tho' space may divide, you will ever seem near.
The requital of love is earth's greatest bliss;
And heaven, perhaps, has none greater than this.

May God give you strength as your days may increase;—
Your labors of love bring you gladness and peace;—
The safe path of virtue bring joy to you now;
The rainbow of promise encircle your brow !
From th' base of the hill we oft lift up our eye,
But fear to ascend it—so rough and so high:
But find as we upward its gentle slope go,
'Tis not half so steep as it seem'd when below.

I first thought a single bouquet I would bind;—
With cords of true friendship around it entwin'd;
And hastily sought through the forest and field,
To find the best flowers that nature could yield;
But th' wood was so dense, and the field was so wide,
And flowers so many, I could not decide:
So gather'd all sizes, all forms and all hues,
And lay at your feet,—to select or refuse.

But I've kept you waiting so long, I'm afraid
The first ones I gather'd—though laid in the shade—
Have lost all their fragrance - are scarcely alive,—
If press'd to the bosom, again may revive; —
Or streams of affection, which roll from your heart,
Or the tear-drop of love, from its fountain may start,
Take the tint from your cheek, as it rolls down your face.
Adorn it again with new beauty and grace.

Some of them I gather'd at morning's gray dawn,
Some of them at noontide I picked from the lawn;
And some by still twilight's last lingering ray,—
Which budded and bloom'd through the long busy day.
The last, but not least, but the best of them, grew
And were gather'd at night-time—all dripping with dew:
When the sun of your eye on them brightly shines,
Some of them may prove to be wild weeds or vine.

I trust, in the pile I have laid at your feet,
No hemlock or nightshade or thorn you will meet;
But some deathless flower, 'mong them you will find,
To plant and to tend in the bed of your mind,—
The pure "balm of gilead " to bind to your breast,
To drive out all sorrow, and make your life blest.
That God may direct you through life, to its end,
Accept, as the wish—as the pray'r of your friend.

ACROSTIC.

RELIGION to woman gives beauty and grace. --
Expresses the love of the heart in the face.
Behold these two beauties ! How brightly they shine,
Encircling her life with a beauty divine!
Care, grief may oppress her, and sorrow molest,
Contentment and peace still abide in her breast.—
And all who live holy are happy and blest

ACROSTIC.

AT home and abroad there's nothing so sweet—
Nothing so pleasant, wherever we meet—
Nothing so lovely;—O, nothing we find,
As woman with gentle and virtuous mind !

WRITTEN ON THE LEAF OF AN ALBUM.

THE words must be few, and the sentence be brief,
My wish to express on this limited leaf;
Yet it may be done in one limited line:—
Do good, and your will, to the Father's resign.

WASHINGTON, D. C., Nov. 2, 1883.

DEAR JENNIE:—As this is the first leisure hour I have had for some time, I will spend it in writing a few lines, suggested by my birthday present from you. The first lines written by the aid of the gift shall be to the giver.

While the intrinsic value of the glasses is considerable, I prize them more for their associate value, which they will continue to keep before my eyes, and which is suggestive of many valued and endearing thoughts.

First, They were intended, by the giver, to make clear the vision of my physical eyes, which enables me to see and remember the loving heart and kind hand which presented them. And as they were intended for near and distant vision, so they bring to mind the kindly acts and motives of the present, and those of the far past—but which still live in the present—as well as those the eye of faith and hope beholds in the future. And as these glasses guide my eyes aright, so may a brighter light guide my feet in the paths of duty, wisdom and honor.

In looking through these glasses objects appear differently when seen through upper and lower glass; yet both were designed for good, which reminds me that we do not all see alike—though our motives be the same and of good design. So we are all looking through glasses of various kinds, and not many eyes see alike, even through the same glasses; yet there should be no variance, but those walking on the same road together should adjust and exchange the glasses through which they look, till their visions becomes as one: or, at least, that each may see the rough and thorny places in the road; and if they cannot see alike, each may see what is for the other's good, and point out the poisonous flowers beside the way, which may appear as harmless and as fragrant as the rose;—thus each being a help and blessing to the other. And as the golden frame together binds the glasses—rendering them mutual aids—so may the golden bands of love, which God hath framed, bind your heart and your husband's as one, though your eyes may fail to see all things alike. And as the stays or shaft hold them firmly in their places, so may the grace of God, which links you to the church's Head, hold you firmly in the path of duty, honor and peace, when adverse or evil winds may blow, and threatening storms arise. And as gold is the emblem of purity, and glass of transparency and tenderness, so may your hearts be as pure as the sunlight, your vision as clear as the dew-drop, and your words as gentle as the springtime zephyrs, and as tender as the tones and touch of a loving mother!

I find that often the glass will become clouded—darkening the vision—and will require cleansing: so, sometimes, will the mists of doubt, distrust, disbelief, and other impurities darken our mental vision and sadden our heart; when we should pray for the sun of righteousness to rise with healing in his wings and drive the darkness from our eyes, and doubt and sadness from our heart. And as the golden rim, which arches the bridge of the nose from eye to eye, gives steadiness to the frame, so may the golden bow of hope ever bend brightly over your head, and keep you in a happy and steady frame of mind, until you pass the bridge of time to the golden shore of eternal light; where we will no longer see "through a glass darkly!" And as the glasses require a case for their protection and safety, so may you be clothed and covered in the "whole armour of God, that you may be able to stand, being girt about with truth, and having on the breastplate of righteousness, and your feet shod with the preparation of the gospel of peace; and, above all things, protected with the shield of faith; and the helmet of salvation, and the sword of the Spirit, which is the word of God: praying always with all prayer and supplication in the Spirit, and watching thereunto with all perseverance."

LANGUAGE OF FLOWERS.

Now come and take a walk with me,
Through fruitful field and fertile lea,
Among the flowers, beneath the trees,
Fanned by the spring-time's gentle breeze,
Along the streams where wisdom flows,
And knowledge bends the spreading boughs.
The Coral Honeysuckle (1) vine,
We'll round the Golden Rod (2) entwine,
And o'er the fields with new delight,
We'll gather up the Daises White (3),
Anemone (4), Goat's Rue (5) and Fern (6),
Before the morning shadows turn—
Sweet Violets, both White (7) and Blue (8),
Fresh, dripping with the morning dew—
Flowering Almond (9), Holly Red (10)—
Which on us hope and foresight shed—
Bright Hyacinths (11) and Hollyhocks (12),
Which grow along the garden walks,
The Ivy, Evergreen and Box (13),
On which frost paints no silver locks—
Chrisanthemums, both Pink (14) and White (15),
We'll with the Heliotrope (16) unite;
Moss Rose (17), Bee Orchis (18) and Oxeye (19)
And Rosemary (20) together tie;
The Pansy (21) and Ladies' Delight (22),
And Buttercups (23) with them unite.
But the Syringa (24) we'll let grow,
And cultivate our path to show,

EXPLANATION.—1, Fidelity; 2, Encouragement; 3, I will think of it;
4, Anticipation; 5, Reason; 6, Sincerity: 7, Modesty; 8, Faithfulness; 9,
Hope; 10, Foresight; 11, Constancy and Play; 12, Ambition of a Scholar;
13, Constancy; 14, Cheerfulness; 15, Truth; 16, Devotion; 17, Superior
Merit; 18, Industry; 19, Patience; 20, Remembrance; 21, Tender and
Pleasant Thoughts; 22, Modesty; 23, Riches; 24, Memory.

We'll take the Rose of Cherokee (25),
Which speaks to us in poetry—
The Cluster Rose (26), which merry makes,
The Tulip Red (27), which love awakes,
We'll seek the Scotch Fir's (28) downy fleece,
And Fig Tree (29), as its fruits increase,
We'll not forget the Flow'ring Reed (30)—
Which upward points from dell and mead—
Nor Everlasting (31), meek and low,
Spread o'er the fields like sifted snow.
From Thistles (32) of Misanthropy,
We'll keep our fields and garden free,
We will not pull, but only look
On the White Poppy (33) by the brook;
Nor will we pluck the Pheasant's Eye (34),
Or Barberry (35), but pass them by;
We'll from the Nightshade (36) quick retreat,
And tread the Nettle (37) 'neath our feet;
And from the Moonwort (38) also flee,
And go not near the Judas Tree (39).
We'll lay aside the Mossy (40) wreath,
And twine the Olive (41) with the Heath (42)
And Periwinkle (42½) White and Red,
And wear their richness on our head.
The Poplar (43) we will sit beneath,
By running brook—along the heath.
The Mulberry we'll not despise—
If prudent we would be, and wise—
But eat the fruits, both White (44) and Red (45),
Which hang so thickly o'er our head.
Garlands of Roses (46) rich and rare,

EXPLANATION.—25, Poetry; 26, The More the Merrier; 27, Declaration
of Love; 28, Elevation; 29, Fruitful; 30, Confidence in Heaven; 31,
Always Remembered; 32, Misanthropy; 33, Forgetfulness; 34, Painful
Recollections; 35, Sourness: 36, Dark Thoughts; 37, Slander; 38, Forgetfulness; 39, Unbelief; 40, Ennui: 41, Peace; 42, Solitude is sometimes
best society; 42½, Pleasures of Memory; 43, Talent; 44, Wisdom; 45,
Prudence; 46, Reward of Merit.

We up the hill of time will bear;
Or plant in memory's cultured bed,
To bloom when summer hours are fled.
And as from height to height we go
We'll vie the vaunting Misletoe (47),
And rest when we our work have done,
'Neath Cedar boughs of Lebanon (48),
With wreaths of Amaranth, (49) entwined
With Laurel (50) 'round the deathless mind—
Which o'er life's lasting leaves shall look,
As oft they turn in Memory's book.
Those pages pure—without a stain—
Writ with Time's hand and Memory's pen;
We'll read them o'er, and o'er, and o'er!—
Forever fresh in Memory's store!

EXPLANATION.—47, I surmount all difficulties; 48, Incorruptible; 49, Immortality; 50, Glory.

--------●--------

PRESIDENTS OF THE UNITED STATES.

FIRST in the Presidential line,
Was Washington, in Eighty-nine.
John Adams to us next was giv'n
In Seventeen hundred ninety-seven
The third was Thomas Jefferson;
He came in Eighteen hundred one.
Then Madison—fourth in the line—
Went in in Eighteen hundred nine.
The fifth Monroe—as will be seen—
In Eighteen hundred seventeen.
John Quincy Adams did arrive
And took his seat in Twenty-five.
Jackson—the seventh in line—
Next took his seat in Twenty-nine.

The eighth—Van Buren—next was giv'n,
He took his seat in Thirty-seven.
The ninth we find was Harrison,
Who took his seat in Forty-one.
The tenth was Tyler—Forty-one—
Who fill'd the term of Harrison.
Eleventh one to wear the yoke—
In Forty-five—was James K. Polk.
Taylor—the twelfth one in the line—
Went in in Eighteen forty-nine;
He died, and Fillmore took his place
In Fifty:—thirteenth in the race.
Then came Pierce in Fifty-three:
The fourteenth—as 'tis plain to see.
Buchanan next, in Fifty-sev'n,
Fifteenth was he,—four and elev'n.
Lincoln—sixteenth—in Sixty-one;—
The year the Civil war begun—
Johnson the seventeenth—alive
When Lincoln died in Sixty-five.
Grant—the eighteenth in the line—
Went in in Eighteen sixty-nine.
In Sev'nty-seven, then came Hayes—
The nineteenth—quiet in his ways.
Garfield then follow'd after Hayes,
His term was short;—two hundred days—
He took his seat in Eighty-one.—
Two more, and then the list is done.
Arthur came when Garfield died—
The twenty-first one to preside.
The twenty-second, Cleveland came,
In Eighty-five—the last to name.

OUR DUTY.

NOW with our hungry spirits fed
   With fruits that grow on Eden's shore;—
And waters from the Fountain-head
We've drank—and live—no longer " dead "—
   Nor will we thirst nor hunger more!

With holy shoes upon our feet;—
   Our wounds with " Balm-of-Gilead " bound,
With praises, thanks and solace sweet,
We'll gladly tell to all we meet,
   What comfort—what relief we've found.

We'll take each wander'r by the hand,
   And with him to the fountain go;
In evil hour by him we'll stand,
And point him to that blissful land,
   Where fruits on trees immortal grow!

Such is the duty that we owe
   To Jesus, for His matchless love,
In leading us from sin and woe
To peace and righteousness below;
   And pointing us to joys above!

This duty should be our delight,
   For what our God for us has done,
In leading us from dark to light;—
From pain to peace, from wrong to right;—
   In giving us His only Son!

"Free ye've received; so freely give,"
  Said our dear Master—wise and kind;—
"More good to give than to receive;
As I have liv'd, so ye should live;
  And prove your love, as I've prov'd mine.

For if ye have true faith in God,
  And hope to dwell with Him above;
Then tread the path that I have trod;—
Drink of the cup, endure the rod,
  And prove your faith by works of love."

Jesus, His work on earth begins
  In love!—In love His labors close!
In life oft weeping with His friends,
And when His life of labor ends,
  He prays;—dies praying for His foes!

We, too, should labor, love and pray
  If we His crown of glory share:—
Should love His law; His word obey;
Should keep the "straight and narrow way;"
  We, too, the "crown of thorns" should wear.

WAITING BY THE RIVER.

IT is said, just over yonder,
　　There's a glory-land, serene,
Where we'll look with raptuous wonder;
　　When we view the radi'nt scene.
I am waiting by the river,—
　　Looking to the other side—
For the lulling of the tempest,—
　　　For the ebbing of the tide.

CHORUS.

I am waiting by the river,
　　Watching, waiting on the shore,—
Waiting, watching, for the pilot,—
　　Waiting till the boat comes o'er.

It is said, beyond the river,
　　There's a calm and safe retreat,
Where the waves shall cease forever,
　　And the storms shall never beat!
Think I see that peaceful haven,
　　Over on the other side,
And the life-boat making ready
　　To launch out upon the tide.—CHO.

It is said beyond the river,
　　Want and weeping shall not come;
Nor disease nor death shall sever
　　Those who meet in that bright home.
Now my vision's growing clearer,
　　I can see the white flag wave,—
Plainly read each golden letter,—
"LIFE-BOAT, COMING O'ER TO SAVE."—CHO.

Now I see the white spray flying
  'Gainst the unfurled, swelling sail,
And the oars so swiftly plying,
  As she speeds before the gale.
It is said, just o'er the river,
  In that holy, happy place,
Father, mother, son and daughter
  Shall all meet in fond embrace.—CHO.

Don't you hear the Captain hailing,—
  See the waving of His hand,
As the boat is nearer sailing,
  Near and nearer to the land?
I can see she's richly freighted
  · With white raiment for the blest;
And all those who've watched and waited,
  ·In white garments shall be dress'd.   CHO.

Now I see beyond the breakers,
  (For the river is not wide)
Friendly hands stretch'd out to take us,
  When we reach the other side.
Don't you hear them sweetly singing,
  As the life-boat glides along!
Hark! the chorus loudly ringing;
  'Tis the welcome, welcome song!—CHO.

Now I know we're near the portal,
  By the music soft and clear;
Such as ne'er was sung by mortal,
  Falls so sweetly on my ear!
When we're done with stormy weather,
  And the river we've crossed o'er,
Friend and friend we'll see together,
  Walking up the shining shore!—CHO.

On this side are ills distressing,—
  Angry words and scenes of woe,—
Heavy burdens, which are pressing,—
  Pressing out the tears that flow.
But I'm told, beyond the river,
  Not an angry word is said,
Nor an unkind deed shall ever
  Grieve the hearts which here have bled.—Cho.

In that land are purest pleasures,
  I am told, and boundless bliss;
And the richest, brightest treasures,
  Laid up for the pure in this.
It is said, there crystal fountains
  Of pure waters gush and play;
And the sunbeams, o'er the mountains
  Paint rich rainbows on the spray. - Cho.

It is said, beyond the river,
  There are flowers fair and gay,—
Flow'rs which bloom and blush forever,
  Blooming, blushing by the way.
O, what joy to tell the story
  Of that land so bright and fair!
God will be its light and glory,
  "And there will be no night there!"—Cho.

DO YOU THINK YOU WILL BE READY.

DO you think you will be ready,—
    Ready when the boat comes o'er ?
Have you helped the faint and feeble ?
    Have you done aught for the poor ?
Have you sought the blessed Saviour ?
    Have you met with Him in pray'r ?—
Then the pledge of love He gave you,
    Will be precious over there !

There's a beauteous city founded
    On the richest gems, we're told,
With fair jasper walls surrounded,
    And the streets of purest gold:
Through white pearly gates 'tis entered,—
    Which shall not be shut by day,
And the throne of God is centered
    In the midst, and lights the way.

On this side there'r sin and sadness,
    Pain and anguish, death and gloom:
And there is no home of gladness,
    But afflictions sometimes come.
But 'tis said, just 'cross the river
    There's a gentle, loving hand
That will wipe away forever
    Tears and sorrow from that land.

As you stand beside the eddy,
    Looking to the other side,
Do you feel that you are ready
    To launch out upon the tide ?—
Do you think in retrospection
    You will ever heave a sigh,
As eternal recollection
    Bring the past before your eye ?

COMFORT FOR THE WEARY.

SOMETIMES, as we journey 'long life's rugged road,
We wish we could lie down and throw off our load,
And—free from all labor and grief and dismay—
Could sleep till the dawning of some brighter day !

Our feet get so weary—our heart so dismay'd,
We wish we could lie 'neath the green willow's shade
We listen and long for the message to come;—
The message to call us from earth to our home.

Sometimes we think we can see just ahead,
A place in our journey more easy to tread,
But when we get to it, it seems just the same—
As rough and as steep as from whence we just came;

And th' burden we thought we should throw to the ground,
We cannot get off, for so tightly 'tis bound!
We hope and despond, and in this changeful way,
We go on life's journey from day unto day.

But always when looking our past journey o'er,
We found that the way had been trodden before;
And all of the hopeful and faithful were blest,
And 'neath heavy burdens, found comfort and rest.

Then let us arise from this slough of despair:—
On Him who is mighty, we'll cast all our care;
He says, " If your burden is heavy or great,
O, come unto me!—I will carry its weight."

When darkness surrounds us, and doubt gives distress,
We'll reach out our hands, and our fingers we'll press
In th' prints in His hands, and the wound in His side;
And know it is Jesus who lov'd us—who died !

"My Lord, and my Master! forgive," I'll exclaim;
O, let me go onward, and work in Thy name.
I'll trust Thee—believe Thee—my Saviour! my friend!
For Thou wilt be with me through life, to its end.

The passage is short, and the journey soon made.
The way has been open'd;—the track been survey'd:
The Saviour pass'd o'er it—left lights on the shore,
To burn till the very last pilgrim is o'er.

He fathom'd its waters with line and with rod;
Survey'd all its coasts, as through Jordan He trod—
Robb'd death of its terrors; illum'd up the grave,
And prov'd by His triumph, His power to save.

But let us remember the sorrows He bore;—
The toil and the conflict ere ent'ring death's door.
He never complained, or murmur'd or shrank,
While the dregs of the cup, to the bottom He drank.

So we will be faithful, and labor and wait;—
The field may be large, and the labor be great,
We will bear and forbear—in faith be content:
The message will come when our stength is all spent:—

The message, the message, how sweet it will sound,—
"In all of thy work thou hast faithful been found:
Thy conflict is ended—thine armour lay by,
And come; you are call'd to the kingdom on high!"

O, yes! when the feast of fat things is prepar'd—
The table is spread, and the bounty is shar'd—
When we, with our Leader, in triumph shall meet,—
O, then will the fruits of our labor be sweet!

Our bread shall be gather'd, tho' far it be driv'n
By winds, and by storms it to atoms be riv'n:
If sown in good faith, 'twill be gather'd again;
And none of our labor shall e'er be in vain.

Our hands then—so weary—from labor shall rest;
Our head may recline on the Master's warm breast;
Our feet—which have trodden o'er life's rugged road—
May there be at rest—there reliev'd of their load !

Our eyes which have wept here shall weep not again;—
No tear shall be shed in all heaven's domain.
Our heart—which has sorrow'd, in doubt and despair—
Shall joy, for no sorrow nor grief shall be there !

All of life's mysteries shall there be revealed,—
The hand which has hid them, no more be concealed,
The tongue which has murmur'd, shall there sing God's
      praise,—
Exclaim, "O, the wisdom and depth of His ways ! "

———◆———

HE SHALL SAVE HIS PEOPLE FROM THEIR SINS.

We learn from the Scriptures, that Jesus shall save
His people from sin, and from death, and the grave.
We find it recorded in second of Luke,—
Confirmed by the writings through all of God's book.

"Fear not," say the angels, as loudly they sing,
"Glad tidings to you and all people we bring;
Let glory to God in the highest, ascend,
And peace upon earth; and good will unto men."

Then trust in the Saviour, and let us not fear;
But love Him and serve Him:—He'll ever be near.
He says He will save us; His words they are true,
And what He has promised He surely will do.

"COME UNTO ME—I'LL GIVE YOU REST!"

YE heavy laden, who bow down
Beneath your load, and ne'er have found
A helping hand, when sore distress'd,—
Come unto me—I'll give you rest!

Ye troubl'd souls—with lashes wet—
Who seek repose, but fail to get
The comfort which will soothe your breast,—
Come unto me—I'll give you rest!

Ye tired and worn—whose weary feet,
From day to day sad steps repeat—
And in your work have ne'er been blest—
Come unto me—I'll give you rest!

Ye restless souls, who spend the night
In sleepless hours, till morning light,
And morning finds you still unblest—
Come unto me—I'll give you rest!

Ye hungry, weak, forlorn and poor,
Who beg your bread from door to door—
Refus'd by those your prayers molest—
Come unto me—I'll give you rest!

Ye rich—whose coffers overflow,
Whose every pleasure—mixed with woe—
Gives to your life no happy zest,—
Come unto me—I'll give you rest!

Ye who have lost your wealth and friends,
And in the world find no amends,
Come now—my love, my pow'r attest:
Come unto me—I'll give you rest!

Gentile and Jew, and bond and free,
Come bring your sorrows all to me;
From north, from south, from east, from west,—
Come unto me—I'll give you rest!

Come each; come all the world, and find
Rest to your souls, and peace of mind.
I'll bear your burdens on my breast:—
Come unto me—I'll give you rest!

IT MATTERS NOT.

IT matters not, though sorrows reign,
    And worldly prospects blast;
If we but fight—the battle gain,
    And wear the crown at last!

Though cares oppress, it matters not:
    It is enough to know
That all our cares shall be forgot;—
    All tears shall cease to flow!

When this shall be it matters not:
    The Scriptures plainly tell
(Then, O, why grieve, if we believe?)
    God rules, and ruleth well!

It matters not:—God knows the best:
    We'll trust, and onward go;
And if at last with Him we'll rest—
    Enough for us to know.

ILL OFT IS GOOD, WHEN UNDERSTOOD.

IN life's measured journey we can't always hope
   In smoothest of places to walk or to dwell,
Nor pluck the choice flowers which 'long the way ope,
   And leave none for those who may like them as well·

As briers oft grow where the berries hang thick,
   And thistles oft grow on the richest of land,
We cannot expect the best berries to pick,
   And never a brier come close to our hand.

While mountain and valley and broad spreading plain
   Compose the round earth—where our lot 'tis to be,
On no one of these can we hope to remain,
   But pass through the changes we find in the three.—

Each one gives its pleasure, and each gives its pain;
   God made them, and doubtless He made them for good:
The sunshine and shadow, the drought and the rain,
   They all have their uses—though not understood.

So life has its shadows, its ups and its downs,
   And from them we cannot expect to be free:
While some bring us laughter, and others bring frowns:
   We'll praise and give thanks when their uses we see.

So we will be thankful for good and for ill,
   Tho' they may bring gladness or grief to our breast,
We'll bear all with patience, and bow to the will
   Of Him who directs them;—He knows what is best.

THE JOURNEY OF LIFE:

AN ALLEGORY;

OR,

FACTS IN FIGURES.

———

Written for and dedicated to my children: with a view of interesting, warning, guiding and blessing them, and all travelers on the journey of life, in whose hands this story may fall.

———

CHAPTER I.

MY DEAR CHILDREN:

As this is my birthday, and I wish to commemorate it in a way that will be remembered with pleasure and profit, I communicate to you some of my varied experience, thus far, on the journey of life, hoping you may be induced to follow the good and avoid the evil; and praying that heaven's blessing may rest upon your pathway as you follow on. What has blessed me in life will bless you, as our interests are so closely linked that they are one.

Two score and twelve years ago I started on the journey of life. To-day I find myself seated at the fifty-second milestone; and in looking back over the road I have passed, I can distinctly retrace my steps to the fifth milestone; beyond which, only here and there, I can indistinctly see some green or barren spot; some piercing thorn, or blooming flower. While journeying the first twenty-one miles with father and mother, (whose names I love and revere, whose lives I honor, and whose feeble forms and tottering limbs can scarcely bear their weight, and who have passed the number of miles allotted to travelers on this journey, and well nigh reached its end), I received from them many words of advice and examples of virtue. The first miles they carried me in their arms, taught my tottering feet to step, and helped me over the briers and thorns, through the mazes and mists, and cheered me in the sunny hours of morn;—which seemed to tell of a smoother journey, and brighter noon and eve. In those morning hours I often tried to walk alone, and with loosened hand, would lag behind, or go ahead, and turn aside from the road in which they directed me to go; and would pluck forbidden fruit, and poisonous flowers by the way; when, with pierced hands and bleeding feet, I would call to them for help; or by them be sought and extricated from the crooked labyrinths and "deep tangled wild wood," or the rocky cliffs, that were in every diverging path.

As I passed from fifth to sixth, seventh, eighth, and along to the twenty-first milestone, I hoped each succeeding mile would be smoother, and freer from cliffs and clouds, and tempting sights and crooked lanes and paths, leading from the straight and travel-worn highway. But I found them all along the road; and traveled far before by experince, I learned the lessons taught me at the beginning, and as from mile to mile I came. And as those traveling on this road are, by precept, example and experience, supposed to be able, from the twenty-first milestone to pursue their journey alone, without the watchings of the parental eye, or the leading of the parental hand, with my father's and mother's blessing I started from there alone. They have passed on, with steady step, over hills and valleys, rocks and rills, through bright and gloomy hours, and have reached the eightieth milestone: and weak and worn and weary, there, for awhile, they rest, and wonder how far to the end? And though their eyes be dimmed by the beaming rays of the sun of many summers, and yet damp and swollen from the tears of many hardships; with yearning hearts and hopeful, they linger and look back upon the road to see if our eyes — dazzled by the shining sand and glittering dust—will see the laws and guide-boards, placed by them, and others who went before them, all along the road, saying, " This is the way; walk herein:" and at every diverging path, saying, (with index finger raised) " Go not in the way of the transgressor." I say our eyes; for their care was not for me alone: but also for my brothers and sisters, with whom hand in hand I walked; and some of whom are some miles in advance of me upon the road, and some are following on: while others faint and weary on the way, rest from their mortal toils. And as we look back upon the past, here and there we see a spot where our hearts have bled, and eyes have wept! and from where, with one less in our number, we have been compelled to journey on, and leave one of our loved ones by the way!—telling us of the uncertainty of life, and of the distañce we may be permitted to travel on its highway. But one mile back I see a mound, still wet with mingled tears of love and sorrow, where sleeps the brother of my boyhood, the companion of my youth: the memories of whom are too many and too dear to speak to the busy and jostling throng upon this crowded highway; but will be spoken of in tenderness and affection when we come to a more sacred and secluded place. And while we mourn, and miss him as a brother, two bereaved hearts, who rejoiced in his virtues, miss him as a son. They no more look for the Sunday-afternoon visit, nor feel the warm and cordial shake of his hand, nor hear his cheering and familiar voice, " How are you, father ?—mother ? " Nor will they again, till he meets them,

Where no parting is, nor tear is shed!

And while they miss him as a son, and we as a brother, there are little and lonely ones who miss him as a father; and who weep for the loss which earth cannot restore; and one whose staff is broken, and who mourns for him in widowhood. May God bless the widow and the fatherless children! Whether I may pass the fifty-third milestone —beyond where he sleeps—I, nor none upon the road may know.

CHAPTER II.

After I left my parents I did not walk far alone.   At times I felt lonely, and wished for some congenial traveler to accompany me.   I met and passed many: but our minds did not seem to be congenerous.   About the twentieth milestone my attention was attracted by a damsel, of fair form, sprightly and expressive eyes, with quick and firm step, with whom I became acquainted.   In our passing and repassing, we met frequently, but not familiarly.

I had noticed, as we traveled on from the twentieth to the twenty-first milestone, several gentlemen who had addressed and engaged in conversation with her; and who seemed desirous of keeping her company; who she seemed to reject.   I noticed a man of fine appearance, who seemed to be acquainted with her, going at good speed, in a coach, with servants in livery, who, as he overtook her, addressed her and entered into conversation: in which her words were few and positive.   He made several attempts to stop the coach, but she walked on with steady gait.   He at length stopped the coach, ordered the footman to alight and open the door, which he did; when the gentleman invited her to get in; offering to assist her— . saying he would take her as far as she wished to go on the road, or if she would go with him, he would take her to his home, which was fine and filled with the necessaries and comforts of life, as far as I could judge.   But she declined his offer: he insisted with many other inducements; but she still declined: after which he rode off, and I never saw him afterward. I learned, however, that when he arrived at home, he sent her several communications; none of which she answered, but the first. It is true, I felt somewhat sorry for him: but my sympathy was not as great as it would have been under similar circumstances afterward, as now: having had somewhat of the same experience myself.

On seeing her actions toward him, and others, I felt greater timidity in addressing, or showing any inclination to accompany her: though occasionally, when the twilight hours approached and the shades of evening prevailed, and that part of the road being lonely, I would offer my company as a friend; the acceptance of which made the time pass more pleasantly to us both.

Having suffered from ill health for the two previous miles at that time of my journey, I would often lag on the road; and becoming weak and weary, would often have to lie or sit beneath some shady tree during the heat of the day! The doctors visited me, and administered medicines of various kinds; which seemed to do me but little good. In fact, from the expressions of their opinions, and the opinions of others, it was not thought that I would continue my journey more than a mile or two further on the road. And though I was willing that the journey should end, I did not apprehend any danger that it shortly would; being convinced that there was much good I could and would do on the journey of life. During these miles I made the Bible my almost constant companion. I read it by the wayside; prayed for its influence; became familiar with its pages; comforted and delighted with its teachings. It drove away the fear of the grave, and made me. as it were, familiar with death; as my eye followed Him who passed through and conquered them both; receiving no wounds nor scars other than those that took Him to their gates. I often thought I would like to follow Him through, but left the time to God's wisdom and will.

Dnring those days, when the Artist of nature had blown His breath upon the autumn flowers, and was wiping off the rich tints which He had so beautifully and delicately penciled;—and was painting the forest trees in brown and golden hues, this lady disappeared from my sight, and reappeared no more until He had lifted the white robe of winter from the hills and the plains, and in its stead had spread out the carpet of green—tacking it here and there with a lily or a daisy: and had unlocked the rivers and the rivulets, and sent them sparkling and dancing on their courses;—bounding along the banks; rolling over the rocks, while receiving kisses from the smiling sunbeams: and had spread out His sheets of music over every glen and through every grove and by-way; the notes of which the untutored songsters were warbling to His praise. She had taken a voyage to visit her friends; during which time I journeyed on alone,—having partially regained my strength:—no communication having passed between us during her absence, though feeling confident that we would meet again, and share our joys on the journey of life; but leaving it all in the hands of Him who will direct the steps of those who will put their trust in Him.

CHAPTER III.

After the return of this lady, we met again near the
twenty-first milestone. So we walked and talked together, and found our thoughts and words congenial. I
offered to unite my hand and heart with hers, as one; divide our burdens, and go to the end of our journey together. This seemed to be a great surprise to her;—she
not dreaming that I had ever thought of anything of the
kind, saying that she had not. But after several talks on
the subject, she said she would accept the proposition,
provided I would wait till we reached the twenty-sixth
milestone. But after a reconsideration of the matter we
agreed to unite, and start together at the twenty-second
milestone, which we did. We often exchanged burdens,
which seemed to make them lighter. And when to steep
and rugged hills we came, we at the base would lay a
portion of our burden down, and both, with willing
hand, would carry the other portion to the top;—return,
and with unwearied step, again ascend with what would
try the strength of each or either when alone. And thus
from mile to mile we came;—often kneeling together by
the way, and asking strength and wisdom of Him whose
eye beholds from beginning to end, and whose hand directs the true and trusting, the weary and the weak.
And often when the king of day would leave us, to light
and cheer the travelers in other lands, and hide from our
eyes his glory, by the falling of the curtain of the night,

and when we were permitted to see his beauty only through the golden eyelets and woven work by which it hangs, would I bow in secret prayer beside her — who slept to rest her weary feet and renew her strength for the burdens of the coming day, — when the machinery of the skies would again turn its ponderous wheels, and roll and lift night's spangled curtain from our view, call in each nightly sentinel from his post, and the king alone in strength and beauty shine!

When we reached the twenty-fifth milestone our hearts were gladdened by the gift of a beauteous babe. That boy we loved, nourished and watched through infancy and youth; and saw, or thought we saw—as parents always see—signs and promises not common in those we meet on the journey of life. His noble form, his truthful word, his honest acts, filled our hearts with hope, and brightened the sky of his future. His little feet soon learned to walk the road with us, and then alone. We smiled to see his independent and manly step; though sometimes he lagged behind, and other times he went ahead; but kept within our sight, or calling distance, until he reached his nineteenth milestone; where he turned suddenly from our sight, since which his face I have never seen; nor listened to his voice. Now and then a message comes which tells me he is not lost: and though often he seems lost to me, I bear my loss, in hope it is his gain. If our roads come not together ere we reach the end, we on the other side will meet. I know he's passed some narrow strait; some thorny path; some rugged hill. But now he rests, I hope, in some bright spot, with one he loves, and who loves him; each having by the hand a precious babe:— gifts that will prove to them a comfort and help as they journey on, and when they sit down to rest. May heaven bless the western home of my first-born!

Three miles from where we found our boy, a little girl was given;—a bright face little cherub, whose sparkling eyes and slender form and active limbs we loved to look upon. Her eager and impatient feet soon undertook to walk alone: and when she saw our smile of pride and approbation, it quickened her efforts to excel. And being of energetic turn, she sped with earnest step past each milestone—anxious to see the next. Before she reached her sixteenth mile her tender heart was won by one who had gone some miles before her, but returning, took her by the hand, and helped her on: and joined with her, as those who join, no more to sunder. They had traveled about four miles together, when she presented him with a picture:—a picture of herself:—one which they appreciate and love above all on earth. And though the suns of five summers have fallen upon and warmed it, and the frosts of five winters chilled it, its freshness and beauty have not faded; and its bright and intelligent eye not dimmed. May this gift, as a central magnet, draw their affections closer together, and be to them a life-long prize:— a comfort in old age. May the love and example of Jesus be ever before them, and influence them for good; and the favor of the Lord rest upon them.

We had not journeyed three miles from where this daughter appeared, before another little lamb was given. She was gentle, loving and trusting. An unkind word, or a harsh expression toward her, would seem to crush the tear-drops from the fountain of her affection, and smother and still the unstudied tones of her free and childish melody. She had only to know my wish, and willingly she obeyed. She has passed with us her twenty-second milestone, and with patient hope she looks up the hills for a brighter, smoother path.

Oh! Guardian Angel, let thy flight be near her path. May she hear the rustling of thy robe, and see thy beckoning hand! Wait, Angel, wait, and let the shadow of thy wings fall lightly on her path : and the sweetness of thy holy song cheer her on her way.

And as I turn awhile from the thronged and travel-worn highway, and bow beside this running brook, bear the words of my petition to Him who listens when we pray.

So, on we journeyed, side by side, leading the three charges God had given. And before we had come three miles, another lovely and promising babe was added to our number. As he lay sleeping upon his mother's arm, in his dress of white, one, who passed, spoke of him as looking like an angel: and before he left, asked his parents to call him after him. And after his departure, he sent a beauteous dress, in which the babe was soon arrayed.

His mother, though she loved him as only mothers love, did not go with him far: her ambition being too great for her physical strength, and in pressing forward, was compelled frequently to rest, and finally fainted and fell by the wayside. I often relieved her of the weight of her babe, and other burdens she would carry. Still she could but slowly proceed. And before the babe had reached its second milestone, holding it on my arm, and supporting her with the other, she stopped to lie down; but before I could relieve myself of the babe, her eyes were closed in death. We buried her at the thirty-sixth milestone. She performed faithfully her part of the duties of life. And we trust she is now the watching and beckoning angel of those who once appeared as angels to her.

CHAPTER IV.

Now with heavy heart and weary feet, I traveled on
with my four motherless children. I sometimes had to
leave them by the roadside, or with a friend, and advance
alone, and prepare for them a place, and return and bring
them on their way.

Thus I passed the thirty-sixth, thirty-seventh and
thirty-eighth milestone; and through those miles I met
and talked and walked with many maidens on the way.
Some handsome, some intelligent, some in gay and showy
attire, some modest and plain; some in high, and some in
humble life. The rich were not congenial, the handsome
not discreet. The intelligent had many admirers. So I
found my greatest joy in the company of my children. But
near the thirty-ninth milestone I observed a damsel, who
seemed to pass many on the road; and, as I approached
her, I observed her eye and tread indicated earnestness and
energy. And as she seemed to have no particular company
—though many acquaintances—we fell in, and walked and
conversed together; and seemed to be of one mind. And
before we had come far, I perceived that veneration, con-
scientiousness, benevolence, hope and trust were promi-
nent traits in her character; and when the shades of night
fell across her path, she bowed to Him who watches
through the night. And when the beams of morning had
chased the darkness of the night away, her thanks ascended for the sweet repose of night. And at the ringing of the Sabbath bells she laid her burden down beside

the way, and turned her feet toward the house of prayer
and praise.   For this I learned to prize and love her, and
would sometimes go with her to the house of God; and
in sweet communion join.

And as we had been traveling alone, we gave our
solemn pledges through good or ill, heat or cold, calm and
storm; over hill and through valley; to go with, and help
each other to the end.

We have walked together seventeen miles, and are
now at the fifty second, from whence my retrospection
commenced.

One mile from where we joined our hands and hearts
we were gladdened by the addition of a tender babe to
our number—too tender, too delicate to face the blasts of
winter, or the sun of summer.   Hence, before his little
feet could tread the smoothest path of life, or bear his
fragile form, God took him where the angels dwell.   Before we had gone three miles,

> Another babe with lovely look,
> Bright eyes and curly hair,
> Came for the one the angels took
> Where all is bright and fair.

May her aims be high, her pathway pleasant, and the
peace which comes from purity, ever rest on her brow ;
and in her may I ever find pleasure and comfort.   And
when we had come about three miles further,

> Two little sisters—Gertie and Grace,
> We found by the wayside, where they lay face to face.
> And here we all halted with happy surprise,
> At the dear little creatures, both the same size.
> We wrapped them up nicely, in white and in blue,
> And started our journey afresh to renew.
> We went but one mile ere we passed by the trees,
> From which there fell blossoms of death and disease
> On the fair brow of Gracie, who closed her bright eyes,
> And slept, as she passed from the earth to the skies.

The other we have brought with us eight miles on our
way: and her loving heart yearns to be ever by my side.

O! can I think her little feet will ever go so far away that my love will not bring her gladly back: or that my voice shall not receive from her a willing and obedient response!

If there is anything that crushes and pains the heart of a parent, it is to raise children and be by them dishonored;—to see the little loved babe for which you cared and prayed; over which you so untiringly watched, and which you so tenderly pressed to your bosom, fondled upon your knee, led by the hand, and delighted to supply every imaginary and real want, and in which you so strongly hoped—grow careless of your kindness, regardless of your wishes, disrespectful to your requests, disobedient to your commands.

CHAPTER V.

And now, my dear children, as I sit here beside the road, resting by this stone, with tired feet, that have walked before you, with arms that have carried you, with hands that have led you and toiled and plucked for you the choicest fruits and sweetest flowers from amongst the piercing thorns, with eyes that have watched and wept over you in every hour of danger,—in sickness and in health, with a heart that loved, and loves you still—a father's heart—that has prayed for and hoped in you, with lips that have kissed and warned you; gather around me and receive, and be blessed by, my experience and instruction. I may not have an opportunity to instruct and bless you one mile hence. You may not all be there, or I may never reach it with you. There are diverging paths and pitfalls; there are lions and serpents in the way: there are tempting sights and glittering sands. O, let them not your steps beguile! I have traveled the road from its beginning; I have passed the places where you now stand, and all that you have passed. My heart now sighs as I look back and see where I was tempted. My hands are now rough and hard with toil—some of which was useless. My bleeding feet bear the marks of many piercing thorns. My form is bent with the heavy and useless burdens I have borne. If I could retrace my steps I would walk in a straighter and smoother path. I would shun the temptations;—I see where they beguiled me—I would sow better seed: and then the bitter fruits which are piled up around me, and which I am compelled to carry, would not be. I cannot leave this load by the way, but must carry it to the end. And in love and pity; and in the name of heaven, I admonish you to guard your steps;—to examine well the seeds you sow. For by the Creator's law it is decreed to grow; and you will be *compelled to gather the harvest;*—to carry the sheaves with burning and bleeding hands; to tread with your own feet the thrashing-floor; and to eat of the poisonous fruit. As I look at the heavy basket, with many bundles, which I have been carrying, on my left arm, I find many packages variously labeled. On one I find written, "Disobedience to parents." I look back, and see near the sixth mile-stone, a hand-board, "Honor thy father and thy mother, that thy days may be long in the land which the Lord thy God giveth thee." From the sixth to the tenth stone I see many little dark spots, where I sowed the seeds of dis-obedience and dishonor. On another bundle I find, "Falsehood." I look back and see near the other board one written on it, "Speak the truth," and other dark spots, disagreeable to behold, where I sowed the seeds of deception. And as I look upon them, I try to close my eyes, but cannot. I try to cover them with my hands, but the basket upon my arm is so heavy it pains me to raise my hands. I look at another package; it is marked, "Dishonesty." I look back and read the sign, written with my father's finger. "Be honest." I look down the road near the other dark spots, and see where I sowed the seeds of dishonesty; and though the spots are small, and the tears of penitence have fallen upon them, and the winds and the rains have swept over them, and the grass has growed arround them, they are still there. I turn over another bundle, and find it marked, "Anger," and I look back and see the rough spots where the seeds have been hastily cast, and where the ground seems parched as by a fire;—I hear the echoes of unkind words, grating harshly upon my ears—upon my soul!—Hasty and unkind words to my brother; my sister; my play-mate; my mother; my children; my wife! Oh! how they lacerate, and cause my heart to bleed! And though I ask, and receive forgiveness from the Father of love and compassion, I cannot hush the sound of the angry words, nor heal the wounds they made. I find another bundle marked, "Idleness." I look near the same place and see the grass beaten down, and the prints of my feet, where I listlessly stood beside the way. I see the unimproved golden moments as they pass, and hear their inviting voice. I cannot reach them now. They are gone, to return no more! And while I attempt to seize those which are now passing, my unskilled hands,—which have been employed in gathering shining and worthless pebbles by the way,—often miss their fruitless aim. I look at the other smaller bundles, and find them severally marked, "Intemperate eating;" "Indiscretion in sleeping, dressing, etc." I look back and see the bent bough from which I plucked the unripe fruit; and where, but thinly clad, I sat or slept in the damp or chilly air. Little I thought, then, that these seemingly little things would affect my strength, my speed, or the length of my journey on the road of life.—We too often learn lessons when the opportunity of improvement is past.—I find another bundle marked, "Doubt and distrust." I look back and find all along, from the twentieth to the fiftieth milestone, places where I had doubted, faltered and lingered; and where I left the straight road and walked in paths which seemed to lead to prosperity; and which were lined with glittering sands; and which in the distance appeared to be shining gold. But I found that "all is not gold that glitters." Though the most of these packages and dark spots are very small —scarcely observed by any one except myself—and mixed with many bright ones, yet I find the smallest give me pain and displeasure.

I noticed in the baskets of some who had passed, and others who were passing, bundles marked, "Intoxication," and "Profanity;" and when I look, and can find none in mine, I feel thankful that I have none to carry.

I have another basket beside me, which I have been carrying on my right arm. I find it not only light, but pleasant to carry; though it is large, and contains many bundles. I find one marked, "Obedience:"—I look back to about the fifth milestone, and see some bright and cheerful spots, where I sat upon my father's, or my mother's knee; and where, with willing steps, I ran at their behest; and where, with loving arms, they pressed me to their bosoms. I find others marked, "Love," "Truth," "Honesty," "Industry." I look back and see green and pleasant places all along, corresponding to these bundles. I see others marked, "Love," "Obedience," and "Reverence to God;" "Prayer," "Faith," and "Trust."

And as I look back to about the fifteenth milestone my eye brightens, and my face lights up with gladness, when I see where I knelt in secret prayer by the way, and where, with a group about my own age, we met together for prayer and praise. I see many a shade tree, beneath which I sat for hours with my testament; and where my bosom swelled with hope and joy; and the tears of gladness and gratitude fell thick and fast as I turned over its pages and read those blessed words—those wonderful "words of light;" words of "life and beauty;" those words only which tell of a merciful and an allwise Father's pitying care, and a Saviour's living example and dying love. I can see here and there,—when the evening shades prevailed, and when the last lingering ray of twilight gave place to the darkness of the silent night, when the travelers had all passed on their way, or were resting their weary feet,—little sheltered spots where, with my book and flickering lamp, I sat, and where I knelt in earnest, faithful prayer, and where, in echoes sweet, the gladdening answer soon returned. Another package is marked, "Charity and benevolence." I look along from place to place and see the little bare-foot, half-clad, hungry boy, as with gladdened look he takes the penny from my hand;—the bright-eyed, tangled-haired, modest girl as she tells of the sickness and want of a widowed mother: (God bless them) the old man with bent form, as with one hand upon his cane he leans, and reaches the other for a penny or a piece of bread. Though what I gave may have been but pennies to me, to them they may have been as dollars: and while they helped them in their need, they do me good to look upon. Some I unheeding, passed; I see shadows resting there: and have often wished to return and do them good. These were not my children, nor your children; but they were some one's children. And some one loves, or loved them. Some of their parents, or grand-parents may have been as high and hopeful in life as we.

When reposing in sleep, near the eighteenth milestone, I had a dream: and in it saw an old man asking alms. He applied to many, and was refused: and as he vanished from my sight he seemed to be my father: and my heart was made sad. The next morning, when at my daily vocation, with a number of men and boys, an old man, the picture of he whom I saw in my dream, came to us and asked assistance. After going to all the others, and being refused, he came to me. I had in my pocket a six-and-a-quart-cent piece, which I had been keeping for some time, and which was all I had. I took it from my pocket,—endeavoring to be unnoticed by the others,—and gave it to him. Some of them having heard him thank me for it, asked, when he had gone out, if I gave him anything? To which I replied, "I did." They said they would not have done so. "Let him work, as we have to do." I see that spot now: and how with pity and gladness my heart rejoices to look upon it. It was but a sixpence. It is worth more to me to-day than many hundred dollars I have spent. These are the little things that render life a blessing.

The seeds we sow—though they be small, and sown in tears—yet, if sown in faith, and watered with prayerful tears, in the harvest time the flowers will bloom to beautify and cheer our pathway, and the golden fruits will make us glad.

Children, don't throw your pennies away, or use them for selfish gratification,—which is sometimes worse. How many souls pine for aid! and how many would be thankful for what we may worse than give away, and what we would scarcely miss if given for good. But with all your generosity, study prudence and economy.

These things will all appear before you as a vision in the twilight hours: and will shine as day-stars under the glow of the sun eternal.

CHAPTER VI.

The basket at my right hand I look upon with delight, and carry with ease and comfort. O, that it were filled with better and richer fruits! And as I again look back upon the road, from whence its contents came, I see the face and form of One,—"the fairest among ten thousand, and altogether lovely;" and hear the voice of One who "spake as never man spake;" saying, "Come unto me all ye that labor, and are heavy laden, and I will give you rest. Take my yoke upon you and learn of me; for my yoke is easy, and my burden is light, and you shall find rest unto your souls."

As I look upon the basket to my left, my heart is sad; and my head droops with sorrow! And as I again look to see where I gathered its contents, I see many diverging roads and temptations. At one of them a messenger stands, and all day long, and through the dark and dangerous hours of night, in tones strong and emphatic, cries, "*The way of the transgressor is hard!*" At another, "Indignation, anguish and wrath upon every soul of man that doeth evil!" At another, "My punishment is greater than I can bear!"

But the night is coming, and I must be on my way. And as I put the basket, to my left, upon my arm to renew my journey, I wish that I could leave it here! But cannot. I look to see if any are coming empty handed; but they all have their burdens. Each must carry his own. I see some bearing palms in their hands; some with beauteous flowers and golden garlands; some with luscious fruits. Their steps are light and elastic; their eyes glisten with gladness and beam with beauty. I ask them from whence their joy and gladness? They reply, " *Whatsoever a man soweth, that shall he also reap.*" And as I look after them tears of repentant sorrow roll from my longing eyes!—not so much for the wrongs I have done as for the good I have " left undone." And as I bow and ask forgiveness for the past, and strength to bear my burden, and to keep me in the future, I hear a sweet and soothing voice, which thrills my soul with hope; saying, " Why weepest thou?" I turn and see an aged man, with hoary head, and pitying eye. But before I can answer—in my glad surprise—he says, " I see you have a heavy burden." " Yes," I replied, " I gathered it by the road; and have been carrying it all along the way. I have stopped here to rest, and to review the past; whereby I may learn lessons that I may not add to my burden in the future." He answered, " In this thou dost well." I asked him how far he had been on the road, and what its condition to the end; and how far travelers usually go? " Three score and ten miles," he replied, " is the distance alloted. Some, in consequence of violating the laws, fail to reach it; while others go far beyond. I have been nearly to the eighty-fifth milestone; and have learned much in these latter miles. Listen to my voice, and I will speak unto thee words of wisdom and counsel. There are," he continued, " in the future, as in the past, many roads leading off the straight highway. Just in advance of you the road forks. The one to the right is the road of life, and peace, and prosperity, and length of days. Enter its gate, and you may lay your burden down. There is a spacious mansion, and there stands an angel of light—a messenger of mercy. If you have resolved to walk the straight road to the end, your burden will be gathered at the gate; your load of sorrow and evil seed thrown into a pile, and consumed by the fire; though your scarred feet and bleeding hands will carry their marks to the end." He then unfolded a map, which he held in his hand, and applied to my eye a glass, which unfolded the beauties of futurity. I looked; and beautiful to behold!—An arch at the end of the gate, having written upon it, "Enter ye in at the straight gate." Within I saw brooks of running water, and wearied travelers, washing from their tired feet the sand and mire, and bathing their parched brows, beneath bending boughs of beautiful shade trees. And further on another arch, green with twining vines, having written on it, "Blessed are they that do His commandments, that they may have right to the tree of life, and enter in through the gates into the city." And as I wiped from my eyes the tears of joy, he gave me a glass of greater power: and as the gate was opened, I saw the road strewn with beautiful flowers, and trees ladened with golden fruit, and vines of luscious grapes, beside green lawns and sparkling waters. I looked again, and behold, another arch, having the appearance of pure gold, spanned the gates of glory! and upon it were little angelic forms in white, and feet with silver slippers; their brows decked with crowns of richest hues; while at their feet lay golden harps, as hand in hand they stood. I listened, and lo! a sound like soft and distant voices fell upon my ears. I listened more intently, and heard distinctly the words,

> "We've been watching, we've been waiting:
>   We are glad to see you come.
> We have welcomed tens of thousands,
>   And for thousands more there's room!
>
> Welcome to the heavy laden:
>   Welcome to the sin-sick soul:
> Welcome to the weak and weary:
>   Welcome to the young and old.

We've been waiting for the lowly:
  We've been watching for the meek:
We've been waiting for the hungry;—
  Watching, waiting for the weak;

Struck our harps with loudest accent;
  Sung our notes of sweet accord;
Beckon'd to the heavy laden—
  Waiting, resting by the road.

Here are groves beside the river,
  Where the sun will burn no more:
Here the boats are ready waiting;
  Ready waiting by the shore.

There are joys we have not told you;—
  Pleasures which for you await,
Which the Saviour will unfold you,
  When you come within the gate.

Here are fathers—mothers waiting;—
  Sisters, brothers, in our home,
Watching when the gates are open'd,
  Waiting here for you to come.

When on th' road we saw you coming,
  We would blow our silver horns;
Wave our snowy robes to warn you
  Not to tread upon the thorns.

When we saw the sad tears gather—
  Burning, dropping from your eyes,
With our hands we'd point you upward,
  Where there are no tears nor sighs.

When you reach the river Jordan,
  We will come to help you o'er:
We have boats to bear your burden,
  Waiting at the golden shore.

We are not tired, though we've waited;
  Watched and waited late and long,
And we'll still keep watching, waiting
  Till you join our happy throng.

And when we saw you sowing tares,
  Our sad eyes would almost weep.
Then we'd bow our hearts in pray'rs,
  For we knew you'd have to reap.

> When we saw the clouds and tempest,
>   Hanging heavy o'er your head,
> We would wave our golden lanterns,
>   That you might see where to tread."
>
> Here are mansions richly furnished;
>   Tables large enough for all;—
> Crowns for each all brightly burnish'd.
>   Don't you hear the Master call?
>
> We've not told you half the story;
>   It would make your journey late;—
> We will sing you songs of glory
>   When you come within the gate.

I stood in silent rapture during the song, and when it had ceased, and as I looked, I saw those composing the angel band stoop to pick up the golden harps that lay at their feet, to wave the rapture back to heaven. And as they were about to strike their harps, I saw two little hands beckon to them to cease. And as they hushed, I saw two little faces and forms—which seemed to recognize me—walk hand in hand down the golden arch, and come near the gate. They appeared to be about a year old;—a little boy and girl. And as they approached the gate, they repeated in musical, but infant tones,

> "Long time we've waited at the gate,
>   Watching every one that pass'd:
> But now we need no longer wait:—
>   Papa, papa—come at last!
>
> Have you brought our loving mother?
>   Are our sisters on the way?
> And our young and eldest brother?
>   T' go from us no more away?
>
> How far my dearest sister twin,
>   Who started with me on the way?
> We will be here to let her in
>   And take her where we sing and play.
>
> Here are uncles, aunts and cousins,
>   Which she's never seen or known:
> Some are in the group here with us,
>   Some are yonder near the throne.

Some repose in shady bowers;
  Some upon the shining shore;
Plucking sweetest fruits and flowers,
  Where they grow forevermore.

Some are climbing up the mountain;
  Some are resting in the vale;
Some are drinking at the fountain,
  Where the waters never fail.

Some are ever in our presence;
  Some are soaring from our sight;—
None will ever stay till darkness;
  In this land there is no night.

They will come when Jesus calls them,
  For His will's our happy choice:
He knows all by name, and loves us.
  And we've learn'd to know His voice.

But sometimes when they are distant,
  And we happy tidings learn,
We our little horns of silver
  Blow; when quickly they return."

I here turned to the aged man, and said,

  "Is this, indeed, the land eternal,
    Of which we often used to sing:
  Where skies are bright, and fields are vernal;
    And where abides eternal spring?

  Is this glass true?—The map correct, sir?
    Are joys as great as here they seem?
  Or will I sadly there detect, sir,
    That this is a delusive dream?"

  Said he, "This is the land immortal,
    Where drops no tear, and heaves no sigh.
  But you have only seen its portal.
    Its bliss is hid from mortal eye!"

Here I could refrain no longer; and handing the old
man the map and the glass, I turned away to weep. And
after I had wiped away the tears, he asked me if I had
read the inscription on the arch. I told him I had not.
My eyes were so dazzled by the glorious sight, and my

ears so enraptured by the pathetic melody of the sweet voices, that I failed to read the inscription on the golden arch. I then looked again, and read, "Eye hath not seen, nor ear heard, neither have entered into the heart of man, the things which God hath prepared for them that love Him!" And through the arch, in the distance, I could see what seemed to be a rich curtain, or veil, having written upon it, "*A far more exceeding and eternal weight of glory!*"

Here the messenger of mercy took the glass and map, and, as he folded them up, he asked me if I had seen any on the highway whose lot I would prefer to my own. At first I was about to reply, many. For I remembered seeing many who had friends and admirers; some with bags of gold; some in rich array; some with chariots and horses, with servants by their sides, who passed me in state; some singing merry songs, and others swaying the masses with eloquence. All with baskets on right and left arms, or in their hands. I thought of my slow march and my low estate: my humbleness of speech, and the long and lonely miles I had traveled: the wants, or imaginary wants, of myself and of those for whom I had to care. I had gotten along with my burden thus far, and knew its weight. I knew not what others were carrying. I remembered when I wept, and some soft hand wiped away the tears. I remembered the desponding and the hopeful hours; the peace of trusting, and the promise to the faithful; the sweetness and hallowed memories of home; the love and sympathies of a wife, the affection and fondness of my children. And I looked up and saw the smile, and felt the approbation of my heavenly Father, and concluded I would not lose them for all I had seen on the road. I remembered the map and the sight, and the songs, and replied, "I would not exchange with any." He replied, "You have answered rightly." We are all pensioners of God; and He has given us that which we can carry better than the loads of others. We can make our burden light; but none can carry it for us: we can add to it, but we must bear its weight."

He then pointed to the deeply marked foot-prints in the road: and asked me if I had noticed them on the way. I told him I had noticed them all along; and had followed them closely from about the fourteenth to the twenty-fourth milestone; and found when I walked beside, or in them, I got along easily. And all who followed them seemed to have light and easy burdens. Said he, " They are hallowed foot-prints. They were made eighteen hundred years ago. They are the foot-prints of the King of the highway: and His path may justly be called, ' The King's highway of holiness.' He had a heavy load to bear, which He took upon Himself, not because of His own sins, but to give us an example,—that we should not weary and faint by the way; but endure to the end. You will find them here and there marked with blood drops; and though the rains and snows have fallen upon them; and the suns of many summers have poured upon them their bleaching beams, they have not been erased, or washed away. It is not the blood of guilt; but of purity—oozing forth from a mighty conflict with the powers of death and darkness. And though the storms of infidelity have beat upon, and the sands of time have rolled over them, they are not obliterated or defaced. Thousands have walked in them, and yet they are distinct. And many who walk in them sing,

> ' His track I see; and I'll pursue
> The narrow way, till Him I view.'

He finished His course, and as He passed in triumph this golden arch, ten thousand voices, in loud acclaim, sang,

> Be ye lifted up ye everlasting gates,
> And let the King of glory come in !'

And voices from the heights beyond, cried, ' Who is this King of glory ?' And thousands who were following on, and tens of thousands marshaled by His side: responded in tones that shook the gates of gold, and thrilled the arched heavens with triumphant joy, ' The LORD OF HOSTS; mighty in battle; and strong to deliver! He is the King of glory!' And an innumerable multitude, which no man could number, fell down before Him: exclaiming, 'Thou art worthy, O Lord, to receive glory, honor and dominion!'"

When these sublime and soul reviving thoughts were presented to my mind, they brought vividly before me some of the happy and hopeful hours in the early part of my journey. I remember well, when tired and thirsty, seeing these words on the roadside, near those blessed foot-prints: "If any man thirst, let him come unto me and drink!" I came near, and lo! sparkling fountains of living waters, clear as crystal, met my longing eyes; from which I drank, and slaked my burning thirst. And as I walked around the fountain, I read on one side, "He that drinketh of the water that I shall give him, shall never thirst." And on another, "Whosoever will, let him come; and take of the water of life freely." And long I lingered near the spot; and drank, and drank again! And tracing the source of this fountain, I found it to be an inexhaustible and ever flowing river of life! And I saw in the King's highway many places where the hungry were fed, the sick healed, the lame made to walk, the blind restored to sight, the deaf to hearing, the disconsolate to hopefulness, the sinner forgiven, rest to the heavy laden, and to the dying, life!

The aged messenger then asked me why I did not follow these foot-prints more closely. By this time I saw that he felt or manifested a deeper interest in my welfare, and appeared as one to whom I could reveal the secrets of my soul; and I related to him the following particulars:—"In early life the influence of my parents, and of others with whom I resided and associated; the influence of the Bible, and, I believe, of God, convinced me that I should prepare myself for the preaching of His word. God had so blest me in my youth, and made me so happy in His service, that I felt it my duty, and desired to do all in my power to enlighten and bless others; and I vowed to God that I would. Many a midnight hour have I walked the floor in tears of joy, praising God, and looking to the happy time when I hoped to break the glad tidings to the unblest, and to tell to all around what a dear Saviour I had found. And I suppose my convictions were made stronger by seeing so many on the way who seemed altogether ignorant of their duty, and destitute of the grace or influence of God. So to this end I studied the Bible prayerfully all the time I found possible. Many hours have I spent, not only in reading, but in prayer, to be guided aright. These were some of the happy hours of my life; happy in hope: happy in anticipation! In this way, and with this view, I spent several years. And whenever I heard an eloquent preacher, or a good sermon, my heart longed for the time when I should be engaged in so happy a work. I often felt as if I would be willing to live in a dungeon on bread and water for ten years if by so doing I could for ten years more preach the truth of God acceptably and effectually." (Here the old man pressed my hand, and looked in my eyes with mingled feelings of approbation, sorrow and hope.) "But being slow of speech," I continued, "and seeing so many who talked with ease and fluency engaged in the blessed work, I became somewhat discouraged, and more so by the discouragement I met with from those who would be my friends. So I concluded that, for awhile at least, I would turn my attention in another direction until I was better prepared.

And when I had reached the twenty-fourth milestone I saw many attractions; and among them beautiful and well tilled and productive farms, with fruitful fields. But still, while some of the attractions were inviting, my heart still yearned to work in the heavenly kingdom; and there continued to ring in my ears, 'Woe unto me! if I preach not the gospel.'

But I was induced to buy a farm, which contained much choice fruit, the cultivation of which occupied the greater part of my attention for several years. And although this afforded me much pleasure, I have never seen really a happy day since. (I do not mean by this that I have seen no happiness since, for I have spent many seasons of sweet communion with God, but have not enjoyed that sweet peace which I would have enjoyed had I lived up to my conviction and desire by doing all my duty.)

> O, it seemed that the step that just here I trod,
> Was one crooked step between me and my God.
> And oft I look back with regret to that place—
> To the steps I know I can never retrace!
>
> Yes, just here, like Jonah, I fled from the Lord,
> And shelter I sought 'neath the shade of a gourd;
> From refuge to refuge I often have fled,
> While God's holy Spirit, 'Come unto me,' said.

While I know, and often realize the comfort and joy of Christ's presence and communion with Him and the Father, I have missed what would have been worth more than the world to me. O, what I have missed! I still live in hope that there yet may be some place in which I can work; some vacancy for me to fill. And this desire, and a conviction of undone duty, is all for which I would ever wish to go over the past part of the road again."

Then said my kind friend, who had listened with such patience and interest to my story, "Thou shouldst have trusted and obeyed God rather than man. For thou rememberest having seen at the fifteenth milestone, 'Trust in the Lord with all thy heart, and He shall direct thy steps;' and at the eighteenth, 'I have never seen the righteous forsaken, nor his seed begging bread.' Now, if you have resolved to go on thus trusting, I will accompany and show you the safe and pleasant places by the way." Here he reached his hand to help me with my load; but which, on trying, I found to be much lighter; and thanked him for his kindness.

So, I started with the aged man—my friend and counselor; I kept close by his side, and listened with pleasure to his advice, as we passed from mile to mile. O, what delight! The fruits we gathered were so delicious!—"Sweet fields arrayed in living green and rivers of delight," so enchanted my eyes that I forgot where I was, and wondered if it were a dream. I seemed to be in company with angels, with harps in their hands, tuning praises to God. O, what fruitful trees! While I was gathering from one, another charmed my eyes: and so we went on from tree to tree, from vine to vine, from fountain to fountain, gathering fruits and sweetest flowers:—richer still as on we went. Lo! here: lo! there:—beauty! grandeur! glory! I was not content to enjoy these fruits alone; and as I drank the sweet waters from the fountain, I felt like ascending some elevated rock, or mount, and crying to the following throng, "Oh! every one that thirsteth, come ye to the waters; and he that hath no money, come yea, buy, and eat; yea, come buy wine and milk without money and without price." "And whosoever will, let him come." The angels seemed to come nearer, and ring from their harps melodious strains of gratitude and praise, which seemed to thrill the air; and from whose lips flowed songs of gladness and glory, honor and dominion to Him who died on Calvary's height, to save the world from sin! I wished I could turn back with hasty feet, and tell the tidings glad, to those who tarried far behind, and who the heavenly way have never known, nor heard such sounds of joy.

After walking some distance, and feasting on these scenes of pleasure and delight, and listening to the blessed words of this man of mercy and wisdom, he, with warm hand and kindly look, bade me, my wife and my children God speed; saying he would meet us further on, and go with and guide us to the golden gate: when he vanished from my sight.

These figures, how like facts they seem!
Is this, can this be all a dream?
If all a dream, how can we know
But life, with all things here below,
Which seems so real, and so true,
Is but a dream; a shadow, too:—
A fleeting shadow, only cast
Until the dream of life is past?

If but a dream, it will be well
To think, and on its lessons dwell;
Such metaphors the Saviour chose,
In teaching friends, and warning foes

CHAPTER VII.

And now, my dear children, as I sit here by this fifty-second milestone, not knowing whether I shall reach the next, or if I do, not knowing whether I shall have an opportunity of communicating to you from there,—I send you this letter of love, hoping that the advice of my aged and wise counselor, with my past experience, may impart to you lessons which will greatly help you on your journey; cause you to shun the temptations by the way; render your journey pleasant, and at last take you triumphantly through the golden gate.

In your short journey, the clouds have sometimes darkened your sky: you have been pierced by thorns: you have sometimes trod on quicksands, and caught at shining dust: you have sometimes stepped in the foot-prints of the deluded. False hope, with half-fledged pinions, has sometimes flown before you. Unkind words, at times, may have lacerated your hearts; lions have prowled in your pathway; deceivers have wrapped around them the robe of friendship and innocence. (I speak from experience: for I came all along the road.) But with all these temptations by the way, you have withstood them, while many have fallen before them. If you are carrying any burden you would like to lay down; if you are drinking any bitter water; if your pathway is rugged: if your sky is clouded, find the foot-prints of Jesus—you can tell them by their surroundings—ever keep them in sight: read His word; resist temptation, and it will flee from you. Ask the Father to help you; speak kind words; be earnest; be diligent; improve your time; let not the hours hang heavily on your shoulders; cultivate trust, faith, meekness; forgive and help each other; shun false pride. Sow no seeds of sorrow, to gather, as you ascend the roughest hills. Be systematic in your habits. False lights often glitter near your pathway to draw you aside. Let the lamp of truth brightly burn.

Oh ! let not the morning hours glide swiftly by,
And noonday overtake you with clouded sky.
For if the hours of morn and noon are bright,
They'll lend their glory to the evening light,
And then the sun's departing crest,
Will fall, and on your bosom rest.

And though at times your journey may be rough and steep;
And you may have to lay your burden down and weep,
They'll not be tears like those that gladly would give vent
To sore and sobbing hearts, when life is illy spent.
But tears that will attract affection from the skies,
And draw the angels down to wipe your weeping eyes,
And take your galling burden, with its mighty weight;
And lead you glad and safely through the golden gate.

And tho' at times your feet be tired and sore;
And you may almost wish your journey o'er,
They'll not be sore like those that early trod
The path that leads from virtue and from God.
But sore like His who rested at the well,
From whose lips words like flowing waters fell.
Like His who stood beside the grave and wept
With those who sorrowed when their brother slept;—

> But tired like those—tho' holy, pure and clean—
> Were washed, and kissed by loving Magdelene.—
> Like those which trod the upward, shining way,
> And bore the heat and burden of the day.—
> Like those that run the race, (but resteth now,)
> And won the crown that decks the Victor's brow.

I have made my letter long: it covers much ground. And if you will learn the lessons it is designed to convey, it will do you good. Many thoughts in it will recur to you, as I pass from mile to mile, on the remaining portion of my journey. And when I shall have passed the last milestone, and permitted, through God's mercy, to see in reality what I have seen in vision, you will remember much of this. And as you ascend the heavenly way, and pass from mile to mile, you will still remember the lessons. And heaven grant that you may not remember them with sorrow, but with joy and gladness: which is the earnest and affectionate prayer of

YOUR FATHER.

Since writing the foregoing, I have traveled some miles on the journey of life, and beheld many scenes of pleasure and delight, and spent many days of joy and gladness. Many changes have taken place with myself and family. I have sat by the wayside at balmy morn, at heated noon, at tired twilight, at late eve, and at quiet midnight, and have written many anthems of praise, songs of rejoicing and exhortations of warning; and have posted them on the trees, landmarks and guide posts, and have scattered many by the wayside and through the fields. And occasionally, for the pleasure and amusement of those whose attention I could not gain by plain truths, stern realities and living examples, I have engaged in a little mirthful amusement, which, while I trust, will not retard the progress or mar the peace and pleasure of any, may attract the attention of some who, while looking at it, may see the truths and beauties with which it is mixed. While my tongue has not been gifted with eloquence, and I have not been able to move the multitude by my humble speech, I trust many hearts may be blessed, and many hands made strong by what I have written. I have done what I could. Others with greater gifts could have done much better. And if those who may follow on can but read on my last milestone—written by Him whose judgment is just—"He hath done what he could," I shall be satisfied. And may this be the epitaph of you all.

And now, Rebecca, my dear wife, with whom I have been traveling the ups and downs of life for many years, may the Lord, who has blessed you in the past, still continue to bless and comfort you to the end. In Him may you find sweetest peace, both in prosperity and adversity. Sometimes we have looked at things by different lights, and what has seemed to be obscure to one appeared very plain to the other,—we thus being to each other mutual aids and helps: and when the shadows of this life shall have passed, may we rest where we will no longer see "through a glass darkly," but understand the mysteries of the past.

Thomas, my first-born, though I have not been permitted to see you since first you left us at your nineteenth milestone, and though now separated by many hundred miles, my mind's eye often rests upon you, my affections hover around you, and my prayers ascend for your welfare. I trust the time is not distant when we shall meet face to face, and clasp hands with more joy than when we parted. May the Lord bless you, your wife and children. In Him may you ever find strength, rest, peace, consolation and eternal life.

Jennie, my second child, it gives me much joy to know that you and your husband have turned your attention and your feet towards the things which make for your present and eternal peace, and that you find much delight in the service of the Lord. May He continue to bless you both, with your little daughter Jennie: may she grow up to be a comfort and a blessing to you both, and with you ever be precious in the sight of the Lord.

Martha, my third child, for whom, in infancy, I besought the guardian angel to protect your tender heart, and guide your willing feet, you have chosen your companion for life's journey; and I trust it is a happy choice, and that the happiness will be of long duration. You are many miles from us, but yet seem so near. Though I cannot look upon you with my natural eye, I often see you in visions. May the blessing of the Lord ever rest upon you, and His spirit guide you, your husband and your dear little son Chester—that pretty, bright-eyed, curly headed boy. May the future develop in him all that his intelligence now indicates. May the precepts and example of his indulgent father and mother lead him to be an honor and a comfort to them, a blessing to the world, and a bright jewel in the heavenly kingdom.

Willie, my fourth child, you have ever been near me in my march, and have seen, and shared in many of the varied scenes and conditions of my life. I have often knelt with you in prayer, and prayed for you, when absent, that your warm affections and tender heart might be guided and led in the right direction, and that our mutual cooperation would result in good. May the Lord strengthen you in all your resolutions for good, and enable you to see that the path of virtue is ever the path of peace and happiness, and bless you now and forever!

Katie, my sixth child,—the little girl with "bright eyes and curly hair," who came in the "place of the one the angels took,"—though you have not yet passed a score of milestones, yet you have assisted me in my work by recording my march from mile to mile, and in selecting some of the choice flowers, and in detecting and pulling out those not attractive; and in making more legible the handwriting which I hastily did, as on speedy wings the thoughts swiftly came, and which I had to catch as they flew, or let them go forever.—Thoughts often come in flocks, and require a quick and skilful hand to grasp and hold the best.—May your mind select and hold the choicest your hand has written; and their influence be a blessing to your life. And as you look forward and aspire to the heights, may the spirit of the Lord be your guide and comfort; and His strong and bountiful hand hold you up and supply your wants, and make your pathway peaceful and prosperous. May you gather and save some of the best seed to sow and bloom along the distant miles of your journey in beauty and fragrance!

And Gertie, my youngest child—whose heart is warm and tender, and whose life is made happy by reciprocated love—may the ties which bind our hearts so closely and warmly together never be weakened, but stronger grow its hold, like the vine which wraps more closely around the oak as its age increases: and though the branches may reach out and entwine the neighboring vines and attracting flowers, yet the roots ever cling to the roots of the supporting oak; and both partake of the same nourishment:— so may we both cling to the "root and offspring of David," and be guided by the "bright and morning star," and partake of that same spiritual food, and drink of the same living water; and thereby grow more like Jesus, and share in His love and mercy now and evermore.

And finally, may we all, as we further procceed on our journey, be united in love and good works, which will bring us the most valuable of all things that which we seek, that for which we hope, that for which we work, that for which we live—happiness here, and happiness forever hereafter. And to this end may we go on our way rejoicing,—trusting in the Lord, and ever saying, "Thy will be done, and thy name forever glorified "

DEAR CHILDREN:

In the preceding allegory I spoke of your uncle Henry—who started on the journey of life two years before myself, and whose journey ended at his fifty-fourth milestone—the memories of whom I said were too dear and too sacred to speak of at length, on the crowded and jostling highway, but would be spoken of in a more secluded and suitable place. He was the eldest brother of five, and the one with whom I spent most of my youthful days—the next brother after me being ten years younger than myself.—And along the banks of the "Rock Creek," of which he so touchingly speaks in his short ode to that little stream, we spent many pleasant hours together, in fishing, bathing, gathering wild flowers and building air castles for our future life. On its green and shady banks our dear departed father often led us by the hand in his pleasant walks.

Though my brother Henry was frank, honest and moral—neither one of us having been habituated to profanity, nor many of the vices which boys are usually so prone to indulge in, for which I thank my good parents— yet he was not impressed religiously so early as I; but engaged in more of the youthful pleasures of life. But his moral and religious impressions became very strong and

permanent in after life; and he devoted much of his time
to the service of the Lord, as may be inferred from his
writings on the following pages.

He had a warm, generous, loving heart; and I always
loved—as I have often heard others say—to feel the cordial,
earnest shake of his hand; which comes only from a feeling heart.

I'll write a few thoughts, as they come to my bosom,
  Which, if not now written, forever may flee ;—
The world might not miss them, e'en though it should lose them;
  Yet they are of interest to you and to me.

O, Brother, dear Brother, how strongly in childhood,
  Our gladness and sorrow together were tied!
How often in youth—in the bright days of boyhood,
  Our grief and our gladness we used to divide !

But long years ago all those bright days departed :—
  And we might—like many—have proven the truth,
That long before this we'd have died broken hearted,
  With nought else to strengthen than we had in youth.

But, O, what delight! O, what strength! and what pleasure!
  We found on the road, as God led us along.—
Too deep was the gladness, and too high to measure,
  Which filled us, and often flowed over in song.

But mixed with our gladness, we often had our sorrow—
  Far deeper, sometimes, than our words ever told—
But never so deep, but that we in the morrow,
  Could see through it all some bright rainbow of gold.

The words to our tongues yet have never been given,
  To tell all the heights, and the depth of God's love !
But when we shall meet with the ransom'd in heaven,
  We'll learn sweeter words from the angels above !

O, Brother !—now parted—we see in thy writing,
  The bright sparks of glory which sprung from thy soul :
But what shall it be at that happy uniting,
  Where anthems, sweet anthems, forever shall roll !

HOW I CAME TO JOIN THE CHURCH.

Copied from the Writings of J. H. Boyd.

On the first day of January, eighteen hundred and sixty-four, I resolved within myself to—as we sometimes say—"turn over a new leaf." That is, I resolved to lead a different course of life from that which I had been living. Though I had ever been living what is generally called a *moral* life. I supposed I was living with a conscience void of offence toward God and man. But I came to the conclusion that *morality* is not godliness: and is therefore not profitable unto all things, neither having the promise of the life that now is, nor that which is to come: but is only a phantom that leads too many into the "slough of despond." I was living a negative sort of life: doing many things that I ought not to have done, and leaving *undone* many, *many* things which I ought to have done. And though I did not do myself what I ought to have done, yet I endeavored to teach those over whom I had the care to do that which I conceived to be right in the sight of God. I taught my children early to fear God and keep His commandments. I taught them to read and reverence His holy word. I sent them early to the Sabbath school, and urged upon them the great importance and benefit of attending church. These duties I taught them more by precept than example. While I would say to them, "Go," I did not always lead them. And I began to notice that precept had its influence on them in their younger days, but as they grew older, example was the

more potent teacher. So I resolved to try and give them
a good example as well as give them precepts. And so,
as I have said, on the first day of January, eighteen hundred and sixty-four, I resolved to change my course of
life, and try to serve God more acceptably in the future
than I had done in the past. The first step I took towards
that end, was that on that first of January I took my
family Bible to the breakfast table and therein read a
chapter to my family before eating; and continued that
practice each morning afterwards. And when I would read
a chapter, if any of my children, who could read, were not
present at the breakfast table, I would put the Bible at
her place, so that, when she came she would read a chapter.
In this way we would have several chapters read by different members of the family before breakfast was over.
And since that time to the present, I have not, with but
some few exceptions, eaten my breakfast before having
read one or more chapters of the word of God.—I say not
this in any spirit of boasting: but that it may have its influence for good. I also resolved for the future to attend
church more regularly than I had been doing in the past.
And as I had previously visited nearly all of the different
denominations of Christians, in order to find which of
them preached the most of the truth of the gospel, as I
understood it: and among others I visited the "Disciples"
church, corner of Paca and Lombard streets, where I had
once heard the late Alexander Campbell preach a very interesting and instructive discourse of over two hours in
length. The next time I went there Elder George Austin
spoke. The theme of his remarks was, "Blessed is the
man to whom the Lord imputeth not sin." And I was
greatly edified by his remarks; in the course of which he
made the following declaration, in that measured style
peculiar to himself. Said he: "I am no preacher, I am
no teacher, yet it is impossible for the truths, of which I
am speaking, to fall upon the ears of any thinking, any intelligent mind without having their influence, without

bringing forth their proper fruits." And I must say that they had their influence on me; so much so that I resolved to become a regular attendant to that congregation. And when I became a regular attendant Elder D. S. Burnet was preaching there; whose arguments, delivered with such rare eloquence and zeal, were so irresistible, that I was "almost persuaded" to become a Christian. And as I had been attending there quite regularly, Brother Burnet noticed that I was a stranger among them, and he enquired of some of the members who I was, and where he could find me. He was informed, and called to see me at my place of business.

His manner of approaching me, and our first, and exceedingly pleasant interview, I long shall remember. Even the charming intonations of his voice, when he said, " This is Mr. Boyd, I believe," are still fresh in my memory. And when I had answered affirmatively—extending my hand to him, and calling him by name—he further said, "I am very happy to meet with you." I requested him to be seated. This being done, we had a very pleasant conversation about the church and religious matters. And when, among other things, I told him of my intention to join the church, he said, "I am happy to find you in such an interesting state of mind."

This was the first time that I had met with Brother B., to speak to him. On leaving, he gave me a pressing invitation to still come to the church, and carry out the purpose of my mind. I told him that I intended doing so. On the next Lord's day I again went to the church, but did not go forward to make the good confession. During the week Brother B., again called to see me, and during the interview he said that he was going to introduce a new style of preaching; which was by a diagram illus- trative of the old Jewish Tabernacle, with the laver, and the inner and outer courts. And he requested that I would do some little fixing in connection with it, which I did. And the which being done, he said, " You have made a good job of it, and now come around to the church on next Lord's day and make a good job of that other matter." I answered, "Probably, I will." The next Lord's day came and I went to the church. It was on the first day of May, eighteen hundred and sixty-four; and I think it was one of the most delightful mornings I have any recollection of witnessing. The church, with its environs, was, indeed, to me, a place of " pure delight." Brother B. preached a very interesting and instructive discourse upon the "Tabernacle and the mercy seat." Illustrating the subject by referring to the diagram which he had hung against the wall beside the stand. He made clear to my mind some points which had previously been to me dark.

At the close of his discourse he extended the usual invitation, and I, from my seat, near the door, advanced up the aisle to the front to make the good confession before many witnesses. I was greeted by Brother B., who, at the close of the singing, asked of me the following question, "Do you believe with all your heart that Jesus is the Christ, and your only Saviour ? " I answered, "I do." "And," said he, " is it your purpose, with the help of God, to devote the remainder of your life to His service ? " " It is," said I; he responded, "God bless you." And after consulting with me, he announced that the baptism would take place on the next Wednesday evening.

The Wednesday evening came; it was the fourth of May, eighteen hundred and sixty-four. And I was, on that evening, by Brother B., baptized into the church of Christ. And on the next Lord's day following I was received into the congregation by Brother B., and was declared to be a member thereof, and in full fellowship with those of the Lord's house, and entitled to all of its privileges and blessings.

Thus I became a member of the Christian Church generally, and a member of that particular congregation specially.

On the following Wednesday evening I went to the social prayer meeting of the church; and I enjoyed it. It was the first real *social* meeting that I had been to for a long time, and I say again, I enjoyed it. During the next week Brother B. and his wife called to see me at my place of residence; and in the course of his conversation requested that I would take an active part in the social meetings of the church. I told him as I was but young in the church I would rather put it off for a while. "No," said he, "the longer that you put it off the less you will feel like commencing; if you want to make yourself useful begin at once." "Yes," said Sister B., " the longer you put off commencing, the longer you will want to put it off, and the less you will feel like beginning." "Yes," responded Brother B., "there are many old members of the congregation who have never opened their lips to speak in the church; simply because they did not commence when they first became members. It is not well to put it off." "Then," I answered, "I will try and do what I can."

On the succeeding Wednesday evening I was early at the meeting; and as Brother B. passed in he came to me and said in a low tone, "Brother Boyd shall I call on you to-night?" "I am at your service, Brother Burnet," I responded: at the time trembling with fear, lest I should begin and make a failure. However, at the close of the singing of the hymn, Brother B. called on me to offer prayer, which—though under much embarrassment—I did. After which Brother B. commended me for the effort that I had made; and at the same time he exhorted some of the older members to follow the example of the young brother, and loosen their tongues, which had so long been silent.

After several hymns had been sung, and several prayers offered, Brother B. read a chapter from the Bible, after which he gave out the hymn commencing,

> "I love thy kingdom, Lord,
> The house of thine abode."

Having read this hymn, he said, "After singing this we would like to hear a word from Brother Boyd." The hymn was sung, sweetly sung; I thought how short it was: and I wished that it was five times as long, because at its close I was expected to speak. The hymn having been concluded, Brother B., with that mellow tone of voice peculiar to himself, merely said, "Brother Boyd." In uttering these words the intonation of his voice had the peculiar characteristic of being both inviting and encouraging. So I arose, and looking around at the congregation, I began by saying, "When I look around me and see so many Christian faces; so many older in the church than myself, I do not know that I can say anything that will edify them, yet I will give my experience in the cause as far as I have gone." I then related the causes which led me to the church; the feelings which I had on the morning when I went forward to confess Christ before many witnesses; the feelings which I had when I went down into the water to be buried with Christ by baptism; and the feelings which I had when I arose to walk with Him in the newness of life. And I concluded with an exhortation as to what I conceived to be the duties of Christians toward each other. I spoke fifteen or twenty minutes, and after I had finished, Brother B. arose and said, "I am glad that our young brother has spoken just as he has, and said what he did. It shows that he was guided by the proper motives in coming into the church; and it also shows a disposition to make himself useful in the church."

At the close of this meeting I was very happily greeted by the brethren, as also by the sisters of the congregation; and the remarks of some of them, on that occasion, are still fresh in my memory. One Brother said to me, "You have done what I never have as long as I have been a member of the church." "What is that?" said I. "Make a speech to the congregation," he said. I responded, "I thought you all did that." Our good old sister Benson—who was ever punctual at all of the meetings of the church, but who has now gone to receive her crown of glory—approached me at the close of the meeting, and said, " Brother Boyd I felt very much rejoiced to-night while you were speaking; I appreciated your remarks very much, for we have all passed through a similar experience."

That was a very joyful meeting to me, and will long be remembered. From that time until the death of our much lamented Brother B., there was perhaps no member of the congregation, know all the members thereof if they could testify, that took a more active part in the prayer meetings of the church than myself. I say not this in any spirit of boasting; for God forbid that I should boast of any such things; for I humbly confess, that all that I have done has been but little, compared with what it is the duty of every Christian to do. I state these things that those who are ignorant of the fact, may know my relations and position in the church. I have frequently had the remark made to me, that I seemed to be Brother B.'s favorite; though I never sought to be the special favorite of any man: yet I appreciated the sentiment and the judgment of all good and judicious persons.

In the latter part of July, eighteen hundred and sixty-seven, on Lord's day evening, Brother B. preached his farewell sermon, commending the congregation " to God and the word of His grace."

As Brother B. had been so faithful to the congregation, and had done so much in the way of building it up, and strengthening it, both by his labors in the church, as well as out of it -for he did not neglect to visit the members frequently, nor did he select some few and neglect the others, but he visited them all—so I thought it would be proper at the last Wednesday evening social meeting that he would be with us, to say some pleasant words of farewell in his behalf, as well as sing a parting ode, which I had written for the occasion, and which was as follows:

CHRISTIANS SHALL MEET AGAIN.

Tho' Christians from each other part,
We shall meet again; ·
Then let not sorrow fill your heart,
We shall meet again.

CHORUS.

We ll trust God's providence,
We'll trust God's providence,
We'll trust God's providence,
And we shall meet again.

And if on earth we meet no more,
We shall meet again
On heav'n's bright and tranquil shore;
We shall meet again.—Cho

We've joyful hours together seen,
We shall meet again;
Where no sad partings intervene,
We shall meet again.—Cho.

When Jesus His disciples left,
We shall meet again;
Of all their hopes they seem'd bereft,
We shall meet again.—Cho.

But He the Holy Spirit sent,
We shall meet again;
Which to their hearts new courage lent,
We shall meet again.—Cho.

And Christians, tho' we drop a tear,—
We shall meet again;—
With parting friends we hold most dear,
We shall meet again.—Cho.

For this good hope to us is given,
We shall meet again;
We'll meet, to part no more, in heaven,
We shall meet again.—Cho.

A few days after this meeting and parting, Brother B. was taken sick; which sickness seemed to have taken a strong hold upon him, so much so that he was compelled to keep in bed. When hearing this, I went to see him, which was on Saturday, the third of August, eighteen hundred and sixty-seven. When I went into his room Brothers Austen and Gilbert were there. I approached the bed upon which Brother B. was lying; he appeared to be very feeble, and when I asked him how he felt, he grasped my hand with both of his, and said, "I feel much better by holding the hand of a good man." I expressed my sorrow at seeing him in that condition, and noticing that he seemed very much affected, I said but little more to him, lest while desiring to do him good, I might do him harm. Presently Brother B. said: "Brethren, as there are several of you present, I would like for one of you to pray." When Brother Austin called on Brother Gilbert, who responded with a very feeling and appropriate prayer. Sister B., who was then in the room, came to me and said, "Brother Boyd, as Mr. Burnet thinks a great deal of you, I would like you to come and sit up with him to-night." I answered that I would with pleasure.

On Sunday evening I again visited Brother B., who was rapidly sinking. When Dr. Knight was called to consult with Dr. Johnston in respect to his condition and the probable result. After they consulted, they decided that it was impossible that Brother B. could recover, and that it would be well to inform him of the fact. When it was decided by those present that Brother Austin should inform Brother B. of the decision of the doctors; which he did. At the announcement of the fact to him, Brother B. turned over and exclaimed, "If I die, I die in the faith of the gospel." On the following day, Monday, the fifth of August, eighteen hundred and sixty-seven, Brother B. breathed his last. On the Wednesday following his corpse was taken to the church, and Brother Gilbert preached his funeral sermon; which he did in a commendable manner. After the sermon the corpse was taken to the depot; and Brothers Morling and Gilbert were delegated to accompany it to Cincinnati.

MEMORY'S EXCURSION.

BY J. H. B.

WHEN memory an excursion takes,
  And views the scenes of former days,
It soon within our soul awakes
  A spirit for poetic lays.

When back to childhood's playful hours,
  Our thoughts are by sweet mem'ry led
Through flowery fields and shady bowers,
  Where nature's sweetest joys were shed,

'Tis then fond mem'ry makes us sigh
  For those sweet hours, which could not last,
And brings a tear-drop from the eye,
  As tribute to the time that's past.

And when, through youth's still later days
  Sweet mem'ry leads our willing mind,
And calls up forms, on which to gaze,
  Was happiness—'twas joy refin'd.

Ah, then! ah, then, what pen can write
  The feelings that sweet mem'ry brings
From those sweet moments of delight,
  Which flew away on rainbow wings.

But when fond mem'ry spreads her wings,
  And back to former scenes she goes,
'Tis not all pleasure that she brings;
  For with the joys she calls up woes.

Then cease, fond mem'ry, cease to roam
  Through all those former scenes of life;
Look forward to a better home:
  The future with bright joys is rife.

VIRTUE'S DIGNITY AMID VICES.

BY J. H. B.

THERE'S nought in this world that's more purely
    sublime,
Than virtue triumphant 'mid folly and crime.
The merits of whom are so seldomly known
Until, like the rose-bud, her leaves are all blown.
Her nature is such, that she's proud of herself;
Yet she boasts not of power, or ill-gotten pelf.
She stands as a guide-post upon our dark path;
She tells us provoke not the Lord's mighty wrath.
And emblem she has in mild Mary and Ruth;
She's the offspring of heav'n, and the mother of truth.
" You never can hurt her," one truly declares;
And she, by her wisdom, shuns all sinful snares.
Therefore it is better to court her mild ways;
She'll give you real pleasure and prosperous days

AN IMPROMPTU.

BY J. H. B.

O FOR a voice that could proclaim
    The glories of Emanuel's name.
    A name like Noah's weary dove
    That brought him, from the olive grove
      A token of a land of rest:

    So Jesus' name brings to the mind
    Of faithful souls, a hope to find
    Beyond the bound'ry of the skies,
    A rest, where pleasure never dies;
      But where they'll be forever blest.

INGRATITUDE.

BY J. H. B.

I'VE seen one man working hard for another,
   Nor asking nor stipend nor pay;
He was treated with all the respect of a brother,
   And allow'd in the family to stay.

But when old time had furrow'd his face,
   And his mind all crazy'd with care,
We've seen him cast off in utter disgrace,
   For to beg for his bread in despair.

And thus it is with the most of mankind,
   Who get rich by the aid of a friend;
They say to themselves, "*Our* coffers are lin'd;
   We'll not give away, borrow or lend."

Hence, thou Ingratitude! hence thou forever'
   Go, fly to some region unknown;
There hide thyself and return to us never;
   For all friendship with thee we disown.

ROCK CREEK.

A little stream dividing Georgetown from Washington, D. C.

BY J. H. B.

GURGLE on! gurgle on! thou sweet flowing stream,
   By whose shady banks so oft I did rove
In the days of my youth; when of nought did I dream,
   But the pleasures of life and the sweetness of love.

Gurgle on! gurgle on! thou dear little brook,
   Tho' never again by thy banks can I rove
With the heart that then lov'd me, for its spirit hath took
   Its flight from this world, to those regions above.

Gurgle on! gurgle on! thou swift flowing creek,
  May thy water still flow for the pleasure of those
Who may roam on thy borders in summer, to seek
For a place on thy sweet shady banks to repose.

Gurgle on! gurgle on! thou rivulet clear,
  Thy sweetness still holds its place in my heart;
If there's any one place under heaven more dear
  To my mem'ry than others, it is where thou art.

A REFLECTION.

BY J. H. B.

YOUNG butterflies, with yellow wings,
  When sporting in the summer sun,
Appear to be right happy things;
  But, O, how soon their race is run.

Just so with maidens, dress'd so gay,
  And with a beau close by their side,
When going to a ball or play,
  And thinking how to be a bride.

But like the butterfly so gay,
  They never think their joys will pass!
They laugh or dance their time away,
  And when 'tis o'er, how sad, alas!

Therefore young maids a lesson learn,
  And yield not to all fancy's pleasure,
But in this life do try to earn
  For future life the lasting treasure.

As I rode in the country one day,
  Near the railroad and turnpike connection,
Two butterflies flew in my way,
  And suggested the 'bove short reflection.

DECEIVE NOT THE DYING.

DECEIVE NOT THE DYING.

BY J. H. B.

A MAN, all broken with excess of life,
Is lying on a bed: and there his wife
Is standing by, to cheer his aching heart,
With some vain hope that they are not to part
Just now. She tries her best to soothe his pain,
By telling him that he'll *get well* again.
His *friends* are there; they, too, will tell
The dying man—"Cheer up, you'll soon get well,"
While in their minds they most assur'dly know,
Within a few short hours he's doom'd to go
The way of all the earth; and none can save
Their fellow mortal from the gloomy grave:
Still they deceive him; leading him to think,
The time is not yet come for him to drink
The dregs of life. And so he'll still conceal
Some precious secret, which he will reveal
To none, as long as there is hope of life;
Not even to his nearest friend—his wife.
And now a friend comes in, and now another;
Perhaps it is a sister, or a brother:
They, too, approach, and by the bed will stand,
Taking their dying brother by the hand;
"How are you feeling?" Thus to him they'll speak:
He gives no answer now—he's grown too weak—
He turns his head, his eyes, and breathes a sigh!
He feels, alas! that he's about to die:
And now he makes a sign for some dear friend
To come still nearer to him, and to lend
A list'ning ear to what he has to say,
Before his spirit takes its flight away.
He whispers low, but can't articulate,
To tell what he desires; he finds it now too late:

He gasps for breath, he tries to say, "Good-bye!"—
His pulse is still, and darkness clouds his eye;
His friends behold the change—they say, "He's dying."
He sighs his soul away, and leaves his friends all crying.
And thus it is so many pass away,
Deceived and flattered in their dying day.
But, O, dear friends, when we shall lay our head
Upon the pillow of our dying bed,
And we're unconscious of our sad estate,
O tell us friends! before it is too late.
If doctors shall decide we're near the brink
Of death; O let us know whate'er they think.
Think not to say the news will brink our heart,
And cause us quicker from this life to part.
What if the knowing should cause us to die
A few hours sooner, when death is so nigh?
What if we should be shorten'd of our pain?
When death is so near, then to die is gain.
Then let us know the worst, whate'er it be;
It may be of some worth, tho' none to me.
For we may have some parting words to tell,
When we're about to bid this world farewell;
And keep them ling'ring in our anxious mind,
As our last words to those we leave behind.
Then tell us—ere our mind becomes too weak—
If death is near; while we have power to speak.
O, let us urge this on our minds again,
And don't decline to tell for fear 'twill give us pain.
'Tis better when our friends are 'bout to die
That they should know the worst, ere death has come too
    nigh.

A SURVEY.

BY J. H. B.

BUT now when e'er I look around,
To see where joy and peace are found—
To see what work will yield the best,
The work of love leads all the rest.

Then may I work in that rich field,
Where sowing love, more love 'twill yield;
And in God's vineyard let me stay
And work.—Eternal life's the pay.

Oh! glorious work to serve my God;
To trace the steps my Saviour trod;
To work for Christ, to aid His cause;
To learn, obey, to teach His laws,

To live more Christ-like day by day,
To bear the cross, to watch and pray;
And leave all worldly cares behind,
For richer, sweeter, joys to find.

O, happy is the man whose trust
Is plac'd in heav'n, for there no rust
Will ever enter to corrode
The treasures of that blest abode.

And may, O God, the joy be mine,
To reach that place and there recline
Forever at thy feast of love,
With Jesus in thy courts above!

And, O my Saviour, may it be,
My greastest joy to work for Thee;
That when this life has pass'd away,
I'll reign with Thee in endless day.

Teach me thy will, O God, to know,
And all my duties plainly show;
And still thy grace to me impart;
Cleanse thou, and purify my heart.

O, grant me wisdom that I may
From all that's evil turn away;
And cause in me thy truth to shine,
And may thy will, O God, be mine;

That when life's journey's traveled o'er,
May hope, bright hope, still go before,
To cheer me when I close my eyes
In death, that I with Christ shall rise.

MARCH ON.

BY J. H. B.

TRIUMPHANT Lord, march on!
　　To conquer and to reign;
　Till all the world one voice shall raise
　　To praise the Lamb,—once slain!

Triumphant Lord, march on!
　Till every knee shall bow:
And every tongue confess Thee, Lord,
　While glory crowns thy brow.

Triumphant Lord, march on!
　Till sin, no more shall roam
Through all the earth, to shackle man,
　And keep him from his home.

Triumphant Lord, march on!
　Till love and peace be given
To all thy people here on earth,
　And discord chang'd to heaven.

"*THE LAW OF THE LORD IS PERFECT.*"

Psalm, 17-7.

BY J. H. B.

THERE needs no lengthy argument to prove
What's written in God's holy book of love.
For whatsoe'er we find inscribed there,
Is always true, and true still ev'rywhere.
But to elaborate—not make a truth—
Is what I now design in rhymes uncouth.
And Thou, my Maker, giver of all good,
Stand by me now, as Thou hast ever stood
By those who ever put their trust in Thee;
And when they need more strength to Thee they flee.
We're told when lacking, wisdom ask of Thee;
I pray Thee, Lord, to give it now to me.
Also thy holy spirit, Lord, impart
To me, that I may write from heart to heart,
That I may so proclaim the words of truth,
And edify the aged and the youth;
That they and I may so behold thy ways,
To walk therein, and thine shall be the praise !
" The Law of God is perfect," it is said
By One to whom was royal honors paid.
This is the theme and burden of our lay;
So you that deem it worthy, list to what we say.
All things that eminate from God's great mind,
Is with perfection stamp'd; this truth you'll find
By searching deep into the laws which He has giv'n
To govern things on earth, in sea, in heav'n.
Whether it be some vast and mighty world,
Which from His plastic hand thro' space He hurl'd,
To travel through those regions of the air,
Where none but God alone can see them there:
Or if it be the smallest living thing,
That floats through ether on its tiny wing;
Yet each, within itself, perfection shows;

But whence it came th' infinite only knows.
And each of these is govern'd by fix'd laws,
Giv'n at their birth by the eternal cause;
And if these laws infraction ever know,
Then all depending on them suffers woe.
And when the mind of man roams through the sky,
And sees vast worlds with speed of lightning fly
Around the sun; and ever keeping place
Through ages, in the grand celestial race;
With fi'ry comets shooting in between
Each others orbits in the heavenly scene,
And yet no danger of a dire collision—
They travel on in such sublime precision—
We'll say with David, then, while viewing this,
"Thy Law, O Lord of heaven, how perfect 'tis!"
And as He gave His laws to worlds and flies,
So, too, He's giv'n laws to men,—more wise.
And having giv'n intelligence to man,
With faculties—His works and laws to scan;
He gave him also, what ne'er He gave to brute,
A moral law;—to which the beasts are mute.
And this law's perfect,—saves from sin and death
All who obey, as long as they have breath.

------◆------

EXHORTATION.

"Admonish one another with psalms, hymns and spiritual songs."

BY J. H. B.

BRETHREN in Christ oft need reminding
That without seeking there's no finding;
Then we should often meet together,
To sing and pray; nor frowning weather
Should ever keep us from the meeting,
Where friend meets friend with happy greeting.
If each would *do*, not shirk his duty,
And serve the Lord in all the beauty

Of holiness; and be more zealous
To advance His cause, and be less jealous
Of another; but be more loving;
How might the cause of Christ be moving.
Then drop all lethergetic madness;
And seek and serve the Lord with gladness.
Grow weary in well-doing, never,
But for His blessings praise Him ever.
And when this life of faith is over,
Our crowns—like dew-drops on the clover—
Will sparkle bright and brighter,
As we approach the light that's lighter
Than mid-day sun.   For God's face shining
On all the saints who're there reclining,
Will make our crowns and jewels glisten,
While to unending songs we listen.
Then let us still be up and doing;
And still the work of love pursuing.

COMPLAIN NOT.

BY J. H. B.

AS to the church one morn I walk'd,
I to myself, both mus'd and talk'd;
Observing many girls and boys,
Pacing to school to seek for joys.

I saw a man within his room,
Who *seem'd* t' enjoy a smoke at home;
But could not tell how much of pain
Was lurking there, within his brain.

I saw a friend approaching me,
He seemed to walk with merry glee;
Tho' in his sad and care-worn face,
I soon anxiety did trace.

And as we met, he never smil'd—
"How do you do?" I said: "My child,"
Said he, "is ailing—quite unwell—
I fear 'twill die,—though hard to tell."

"Hope for the best," said I, and left.
"My heart," said he, "of hope is 'reft."
"Then look to God," said I, "in prayer;
He's merciful, and still may spare."

I passed along and met a boy,
Whose bright eye might betoken joy;
But when with piteous words he said,
"Please, sir, a cent to buy some bread,"

I thought, no matter where we go
In this wide world we meet with woe.
Tho' hard our lot, there's harder still;
Let this console—It is God's will.

AN APOSTROPHE TO RELIGION.

BY J. H. B.

RELIGION! O thou daughter of God,
And heir to immortality arise!
Thou mother of true happiness, O come;
And from thy quiet couch, with sacred steps
Make speedy progress to this stubborn heart,
And at its steely doors for entrance knock;
Or with persuasive words admittance gain.
Therein with bounteous hand love's spirit sow,
And, as the rain the earth, with copious showers
Of thy inspiring zeal, O keep it kind;
That it may be productive of good deeds,
And add new glory to thy righteous ways,
And everlasting praise to God in heaven.

FREEDOM.

BY J. H. B.

WHO that knows what freedom is,
    All its independent joys,
Would again in slavery live,
    Serving cruel master's boys ?

Who that knows what bondage is,
    All its insults—all its ills;
Would not rather die, than live
    To do as any tyrant wills ?

Who that by a kitchen fire,
    Cooking sweet-meats ev'ry day;
Would not rather die, than live
    Hungry—half-starv'd—without pay ?

Who that wasting life away,
    In another's cotton field;
Would not rather die, than live—
    Getting nothing of its yield ?

He that knows what freedom is,
    Let him ever thankful be;
And praise his Maker while he lives,
    For the blessing to *be free.*

A WARNING.

BY J. H. B.

COULD I write some words with power to save
The heedless youth, from an untimely grave:—
To rescue those who early learn to stray
In that alluring *path* which lies along their way.
Then *pause*, young man,—consider well—and think,
Before you enter on its dang'rous brink;

Or, if you've enter'd, quick your steps retrace,
Before its shame is stamp'd upon your face.
Think not t' escape, if you while young begin,
T' indulge in habits known as Onan's sin.
Your Bible read,—in GENESES you'll find
A lesson, worth your bearing it in mind:
To find the chapter,—thirty-eighth,—and then
Read well the verses each, *eight*, *nine* and *ten;*
And ponder well, how God will surely slay
The man that disobeys His righteous way.
Be strong, and from all lew'd indulgence keep:
For whatsoe'er you sow, you'll also reap.
Sow to the flesh, and life will pass away
In sickness, pain and premature decay.
Sow to the Spirit,—flee from sin and strife,
The promise then is yours,—Eternal Life.

ALL FOR SINNERS!

BY J. H. B.

COME all you that long for heaven;
 Join to sing the Lamb that died:
Give Him praise, and give Him glory,
 For there's none like Him beside.

CHORUS.

All for sinners; all for sinners;
 Sinners vile as you and I:
All for sinners; all for sinners,
 Jesus condescends to die.

On the cross my Saviour suffer'd,
 Bled and died that we might live.
All He asks from you, poor sinners,
 Is that you on Him believe.—CHO.

Then believe;—the Saviour calls you:
Calls you from your lost estate;
Heed the words of life He gives you;
Heed them ere it is too late.—CHO.

PRAISE THE SAVIOUR.

An impromptu song of praise.

BY J. H. B.

MOURNING souls lift up your heads,
And hear the joyful story:
Christ the Lord has conquer'd death.
And now He reigns in glory.

CHORUS.

Praise the Saviour!
Praise Him! Praise Him! Praise Him!
Praise the Saviour!
He who died for sinners.

When the world was wrapp'd in gloom,
And none to save or pity;
Then salvation's joyful sound,
Was preached from Zion's city.—CHO.

Jesus Christ, our faithful friend,
Came to this world so lowly,—
Taught that love to God and man,
Would make us pure and holy.—CHO.

O, that all would hear His voice—
Accept the great salvation,
Freely offer'd to us all,
To every tribe and nation.—CHO.

If we put our trust in Him,
  He never will forsake us;
If we're faithful to the end,
  To heaven our home He'll take us.—CHO.

With that happy throng above,
  We'll tell the wond'rous story;
Shout and sing redeeming love,
  And glory! Glory! Glory!—CHO

RETURN UNTO THE LORD.

BY J. H. B.

O HASTEN, sinner, to the Lord,
  And stay not for the morrow;
You ne'er again may hear His word,
  Inviting you from sorrow.

The Spirit will not always strive,
  With those who are invited;
And that which keeps the soul alive,
  Once gone, all hope is blighted.

O, sieze the prize while now you may,—
  Your days are swiftly fleeting;
Death presses on from ev'ry way,
  From Him there's no retreating.

Then fail not to obtain the power,
  The Spirit of Christ, which giveth
New life in ressurrection's hour,
  To live where Jesus liveth.

HARRY WILLIS BOYD.

Died March 9, 1877.   Aged, 1 year, 7 months.

BY J. H. B.

ITTLE Willis how we miss thee,
How we'd love again to kiss thee;
And to scan thy ev'ry feature,
And embrace our darling creature.

But we would not call thee hither
From thy resting place, to wither
And die again; like a flower
Pluck'd untimely from earth's bower.

No, no, sleep on, we would rather
Wait till Jesus comes, to gather
Within one fold, all His dear ones,—
Father, mother and our near ones.

Till then we will cease to sorrow
O'er the absent one—we'll borrow
Comfort from the hope of meeting,
In that happy land of greeting.

TWENTY-FIFTH ANNIVERSARY OF OUR WEDDING.

BY J. H. B.

UST five and twenty years ago to-night,
  Dear Sue! we, hand in hand, stood side by side,
And in each other's presence took delight,
  And I became your bridegroom,—you my bride.

That happy hour I still remember well:
  The then long future brighten'd to our view;
We pledged that we would love as husband—wife,
  And until death continue to be true.

Now five and twenty years have pass'd away;
  And though our path has not been strewn with flowers,
Yet with the checker'd scenes we still can say,
  We've had a goodly share of happy hours.

With many children we've been blessed—just nine.
  Tho' two have gone before us to their rest,
Yet in their loss we will not dare repine,
  While with the other seven we are blest.

We both, perhaps, of faults have had our share,
  But let them all in Lethean waters glide:
And may we still each other's burden bear,
  And should we see a fault, strive it to hide.

These many years have swiftly roll'd away,
  And now our lives are on the downward slope;
How many more are left we cannot say,
  For all our future life is only hope.

And if our future life be short or long,
  May we continue faithful to the end,
And when the separation comes, be strong
  To bear whate'er kind heaven for us may send.

THE DEATH OF "SUSIE."
MY INFANT DAUGHTER.

Composed while going to the grave with the corpse, August 9, 1856.

BY J. H. B.

O SUSIE! Dear Susie! thou art gone from our presence:
    Thy soul has departed its beautiful clay.
It has mounted on high, like the very quintessence
    That exhales from the rose-bud in morning array.

Thy life it was short; tho' as sunshine 'twas cheerful,
    And it gladden'd each heart that beheld it awhile:
But too soon with its dart, Death, alas! brought a tearful
    Eye, that soon from us all did our pleasure beguile.

Yet I hope even now, that thy soul has reach'd heaven;
    And there with the angels art happy with God;
And singing sweet praises with those who're forgiven
    Of their sins, and have reach'd that most happy abode!

ARE WE CHRISTIANS?

That is, do we follow after the precepts and examples of Christ as closely as it is possible for us to do? Have we a strong faith in His promises? That is, are we satisfied in our own minds that He will perform all that He has promised? That if we are faithful in serving Him unto the end, He will give us a crown of eternal life of joy in His kingdom which is to have no end. If so, we ought to be very happy. And if we are not Christians, and thus happy, whose fault is it? Every man has the right and privilege of being a Christian. And if he is a true Christian he will alwaysbe happy. And as happiness is the object for which we all strive, it behooves us, as wise men, to ascertain the most direct path which leads to an object so desirable.—*Found written on a loose leaf in J. H. Boyd's scrap-book.*

IN MEMORIAM.

J. H. BOYD, from whose writings the preceding sketch and poems were selected, spent an active Christian life from the time he joined the church, in 1864, until the time of his death.

On Saturday, August 9, 1880, he, with his wife, went from his home, in Baltimore, to Summit Grove camp-meeting, in York county, Pennsylvania. He took an active part in the meetings on Sunday, and spoke very earnestly and touchingly of the great joy and blessedness of a Christian life and Christian work, and the happiness he had found in them.

From the night air, and a sudden change in the weather, he was taken with a chill on Sunday night; and he returned home on Monday morning; went to bed in the evening, and continued there the remainder of the week.

Late on Saturday evening I returned from the country—where I had been for several weeks—not knowing that my brother was sick—and early on Sunday morning the message came to me, informing me of his illness. I started immediately to see him—having about two miles to go—hoping to exchange some parting words with him. But instead of enjoying this privilege, I found his wife and children weeping around his lifeless body.

Thus, on Sunday morning, August 17, 1880, about eight o'clock, he passed away, to realize the glories of that land which he so often beheld in vision, and of which he so hopefully and joyfully talked and wrote.

He, doubtless, knew some days before his death that the time of his departure was at hand; as one of his latest acts was to get the deed of his burial lot from a secluded place, where he had put it several years previous, and lay it where it could readily be seen after his death.

May his example and precepts prove a blessing to his seven children, and to many others, who may feel the influence of his life.   A. S. B.

"HAVE FAITH IN GOD."

BY A. S. BOYD.

'TWAS midnight, lone, and dark, and drear!
And weary, worn, and full of care,
Sleeplessly on my bed I lay,
As slowly passed the hours away!
I wished the night might soon be gone;
Yet saw no comfort in the morn:
My faith so weak I scarce could pray;
And hope so faint, and far away!

The dreary hours so slowly fled,
As ticked the clock beside my bed:
My mind ran out to many more,
As sick as I—as sad—as poor;
And wonder'd why from heav'n above
No comfort came, if "God is love?"—
And if the words were understood,
Which oft declare, "The Lord is good!"

And yet my heart did not despair,
But looked to God in earnest prayer—
Which must have reached His ear, for He
Soon sent the answer down to me.
For while I prayed some gentle word,
As sweet as mortal ever heard,
Fell on my ear—I hear it now—
"O, troubled soul! why weepest thou?"

I turned my head around to see
Who he that spoke these words could be,
And as I looked, my longing eyes
Met with a sight of glad surprise:—
A flood of light seemed to illume
The darkness which reigned in my room;
And by that light my eyes beheld
A form which half my doubtings quell'd:—

A form as fair as fair could be;
And seemed so kind and near to me:
So near, I reached my hand, and lo!
I felt some soothing, hopeful glow:
So kind I told him all my grief—
Trusting he came to my relief.
His eyes were soft, persuasive, bright,
That looked on me in that dark night!

Said I, " I'm sick, and weak, and tired;
Yet heavy burdens are requir'd
Along life's rough and dreary road;
And oft I sink beneath the load!
My wealth is small; true friends are few,
Yet each for each would gladly do."
Said he, " I've come to be your friend,
And bear your burden to the end."

" These words fall very sweet," said I,
" Upon my ear; in days gone by
I've read, and in them solace found,
A balm for every bleeding wound.
But now—with faith so weak—I cease
To feel the wanted joy and peace."
Said he, " Have faith in God: and find
Rest to your soul, and peace of mind."

“ I try to trust in God,” said I,
“And on His promises rely:
But still a thousand ills I see,
Which makes God’s love a mystery!”
“ Have faith in God,” he said again,
“And He will sometime make it plain.”
As these sweet words fell on my ear,
My darkened vision seemed more clear.

But then I thought of those whose eyes
Were wet with tears; whose sobs and sighs
Found no response; but only found
Their grief prolonged through all life’s round:—
And then I said, in tearful mood,
“ Why are these things, if God is good ? ”
And as I asked, I deeply sighed !
“ The Lord is good,” he still replied.

To know his name was my desire;
Then, “ Who art thou, may I enquire ? ”
I said—as hushing my sad sighs,
And wiping tear-drops from my eyes.
“ Dost thou not know me ? ” then he said,
“ Yet from my hand you’ve oft been fed:—
I’m He whose feet for you have trod
The roughest path.—Have faith in God ! ”

I lifted up my weary head—
Made lighter by the words he said—
When to my bed he nearer came,
And whisper’d in my ear his name,
And laid his soft hand on my brow,
And said, “ Dost thou not know me now ?
Reach forth, and feel my hands, my side:—
Have faith in God: He will provide!”

I could not speak—my soul so wrought—
And as I sat, with gladden'd thought,
He said, "I'm He whose word imparts
The sweetest joy to saddest hearts;—
Who broke the seal, and conquer'd death;
Breathed into clay immortal breath,
And captive death's strong victor led!—
Have faith in God!" again He said.

His hand He lifted from my brow,
And said, "Dost thou not know me now?"
I bowed my head in glad accord,
And said, " 'Tis Christ, my risen Lord!"
He took my hand—bade me arise;
And with His fingers touched my eyes;
When plain I saw; and understood
These blessed words,—"The Lord is good!"

"Have faith in God," He said again:—
"Take courage from the thousand men—
Who suffer'd hunger, pain and loss,
And counted all the world as dross,
That they might gain the priceless goal
God has for every faithful soul:—
Through tribulation deep they trod,
Supported by their "faith in God!"

"O, Son of God! O, man divine!
Increase my faith; that it, like thine,
May cheer my heart, and give me strength,
To press unto my journey's length.—
Come often, Lord, beside my bed;
Lay thy soft hand upon my head,
That I beneath the chast'ning rod,
May still look up, with 'faith in God!'

Will all the work I've left undone,
And victories lost, I might have won,
Make less my joy—make less God's grace,
If faithful I pursue my race?"
"O, no!" said He, "God's grace is free!
And He can give as much to thee,
In evening hour with work well done,
As t' those who wrought 'neath noonday sun.

But wait not till the evening hour—
Till dark'ning clouds around you lower—
Till faith grows weak, and hope's half flown,
Ere you your wants to me make known:
Call on me early;—I'll be near,
And keep your pathway bright and clear.
By faith the darken'd way I trod;
But now 'tis light.—Have faith in God!"

"Then all my care on God I'll cast,
And ask Him to forgive the past!
And now my soul finds peace and rest,
In trusting God.—He knows the best!"
My blessed Saviour, and my Lord,
Here breathed on me His parting word;—
So sweet! so brief! now understood;—
"HAVE FAITH IN GOD; FOR HE IS GOOD!"